I0762153

EXECUTIVE JUNGLE

"Only a seasoned professional with the brilliant insights of a David Levy could show us what goes on behind the scenes in the upper echelons of the often down-and-dirty business of the television and motion picture industries. *Executive Jungle* is a superb work and I highly recommend it to anyone who wants an in-depth look at the way the key players operate behind the scenes. Well done, David!"

William Froug
Author of *Zen and the Art of Screenwriting* and *Screenwriting Tricks of the Trade*

EXECUTIVE JUNGLE

A NOVEL

DAVID LEVY

Essex, Connecticut

Prometheus Books

An imprint of The Globe Pequot Publishing Group, Inc.
64 South Main Street
Essex, CT 06426
www.globepequot.com

Library of Congress Cataloging-in-Publication Data

Levy, David, 1918–
Executive jungle / by David Levy.
p. cm.
ISBN 978-1-57392-245-6 (cloth)
I. Title.
PS3562.E927E94 1998
813′.54—dc21 98-37788
CIP

ACKNOWLEDGMENTS

Many people are involved by the time a book has reached completion from its first inception in the mind of an author to its final publication, but that is only to be expected over time if a work has any life to it. I want to thank all those who have read previous versions of these stories and shared their thoughts with me. In particular I want to thank Penny Rieger for her patience and time in preparing drafts of many of these stories. Charles Lee, my brother, has been an invariable source of critical input and patience through my many revisions. Eugene O'Connor at Prometheus Books contributed several excellent ideas as to structure and content, and was patient with the sometimes difficult process of assembling a final draft. My son Lance Lee carried out the final editing and revision at my behest while I was ill, and contributed Prelude and Envoi with my review and thanks.

CONTENTS

PRELUDE

William Burns thought he had interviewed enough aspiring young men for work at Otis & Meade to make surprises impossible. O&M was by far the largest and most influential advertising agency in New York, with a deep influence on the television programming that reflected and in large part determined the tastes of Americans.

But Steven Lane was different. It wasn't Lane's head-turning looks, his six-foot, trim but wide-shouldered frame, his black hair emphasized by the fair, clear skin, or features of an almost Roman strength and attractiveness. Burns reflected it was Lane's good fortune his nose had the slightest of hooks in it to break the impression of a model's perfection, and that there were an intensity and intelligence around the eyes that belied his youthfulness. Nonetheless, Burns could imagine Lane entering a room, especially with an attractive woman on his arm, and heads turning to look at both of them.

No, he had seen handsome men before. There were enough here at O&M. Nor was it the young man's hunger to get ahead: that was more common than starlets in Hollywood. It was his coolness. To be sure, Burns expected that everyone wanted to appear at once able, eager, and collected. But with Lane he sensed the coolness was innate. This young man would walk away from Otis & Meade if the deal wasn't to his liking despite his eagerness to shake Philadelphia and become part of an agency that was one of the great players in the media.

Even more unusual, this was the third time they had met. It usually took two meetings: one to dismiss a potential prospect after a face-to-face review, two to hire one. To be in a third bargaining session was, to say the least, uncommon.

"I'm afraid I can't really offer more, Mr. Lane," Burns said. "I've reviewed your accomplishments and discussed this with the firm. Twenty-two thousand five hundred dollars is really it."

"That's $468 a week, and change. I make considerably more than that where I am, Mr. Burns," Steve Lane replied calmly. He had already talked them several thousand above what he did make. His 'considerably more' reflected his monthly, not weekly, take at Franklin & Reed, the local advertising firm in Philadelphia where he had gone after graduating from the University of Pennsylvania.

"Working at Otis & Meade represents a considerable premium in itself."

"I've already proven my ability, Mr. Burns. *We Philadelphians* is one of the highest rated local shows ever aired in Philadelphia, and my inspiration. *Henry Lee Reviews* is the most popular review and guest show the city has had. And," he added calmly, "I brought *you* Roy Pearson's ***Guess My Life*** and General Foods's interest in it."

Burns leaned back and smiled. There was no doubt Steve Lane was a whiz kid at twenty-five. He knew he had been almost more than staid Franklin & Reed could bear. They had let him loose on television because it was their weakest department, if it could be called one at all: F&R was that classical organization, the big fish in the small pond, the local advertising agency that did well in its home town and carefully avoided expanding beyond its real capacities. Charles Mayberry understood his firm well, and had let young Lane drag them into the local TV market as part of a legitimate effort to expand: but beyond that he would not be led. Charles Mayberry had made that abundantly clear to William Burns when Burns called him on Steve Lane.

"Good boy," Mayberry had said. "Ambitious. Has it. Has too much for us. Frankly, take him before someone else does—or he drags us into bigger markets!" They had laughed.

What Burns didn't know was that Mayberry had sat Steve Lane down in his office and bluntly told him how to deal with William Burns and Otis & Meade.

"Ask for twice what you get here. Don't take their first counter. Or their second. You're as valuable as you think you are in this world."

Steve knew Mayberry meant the world of advertising, of television, of the media, by 'this world': the world of appearances, and the people who manipulated those appearances. He nodded.

"If you come cheap, you are. Take my advice, son," Mayberry said. He was sixty-four, portly, good natured, the kind of man who could make music out of spoons and glasses in family gatherings, or tell a ribald joke among cronies after a Chamber of Commerce meeting. He knew his abilities, his goals, and his limits, and had built Franklin & Reed from a two-man operation into the successful company it was now. But he also liked a relaxed life, one that involved little travel, no close involvement with New Yorkers or, worse, those men lost in clouds of ego and sex and money from Los Angeles. Philadelphia fit him fine. But it was not for the young man before him.

"I saw your *Some Fall Down.* Not bad at all," he added before Steve could reply. "Not bad. A little slow in the second act."

"Thank you very much."

"You're not a Miller."

Steve stared at him. He knew Mayberry liked him, liked him a lot, and he had already heard he had liked his play. Lane had learned not to underestimate Mayberry either. Mayberry understood his place and achievements exactly. He had maintained his choice of lifestyle and the right niche at Franklin & Reed against all temptations to stray. Mayberry was sharp under the genial, rounded surface.

"No. I'm Steven Lane."

Mayberry smiled. That was a young man's answer, one Lane would soon learn not to make in New York. "It's easy to be confused by promise, when young. You have the knack of a writer. But you're a player. That's why you want to go to Otis & Meade, not work calmly here and be able to find enough time to write steadily and then, when successful enough, drop us and just write."

Exactly that thought had crossed Lane's mind. It was equally true he hadn't acted on it. He knew working at Otis

& Meade would make that goal impossible, reduce writing to a sideline.

"You need to be in the hunt, Steve, you need to be a player. Start by acting like one."

Now, as he sat across from William Burns, whom he instinctively liked, Steve Lane let himself sigh. "I guess you have plenty of people already bringing you good work. You clearly don't want me very much." He stood up to go, on fire with uncertainty within, absolutely calm outside. He held out his hand to Burns. "It's been a pleasure to meet you." That was true. Burns was an immediately likeable, jovial man. "I would have loved the chance to meet Mr. Wayne or even Mr. Otis."

William Burns was genuinely nonplussed. Since when did a prospective hire dismiss him? Particularly someone they wanted to hire? Suppose Lane walked out the door? How would that appear to Ted Wayne? Or Otis? Would they think he couldn't bring in the young talent anymore? Worse, had habitual success made him smug, and set him up for a fall? Burns could imagine the rebuke that would bring from Otis! Some of his surprise flashed across his face.

"Sit down, Steve," was all he said. "Give me a moment." And he walked out.

He knocked at Ted Wayne's office. Wayne was scowling over a report.

"Bad moment?"

"No, c'mon in, Bill. What's up?"

"It's this Lane kid. He stood up, offered his hand, and was about to walk out."

"Mean it?" Burns nodded. "Tough little bastard, isn't he?" But Ted didn't look displeased. In fact, he smiled and leaned back in his red leather chair. He was almost too big for the chair: not fat, solid. A big man. "What's he asking?"

"Thirty-six thousand." Ted laughed. "We're at twenty-two. He only made eighteen in Philadelphia."

Ted nodded. He shuffled papers on his desk, and finally pulled out Steven Lane's file. He flipped through it.

"Talented kid. Brought us the Pearson show."

"College friends."

Ted nodded. "See his play?"

"Mayberry said it showed promise."

"Has the sense not to follow his second talent. What do you think?"

"I have other people to see."

"Think Otis will like him?"

"Oh, yes."

"I can use that sort of energy and brains. Tough, too," he repeated, admiringly. "Okay."

And so Steve found himself ushered into Ted Wayne's office and given a hearty handshake to welcome him to the television department of Otis & Meade. Then he found himself being led upstairs and past Florence West, James Hornwell Otis's trim, blond, blue-eyed secretary whose attractiveness did not for a second interfere with her ability, to meet the patrician head of O&M.

Two details only stuck in Steve Lane's mind from that first meeting with James Hornwell Otis and the haze of emotion he fought to contain. One was Otis's pipe: Dunhill, lit, filling the room with a pleasant but pungent aroma; the other was the simple fact that of all those he met that afternoon at Otis & Meade, no one else used a pipe.

Steve regaled Helen with his account of the negotiation with Burns, and the meetings after, even as he broke the news to her he would be living in New York within two weeks. They had wanted him immediately, but he had responsibilities to make a smooth transition at Franklin & Reed, even though Mayberry would have let him go the next day if he had asked. He insisted on being professional: no sudden moves to betray just how young he was.

Helen laughed. They were in a comfortable restaurant, with a table in a dim recess. She wasn't sure what to think as Steve jumped from one incident to another, retailed this impression and that, leapt back and forth between Theodore Wayne and William Burns and James Hornwell Otis and Hendrik Taylor, who would be his immediate superior, and O&M's location on 42nd Street and the sheer, galvanizing energy of New York. He was happy: she was happy.

"I'll have to spend a lot of time making arrangements," he was saying enthusiastically, "not just at F&R, but in New York, finding a place, a place big enough for us," he added. She smiled. "We won't see much of each other for a while."

"I understand." Helen didn't add that if it was to be a place big enough for both of them, then there was more that needed to be said, much more, or that she should be doing some of the looking.

And later, when they went up to his small apartment for a nightcap, Helen didn't say anything about all the assumptions Steve made about a future they would share without ever discussing it with her. She didn't say anything about the fact they had met as freshmen at Penn, and were still just dating. She knew his career was all-in-all to him, and tonight was his big night, maybe his biggest. And, after all, he was including her in it.

She straightened her hair in the bathroom, taking a

good look at herself. She was twenty-five, too: nice looking. Rich, brown hair, lively brown eyes, a beautiful complexion. She knew men found her attractive—not beautiful, but nonetheless someone to look at. She was soft in manner: she couldn't help that. And bright—she couldn't deny that, either. She was no stay-at-home, but an editor for a local publishing firm, and a good one, She had a future. She was self-supporting. She was Jewish.

Helen knew that didn't matter as much as it had once. That had never been an issue with Steve, either: he seemed blind to ethnic and racial divisions, despite his mother, who never lost the prejudices of the once poor. Her parents weren't blind to those either, and had always been nervous about Steve. "He has the manners of a WASP," her father growled once.

"Oh, Daddy," she had laughed, "you mean impeccable manners. There isn't a prejudiced bone in Steve's body."

But the upper echelon at Otis & Meade, as well as the other main advertising agencies, were still repositories of patrician, personally conservative men. If Steve wanted her, so be it: she would handle whatever came her way, even keeping out of the way, if that helped him.

When they found themselves on the edge of the bed, she melted into his arms, withholding nothing. She wanted to be with him. She had loved him from the moment he had run into her at Penn looking elsewhere as he waved goodbye to someone. That had angered her at times: she was too bright to be trapped in a blind, female 'adore on first sight' relationship, but that's what it was with Steve. She was sure he knew it, too. That's why discussions of 'their' future had never been necessary.

Her blouse melted from her shoulders, and there was a

rightness to how her breasts felt in his hands, as if they needed to be there. She did her best not to think of all the other times they had started off so passionately like this and then slowed, sometimes stopped. Steve had not wanted to be trapped, she knew that. Both of them wanted careers, and then marriage and family. And both were too shy, children of the fifties, despite all the present changes, to understand much about birth control, which seemed somehow furtive, and beneath them.

Tonight Helen covered Steve's face with kisses, murmuring his name repeatedly, and urged him on. She didn't care. She wanted to be as memorable a part of this day as the rest of it. His shirt came off easily, and she covered his chest with her kisses, then moaned helplessly as his hand slid down her smooth belly, lower, then lower: she snapped her garter belt free, then helped him push her skirt down, her slip, her panties. She was shaking now, naked in emotion: she had never been so naked before, never so wanted to be so naked . . .

"Steve, Steve darling, yes," she breathed in his ear, and clung, and let him bend her back, let him, yes, let him do what she so hungered for. And when Steve hesitated, and began to pull back, holding her tightly so she couldn't move, Helen ignored shame and begged him not to stop, not tonight, assuring him it was safe, shamelessly adoring him until he clasped her to him hungrily, aroused, and took what was so fully given.

Later she curled into him, listening to Steve replay the day's events at O&M again, and build a picture of the future, talking of show ideas he already had, sponsors he could imagine pairing these with, imagining how he would measure himself against rivals, debating where he would find a place for them in New York, carrying on about the thrill of having Broadway available any night he chose, and of exploring the great restaurants.

"We'll have a fine time together," he added, including her in this stream of consciousness.

Helen knew he meant it, too. She didn't doubt that for a second. When Steve finally trailed off, and slept, she sat up and stared at his face a long time. How difficult it was to love someone like this, so one-sidedly. Quietly she moved from his side. For a time she sat quite still by the window, running the evening through her mind over and over like a favorite movie. After a time the tears started, unheeded. The nights they spent together were always like this, the passion they shared one she evoked, working hard to be as exciting as possible.

But Helen had learned the one thing she needed to know, tonight. Or, rather, she had let herself know what she had known a long time. This was the best it was ever going to be. This comfortableness on his part.

She reassembled all the clothing men found so hard to resist and women part of the necessary chore of being a woman, and quietly slipped out without waking him. She said nothing of her thoughts when she waved him off at the train station that weekend as he set off to find 'their' apartment.

All she said was, "Goodbye, Steve," and uncharacteristically held out her hand. He looked at her, startled. But her face was the same warm, loving face he had known for years, but set now, brooking no response. Nothing more. He shook her hand and got on the train, confused. She watched it leave with the man she loved but who, she knew, found her resistible.

● ● ●

Some months later Steve and Roy Pearson met for drinks at New York's famous "21." Roy was already full of ideas for new shows, Steve full of cautions about the need for a careful, developmental nurturing of his ideas so that *Guess My Life* would prove to be the start of a great career, not a flash in the pan. In the midst of this earnest debate William Burns stopped by on his way to join Hendrik Taylor and Ted Wayne, whom Steve had already saluted at another table.

"Hi Steve. Mind if I join you for a moment?"

"Not at all. You know Roy Pearson?"

"Of course. We're all waiting to see what you come up with next." Pearson, unexpectedly, flushed.

"I was just telling him O&M would naturally be interested, but it has to be a polished idea."

"Does Ted know you're encouraging Roy?"

"Of course! I told him first thing that we were friends."

Pearson excused himself for a moment.

"Things going well?"

Steve Lane leaned back. He was certain William Burns knew exactly how things were going.

"I love it," he said candidly. The older man broke into a wide smile. That was Lane's way. He never did things in half measures, and his reactions were honest.

"You certainly ran us a merry chase to bring you on board." Steve Lane only smiled. "I should tell you, friend to friend," Burns said, "it was a good bargaining." He and Lane had become friends, too, already: Burns liked the younger man, and had had him up to his Park Avenue apartment several times. Lane could also see Burns had had a few before coming to "21." Burns didn't lose discretion when he drank: anyone who did that would have had a very brief career at O&M. But Burns did become a little more open on matters there really wasn't any point in being secretive about any longer.

"You weren't as tough as you think," he smiled.

"No?" Lane thought he had done very well.

"We'd have gone up to thirty thousand, Steve."

"I'd have settled for twenty-five or a little less."

"Then we're both happy." Burns patted him on the shoulder and moved on as Pearson sat down again.

"What was all that about?"

"Just a little reminder to think better of ourselves than we do."

Pearson didn't understand, and Steve Lane didn't explain.

AND THEN THERE WERE THREE

THE THREE WERE BARTON K. HILLS, Theodore 'Ted' Wayne, and William T. Hopper. At that very moment they were in the boardroom collecting papers following the usual staff meeting of the giant advertising agency.

"My extra sensory perception tells me something's brewing," Bart was saying. "Whenever the old man skips a meeting like this he's evolving one of his goddamn plans and the trouble is his work."

"And we've been pretty slow getting ours firmed up," Hopper said, as he toyed with a gold-filigreed pillbox that Otis had given him on his twenty-fifth anniversary with the agency. "What's more, my spies tell me he's been temporarily ignoring Florence West, and whenever that happens someone's goose is being fried and it's not hers, you can bet a long shot. Any bright ideas?" he snapped.

Ted Wayne shook his head in mock disagreement. "She hasn't minded his absence, Hop. That type doesn't go for the nunnery bit. Being the only bachelor among this little band of intrepid conspirators, I decided to chance it once myself, but she's no pushover. In the end she could zing you a thousand ways to one and the old man would follow her zing. She's got him and he's got her. Period."

"When did this little romantic interlude take place?" Hop asked as he took a pill from his box and swallowed it.

"Couple weeks ago," Ted said. "We had dinner, danced at the Embassy Club, I persuaded her to have a nightcap up at my place and then when it was time for sweet music and candles, I suddenly felt I was hit by a battery of floodlights and a military march."

"Meaning?"

"I got an instinctive feeling she was grilling me, that as I softened, she hardened, that as I paid her a compliment, she'd toss me a question."

"What kind of question?" Bart asked.

"Questions about morale, my aspirations, yours. After I got near first base the second time I knew what she was up to. She's a goddamn Mata Hari, and if the warm hands were hers, the icy voice was the honorable James H. Otis. And, boys," Ted added, looking at his watch, "I think my inner warning system suggests we break up this meeting for now."

Some two weeks later, James Hornwell Otis was observing the reflection staring back at him thirty-two stories above Madison Avenue. He seemed amused that his ghostly image could hover there securely above the traffic below. He studied the sardonic image as though it belonged to some stranger; his evaluation was swift and reassuring. The face was firm, even at sixty-three, and the brown eyes were clear. He was proud that he needed no glasses; he was proud of his hair—gray to be sure—but as thick and disciplined as when he had been a Princeton undergraduate. A smile crossed his lips—planning had done it, done everything for him. He had frequently traced it all to the vow he had made at Princeton: moderation at all times; awareness at all times; being prepared at all times. It meant always having a plan.

He turned from his pleasant reverie, solemnly tapped his Dunhill against the edge of the ashtray, making certain that the pipe bowl would not even slightly nick the inscription, "This Stone Came From the Houses of Parliament" set in lead, deep in the center of the tray. For a moment he thought of Churchill's heroic few who had given so much to the many for whom the stone had been designed as a symbol. Then he thought of his three senior vice presidents who similarly had done so much for the many in the company, and especially for him. He glanced at his watch. It was four o'clock and he had made a decision.

He pressed the buzzer once on his desk, waited a moment, and watched Florence West enter, book in hand. She approached the chair beside his desk. In the few moments that she took to cross the room, he was able to grasp a dozen fleeting thoughts that swept in regimented style through his mind. He was sixty-three and she admitted to thirty-eight. She had good legs. He enjoyed seeing her stride, particularly in her new shorter skirt. She was probably in her early forties. After all, she had been his secretary twenty years. And something more for almost all of those years. Modern makeup did miracles, or perhaps it was the mind. Her figure was still trim. "Age cannot wither her . . ." She had great presence; he was sure no one could detect their relationship unless he released her—even now, alone, in his private office.

"I've come to a decision, Florence," he said, scrutinizing her closely, wondering if this enigmatic announcement would give her a start, flood her with hopes that he and Mrs. Otis had finally separated. Florence West had learned her part well; there was no trace of reaction, no flicker of curiosity. "It's about our three young heroes," he added. "I think it's time we gave them wings."

James Otis rose and passed his secretary's chair. "Smell good, Florence," he said touching her cheek gently.

"Thank you, James," she replied.

"I'll be coming by tonight," he said, as he twirled the combination to the private safe set behind the painting he had had commissioned showing him at the helm of his schooner.

"It's been a long time," she said a moment later.

He reached into the safe, found the paper he wanted and returned to his desk. "Perhaps we'll have more time when we set this plan in motion. You do remember the Plan, Florence?" he asked as he pushed the papers toward her.

She glanced at the title page. It read MEMORANDUM FOR THE REORGANIZATION OF EXECUTIVE RESPONSIBILITY.

"Nor custom stale her infinite variety," he said glancing at her.

"You and Ted Wayne have at least that in common," she said. "He can quote Shakespeare, too."

"Did he give you the same quote?"

"Yes, but he also had others."

Otis chuckled. "There's a rare combination, that Ted Wayne. Looks like a fullback, thinks like a computer, quotes Shakespeare. Any other poets?"

"I think I spoiled his timing. I was quoting too early, perhaps."

"Quoting?"

"Asking those questions."

"He's quite a boy."

"I never really found out," she said.

"We'll talk of that later. First things first." He picked up a pencil, tapped it on his chin. "I become chairman and that raises three questions. First, which of the three should be president? Bart? Ted? Hop?" He studied Florence's face. "Well?" he asked.

"You have that famous enigmatic Otis look," she replied. "I don't know."

"Well, I think I do know," Otis replied, smiling. "It'll take a bit of time, but you'll see. The question is, what will the other two do?"

At that moment, the three men were once again in the boardroom at the end of another meeting. Ted threw his feet up on the long table. "Gentlemen," he said, "I have a little announcement to make. The time to move is now. We've got the business in our hands. We know it. The clients know it. And you can bet your bottom dollar James Hornwell Otis knows it. We've been chewing this over for months."

Hopper drummed the table. "He's sixty-three. Sixty-four in three months. And then it's only a year."

"Screw," Ted said. "He can count as good as you. Hop, you're basically a pussyfooter."

"Now just a minute. . . ."

"Can it! You didn't last here twenty-five years on guts. You did it on your belly, so don't kid us. We've each done ten years and we know. Now if Bart goes I'm ready. What do you say, Bart?"

Barton K. Hills looked up toward the ceiling searching

every crevice of the mahogany board room for a clue whether to move or not. He was famous for caution—which often merely covered up his own deficiency in decisiveness. At forty-four he was the youngest, and yet his premature loss of hair, the deep lines etched into his mottled face gave him the substantial look of a conservative, older man. That seeming strength was an illusion. "Hop," Bart said, "kindly stop drumming the table, if you want me to think."

William T. Hopper gritted his teeth. He was sick of being ordered around, sick of toadying to Otis, sick of being brushed off by Wayne, sick of hearing Bart constantly praised for his thinking things through. He felt his own seniority merited more recognition by everyone. He tugged at the Italian silk handkerchief in his breast pocket carefully selected to complement his tie, not to match it. That was for the Ted Waynes of this world. The men who really didn't care to dress smartly, or didn't know how. The rubes.

Bart turned to Ted. "Do you really think we can pull it off?"

Wayne smiled that engaging smile of his. Disarming, people said, but Ted Wayne smiled that way to hide his snarl of contempt for the buck-passers, the men who couldn't make the hard decisions. He was not only the *only* bachelor of the three; no female had been able to grind him to a halt, to exhaust the tempo and fervor of his drive. He hunched forward at the table, his large frame seemingly poised to leap forward. "I know we can, if we do it right."

"And how do we do *it* right?" Hop said. "That is, if you don't mind letting us in on your secret."

"Hop, let's cut the cutes, okay?" Wayne said. "We stick together, that's how. We tell him we're prepared to leave the company. We know and he knows the company can't stand that kind of break. We buy him out, he retires, and we give him a big sentimental party and toss in Florence West for keeps."

"What about keeping him on as a consultant?" Bart suggested.

"Okay, we keep him as a consultant," Wayne said agreeably.

"What about the company name?"

"We keep the company name. Otis & Meade, Inc. He deserves that much. He did a lot of the building, and we don't forget it," Wayne said.

"He hired me," Hop added.

"He made other mistakes, too," Ted said with a smile.

Hop rose abruptly from his chair.

"Sit down, Hop. I wanted to get a rise from you and I did."

"Ted, I'm not sure that I want to sit down. I'm not sure I like you. I'm not sure the plan is any damned good."

"Got any ideas that are better?"

For a moment, the three sat in silence.

"I guess we're coming very close to a decision, aren't we," Bart said.

"The company's his, Bart," Ted said. "He can do anything with it he damn well pleases. It's all a matter of timing. We either make the decision or *he* makes it. For five years he's sat through every meeting and he's never, but never, given a single clue as to his intentions. The business has stood still. He can dissolve it, sell it, or give it away. And we'll be dead little cookies. Yeah—we want him out. We want him out good. And the three of us can do it if we just stick together exactly the way we planned. He resigns.

We call the key executives together—Bart, you've got the list. They vote for a new president. Period. We back up the new president. Period, period."

James Hornwell Otis buzzed twice, signaling his second secretary. When she came to the doorway, he said, "Miss Kling, would you mind asking Mr. Hills, Mr. Wayne, and Mr. Hopper to come into my office."

Miss Kling stopped at Mr. Hopper's secretary's desk. Glancing back at Otis's office, she whispered, "Never changes, just the two of them, Marge, sitting there lovey-dovey. Where're the three little bears? Boardroom?"

Marge snapped her chewing gum. "Where else? Meetings, meetings. When any work gets done around here beats me."

Miss Kling knocked gently on the door of the boardroom and opened it almost instantly. "Boss wants to see you, gentlemen."

The three men pulled together their papers and walked down the heavily carpeted hall, with Miss Kling following politely behind. "You can go right in," she said.

As they entered, Mr. Otis indicated by a wave of his hand that they were to be seated. Florence West leaned forward in her chair. "Anything else from me, Mr. Otis?" she asked.

"I think it might be appropriate for you to stay, Florence. We don't have secrets from Miss West, do we, gentlemen?"

Florence turned her head and permitted a half smile to escape her lips as she gazed at the three men. Bart had seated himself in his usual slouched manner as though he were part of the big wing chair. Ted Wayne was relaxed on the sofa, idly thumbing through a book left on the end table. Hop was sitting in the hard-backed little Victorian chair, caressing his pillbox.

Mr. Otis picked up the document an his desk. "As you know, gentlemen, I believe in planning. This document written two years ago and—" he added turning toward Florence, "Miss West well remembers the work we put into it—is ready to be put into effect."

Hop gripped his box tightly. Bart frowned thoughtfully. Ted used the toe of his shoe to straighten the magazines on the coffee table before him.

"This paper is entitled MEMORANDUM FOR THE REORGANIZATION OF EXECUTIVE RESPONSIBILITY. Now I'd like to detail its conclusions."

There was a prolonged silence.

Suddenly Ted leaned forward. "Excuse me for interrupting, Mr. Otis, but do you mind if I say something?"

The old man smiled. "Not at all, Ted." He gazed hard at the broad shoulders of the younger man. In his heart he was certain that, given half a chance, Ted Wayne would drive him straight into retirement.

Ted looked at Bart, then at Hop. "Don't we want to say something now? First?"

Bart rubbed his chin thoughtfully. Mr. Otis's voice cut through. "What do you want to say, Ted?"

Ted stared at Otis. This was the moment and both men knew it. Whatever was to be said had to be said as Ted put it—now, and first. Hop broke the silence. "Ted," he said, "I do think it's proper that we allow Mr. Otis the courtesy of being heard first. After all, it's his meeting."

"Thank you, Hop. If you don't mind, Ted, I'll proceed."

Ted Wayne stood up, sucking in his breath and tightening his belt one notch. He walked over to the window where he could observe Mr. Otis. One day, he thought, one lousy little day. You talk, talk, talk plans, and then one lousy day he springs his. Before yours is ready. Before it's solid. Unbreakable. Unshakable. Ted turned and looked at Hop, then at Bart. "Go ahead, Mr. Otis. Sorry I interrupted." He sat down on the window ledge.

"Except for Tony Gordon who is a fixture at O&M, you three are the main cogs in the company, and I feel the time has arrived to give full recognition to your talents and contributions. I have decided, therefore, to create the new post of chairman of the board, which I will occupy for at least a brief period, primarily to effect a smooth transition of authority from myself to a new president. Tony, of course, as everyone at O&M knows, is our only senior executive vice president, and has made it clear to me and to everyone else, you three included, that he wants no further responsibilities."

Mr. Otis smiled and glanced at the three men. Hop was an image of frozen correctness. Ted was the picture of a man about to be angry. Bart had the look of a brooding scholar.

"I have not been unaware of your interest in setting up a new management—you would have been derelict if you had not also speculated on its form or need. Of course, you have to have a plan. I have observed you three under all kinds of pressure as I observe you now. All three of you cannot be president, but as the major stockholder, I can designate one of you—unless, of course, any one of you shares the belief that it should be someone other than one of you. Is there any such doubt? Hop," he gestured, raising his hand, "any other candidate?"

Hop shook his head.

"Ted?"

"Mr. Otis, he would have been in this room if you felt it desirable."

Mr. Otis smiled. "Bart?"

Bart slowly seemed to emerge from the depths of the chair.

"Mr. Otis," he said in a voice that seemed to be strangulated whisper, "you are the only one capable of making this kind of judgment."

"Very well. I feel that we need a president of vigor and mental courage, a man who can balance differences of opinion, a man who can exercise judgment based on a storehouse of experience and innate wisdom. And a man who can be backed up by a team. You three are the team. Tony Gordon, of course, stays in place.

"Therefore, as president, I name you, Bart. As executive vice president, William T. Hopper. As executive vice president, you, Ted. I want to congratulate each of you."

The three men sat in silence. Mr. Otis rose from his chair.

"I know this has been something of a surprise," he said, gripping each of the men by hand. "I'm having a little lunch set up in the dining room, and after you've had a few moments to talk about this, I wish you'd all join me."

He strode out of the room followed by Miss West.

Bart shifted uneasily in his big chair. "Got an aspirin in that pillbox, Hop?" he asked reaching out a hand.

Hop flipped open the box. "Sure, Bart. The large white one," he said, passing over the pillbox. Then, drawing a deep breath, he said, "Well, it's all done, and I for one am damned. Congratulations, Bart."

"Thanks, Hop," Bart said with a friendly smile, "and congratulations are due you."

Bart glanced over at the powerful figure of Ted Wayne staring impassively across at the chair so recently vacated by Mr. Otis.

"Ted?" Bart said as though his acknowledgment of the other would ease the change.

Ted turned to face the other two. "The smart old bastard went and did it all right, like you said, Hop, and he managed to pull every nerve and hair he could grab in doing it. We're washed up. Finished."

"Now isn't that a little bit of an odd reaction just after he's announced his retirement and put Bart in as president?"

"Apparently you didn't get to listen very deeply, Hop, which doesn't surprise me. Mr. Otis didn't change anything except a bunch of titles, and he didn't say he was resigning or retiring."

"I thought I heard him say that Bart was the new president. *Our* new president," Hop added. "And I must say I'm pleased for Bart. And I'm pleased, for that matter, for myself. Even in our own plans—"

"What do you mean 'our own plans,' Hop?" Ted snapped. "What plans? We had a chance here and you went and blew the whole goddamn idea with your jellyfish talk that this was his meeting and we had to hear him *first.* We heard him first and look what happened?"

Hop smiled. "Ted, it wouldn't be that you were suffering a little bit of acid stomach reaction? We couldn't all be president. And I think we're being quite a bit ungracious when we don't give Bart the feeling that we're one hundred percent behind him."

Ted carefully placed his fingers in a cathedral shape pondering each of the others, "Okay, so Bart's president. But you forget one little matter. He's Mr. Otis's president."

"There are many roads to Rome, Ted. We had one and Mr. Otis had one, and we both came out with what we wanted," Bart said quietly. "A new organization."

"The same old fertilizer if you want my candid opinion, Bart. I wanted every key executive in this place to have a word. Bart has the list. Where do they come off?"

Hop smiled indulgently. "Are you saying that they won't be happy to find they have a new president?"

"I'm saying that maybe they would have had their own ideas. And I'm not at all sure that Bart would have been their choice. Or me. They could have chosen someone else."

"I gather that you do not think they would have chosen me," Bart said, a note of asperity in his voice.

"Maybe. Maybe not. Maybe Hop on the grounds of seniority, perhaps." Ted turned to face Hopper. "I don't think you'd have made it, Hop, on any other grounds. And I don't think you're going to be the leader of a referendum. I know your kind of guts, Hop. Great with clients. Great with the 'on the one hand and on the other hand' act. But you tell Mr. Otis to stuff his clever little MEMORANDUM FOR THE REORGANIZATION OF EXECUTIVE RESPONSIBILITY straight up little Miss West's rear engine? Not a chance. Not you."

Hop stood up. "I think, Ted," he said icily, "that I've had enough of your snide lectures. Everything has to go your way. If it doesn't, you voice your spleen on everyone in sight. If Mr. Otis had appointed you president, or, for that matter, made you the number two man instead of me, I would have congratulated you immediately instead of all this postmortem whining."

Ted smiled. "Of course you would have, Hop. But you two know I never cared whether I was president. I only wanted Otis out so that things would change. If he had named me president or senior executive vice president you're absolutely right—you would have been clinging to the side of the ship just to stay afloat. Now I suggest that you run along to the dining room. Mr. Otis is waiting. Run in and tell the old man how smart he was to pick Bart and how you pledge your life, your fortune, and your sacred honor to support him. Run along, Hop."

Hop strode to the door, glanced at the other two, and walked out.

Bart stretched himself as though it were his turn to prepare for a different kind of thrust.

"He means well, Ted."

"If he heard you say that he'd go home and cry. Hop may be a weakling, but he knows the score when he hears it and you just put the kiss of death on him."

Bart's fingers were now tightly clasped. "Ted, we've got to go in in a few moments. Let's talk a bit first. I'm sorry that it didn't work out precisely the way we were talking. But just as you say, it never got a chance. Hop did put his foot into it when he told Mr. Otis that it was his meeting."

"You didn't stop him either, Bart."

"I just didn't know the old man was going to go that far. None of us did," Bart pleaded.

"That's precisely why I didn't want him to have the chance to talk at all. You helped give him that chance, Bart, by remaining still."

Bart moved over to Ted and put a hand on his shoulder. "It's too late to talk about what any of us should have done. 'There's a tide in men's affairs.' "

"You talk a pretty streak, Bart, which is probably one reason you charm the old man. But look, you and I know. *We* know," Ted emphasized.

It was Bart's turn to draw away and pull himself erect as though sentence were about to be pronounced.

"Would you mind clarifying for me what *we* know?"

"We both know you're cut from leftover cloth," he said bluntly. "We know that your principles are designed to have great tensile strength so that you can bend to the right and to the left. We both know that you're an intellectual vacuum surrounded by the wisdom of others, dead and living, whom you quote brilliantly and too frequently. Period."

"Will you tell me why in heaven's name, if you had such a low opinion of me, and I presume of Hop, too, you teamed up with us?"

Ted chuckled. "That's easy, Bart. Because you were the best around. And because I knew it, had to be with the two of you or not at all. Now with your new chairman, you are three again. And if I were you, I wouldn't keep him waiting too long either. He's not used to presidents cooling his soup."

"You're a goddamn son of a bitch!"

"First true reaction you've had all day, Bart. Now, if you don't mind I want to pick up my hat and on the way out pat Florence West's well-tailored tail and blow."

"And what does that mean?"

"It means that you can send my last check to my home address. I'll be in Bermuda this afternoon sweating all of you out of my bloodstream. Goodbye, Bart, and good luck."

Bart Hills watched the towering figure of Ted Wayne stride out of the office. He heard the sharp intake of breath from Florence as Ted passed her. He had mixed emotions. Ted had been his only real competition; everyone with a half a brain knew that. Ted was a combination of strength, sagacity and knowledge. And Bart knew he would miss him. He did not like being the bearer of the news that Ted Wayne had resigned.

● ● ●

Bart had been right. Mr. Otis had registered strong irritation that Ted had resigned so abruptly. He had reminded Bart that he had always judged the three top executives as a single, powerful unit. He had been, he'd said, surprised to find that his estimate had been wrong.

But in the privacy of his own office Otis had a different view—and he exposed those views to Florence. As time had passed he knew for certain how badly Ted was missed. His drive and his courage were the ingredients that made him the unique person he'd been—even a threat to his own deep-seated desire to stay on top. He knew that now that Bart had come face to face with the realities of running the company he felt exposed and vulnerable. The only real threat to Bart was Hopper. It wasn't that Hop wasn't bright, or lacked shrewdness. Mr. Otis knew, too, that he was cunning. And it had not escaped him that Hop had bypassed Bart on more than one occasion, using as his pretext the pressure of time and the need for decision that only, he, Otis, as chief executive officer, could provide.

Bart had had similar thoughts. He stretched himself across his reclining chair. His wife had given it to him so that he could meditate—at least five minutes each morning and afternoon. Ten minutes a day isn't too long, she'd reminded him, when Einstein had devoted a lifetime to it.

And so he meditated and the decision formed in his mind. Hopper was no Ted Wayne—but he was only a step from the throne and he wasn't afraid to run around him; Hopper's presence was, in fact, a threat to his own security and title. He knew there was no one else he himself would project into the spotlight—not until he had the company firmly in hand, and that meant the actual retirement of James H. Otis himself, now some eleven months away. Anything could happen in eleven months and there was no sense in gambling. Not now. Not without Ted on deck. It was there to see and waiting to be done: Hopper would have to go.

Mr. Otis had been concerned in expressing his reactions to Bart's decision. "You feel this is a necessary recommendation?"

Bart took his customary time in replying to Mr. Otis's questions and observations. "Yes, and the most difficult decision I've ever made. Hop has so many assets, so many virtues."

"But none sufficiently valid to induce you to hold him," Mr. Otis said quietly.

"No single one that makes him clearly indispensable, not that any one of us is, I hasten to say," Bart added, slowly, measuring his words. "I think he's given his best, and in today's whirling world he simply can't move fast enough—his best just isn't good enough."

"When are you going to tell him?"

Bart sighed. It was over and he'd won. The telling would be painful, but it would be easy now

"Tonight."

He returned to his office pleased with the way it had gone. The old man hadn't been too surprised and hadn't made any real issue. Bart invited Hopper to have a cocktail with him in the Tower Restaurant above the office. When they had been shown to a table, Hop said, matter of factly, "Saw you huddled with the old man today. Any problems?"

Bart sipped his whiskey sour. "No—no problems that we can't explore and solve."

Hop frowned. "That's pretty enigmatic. Sounds like the kind of opening Ted used to make just before he belted you. Wonder what Ted is up to now?" he asked cheerfully.

"Paris, last I heard."

"He'll be big on both banks. Mind if I have another? You're a sipper, but I'm afraid I'm a drinker."

Bart was staring through Hopper now, adding him up. He has three kids, Bart thought, all past school age or the last one about to get through. His home must be paid for, at least it should be. Hopper had had twenty-five good years to sock something away. But you never knew really. The whole question now was how to tell him. Straight out, or try to lead him into it by a little circumlocution. So that he would recognize the message himself without requiring too much spelling it out.

"Ted probably is having what my kids call a ball all right. Maybe he did the right thing after all."

"How do you mean?" Hop said, lifting his second glass in a silent toast.

"Having the courage of his convictions. Acting on them."

"I'd say he was irresponsible. A damned impulsive gesture. And look what it's done for him," he said disparagingly. "He's probably in some dive in Pigalle and we're up here," Hop said indicating the whole expanse of New York spread out like a jeweled rug far below them.

"He may come back refreshed. People have a way of doing that with a few months on the loose. They get a new point of view—have a whole new approach. To life. To business even."

"You seem to have a barrelful of medals for Ted Wayne tonight," Hop said. Bart noticed that Hop had started drumming on the table with his fingers. "You miss him?"

Bart continued to focus on the nervous beat of the fingers approvingly. A little bell, he was sure, had begun to ring in Hopper's head.

"Sometimes."

"Why?" Hop demanded.

"I'll have another drink, too, if you don't mind." He caught the eye of his waitress and raised his glass. "One more of these, please?" Then turning toward Hop he said, "Want another?"

"Not yet, thanks." The waitress left. "Now, what about my question. Why do you miss Ted?"

"I hadn't thought of him really for some time—but I guess he's actually been on my mind." Bart pushed his chair back. This could be the moment, he thought, the way to tell Hop. He would do it by telling him why he missed Ted. "Well, I guess it's a combination of things, manners, attitudes and all of that. Imagination, maybe. Follow up, to be sure. Drive. And awareness. He was in tune with the times—he had a kind of inner sense that separated him from most people. He comes closest to being another Tony Gordon. A younger version, of course. We need that kind of restless energy. I guess that's why I miss him."

Hop looked across at Bart uneasily. "You trying to say something?" Bart remained quiet. Hop persisted. "You are trying to say something," he said. His face appeared tense, the muscles in his jaw were beating rapidly as he clenched his teeth. Bart let the silence lengthen. "Bart, I know you pretty well and you know me." Hop hesitated.

"Go on," Bart said.

"You just don't start praising that, that," he fumbled, looking for the right word, "that deserter Ted Wayne clear out of the blue without some reason. Everything you do has to have a reason."

Bart removed his glasses and began to wipe them. He could only see a blur before him and he felt the final thrust would be easier this way. "It has a reason, Hop. I have to compliment you. You're a discerning fellow."

"To hell with the compliments. What's the reason?" Hop asked as Bart peered through his glasses to see if any fogginess remained. "You think Ted would have been better than me, is that it?"

Bart smiled approvingly. He would now deliver the final thrust. "He probably was better than both of us."

"Meaning?"

"Well, we can't take him hack . . ." Bart let the message hang in the softness of the room.

"Are you by any chance trying to tell me that you want to get somebody else in? To replace me?" Hop whispered as though the words were unbelievable.

"I said you were a discerning fellow, Hop, and now you go and prove it."

Hop's hands suddenly stopped drumming and tightened up. They had become hard and ominous looking but Bart knew it was reflex only. "Discerning hell. I'm a dumb bastard, that's what I am. How much time are you giving me?"

Bart smiled easily."You should get away, Hop."

"Like Ted."

"Not at all. You've earned it. Take time. And we'll do everything right in any event. That's always been policy. We'll just say you're going on vacation and we'll work out the kind of announcement you'd approve."

"What happened to us, Bart? You. Me. Ted. We had it made six months ago. How do you explain it?"

Bart called for the check. "Explanations are never satisfactory, Hop. You know that there isn't one that would ever satisfy you. You also know without my saying it that you can count on me to help in any way I can. We can still be friends, I hope." Then to ease his own position, he added, "Mr. Otis hopes you'll feel that way."

Hop tapped his silk handkerchief. "So, Mr. Otis knows. Well, of course, you wouldn't make a move like this on your own." Hop stood up. "Thanks, Bart. I may have to call on you. I'll stop by in the morning and we can make the arrangements."

"Can I drop you off anywhere?"

"No thanks. I was going to stay at the club, but I think in view of this news, I'd better call Margaret and go home."

The next morning Bart had advised Mr. Otis of the manner in which Hop had taken the news. "He didn't appear angry, Bart?"

"No—he seemed to figure it out himself."

""I see," Mr. Otis said. "I don't like to have anyone leave us angry. How much time did you give him?"

"I told him to take his time—a couple of months if necessary."

"That's fine. You did it right. But it's better if he does it fast. These things get out no matter how hard you try to conceal them."

● ● ●

Hop hadn't moved fast. He seemed to slip into a semi-hypnotic state, and scarcely a day went by without his showing up, neat, tidy, resplendently proper, useless and unwanted. "Just want to help out in the transition of my accounts," he'd told Mr. Otis on passing him in the hall.

Mr. Otis had made no secret of his irritation about Hop's presence. Finally, he summoned Bart to his office.

"Bart, on thinking things over, I don't think this Hopper business was handled too well."

Bart shifted uneasily in his seat. "It has dragged, I'll admit."

"Terminate it," Mr. Otis said sharply.

"Terminate?" Bart repeated, taken aback.

"He's to leave tonight and not return. We'll ship his personal things out to his home. That's all I want to say. Now if you'll excuse me, I'm busy." He flipped on his intercom. "Miss West, will you come in, please?"

Bart felt a sudden urge to rebel. He resented the brevity of the order. He resented being dismissed like an office boy. But he knew now that in only eight more months, Mr. Otis would retire. The company would buy him out and he would be president, in fact, as well as in name. Then the three of them, Wayne, Hopper and Otis could burn in hell itself.

Bart thought everything through carefully. Mr. Otis would bear gingerbread handling, but he could be handled; Bart had always felt he had measured his approach with just the right mixture of recognition of authority and the need occasionally to demonstrate a show of independence. Team play, judgment based on experience, courage based on fresh thinking—those were the foundations on which Mr. Otis had built his reputation.

Bart was shrewd enough to handle Florence West carefully; he had even gone to the point of intimating that her future would be secure with him in all the same respects as it had been with Mr. Otis. It had seemed that the whole plan had a biblical tone to it; he would inherit the kingdom, everything and everyone in it.

Bart had studied others in the company and had mapped out a new organization to follow the old the moment when the old had retired. He had not presumed to lay it all out for Mr. Otis; he had felt certain Mr. Otis, who planned everything so precisely, would have his own plan to show and to bequeath. And so the days passed, and as each day passed, Bart found himself wishing he had the thinking of Ted Wayne and even the familiar, if ineffectual, counsel that Hop could offer.

Mr. Otis, too, was waiting. As he did, customarily, on each day, as he arrived at his desk, he drew a slashing line across the calendar page of the preceding day. It was a ritual, one that he secretly hated but was powerless to abandon. He was fond of saying extravagant things—he had told Florence, the night before, that he visualized another world for them some day in some new guise, that he wanted to spend the days ahead in her company—"to the very last beat of time, to the very final edge of space," he had put it. Florence brought in a file as he waited, saying nothing, only smiling that smile lovers kept for themselves in privacy.

"To the very last beat," she said, as if reading his mind.

Last night was still on her mind, too. They had finished dinner, finished the easy banter that shifted from office politics to the latest, serious critical success on Broadway or Off Broadway that might be worth a visit before it closed for lack of a popular audience. His wife never came up, nor bills whether for clothes or doctors or household items, or money itself: they lived in a realm unsullied by the everyday. Once Florence had been too insecure to think of bringing any of those into their relationship: later she valued their freedom from all the usual mundane concerns, and the blend of passion with periods of absence in which she was free to pursue her own concerns with no one to judge or gainsay her. Maybe, if she had wanted children, this relationship would have collapsed years ago, but that had never been her desire. Without the title or office she was at the center of things with James Hornwell Otis at O&M, and she knew if not quite in the center—no one was there except himself—she was certainly within his heart, somewhere.

So when he suddenly opened the door to a future together, she was surprised, and a little taken aback. He was in the armchair, talking freely, with herself seated on the floor, leaning back. Her satin gown had opened, baring a length of leg and thigh she made no effort to hide, while his hands played with her hair, still up, or idly rubbed her neck.

"What do you mean, James?" she asked, letting her head lie back, keeping as cool as she could.

"I mean us, together."

"How lovely that would be. Mmmm, don't stop," she added, as his hands hesitated a moment on her neck. "How together?"

"Your skin is so smooth, even now, as if you were still in your twenties."

She twisted around and rose to her knees, putting her arms around him.

"Flattery will get you everything." Her decolletage was held together by a hand-tied bow. He pulled it free and slowly and confidently ran his hands over her breasts.

"You are still in your twenties." She kissed him, and let

those practiced hands explore her breasts' smoothness, lightly play with their dark nipples until they rose, sensitive—then she pressed against him.

"James," she whispered in his ear, sitting in his lap, letting him slide the gown to her waist. "When will we have this time together?"

"You'll see . . . there will be time enough, and world."

"Will I see it in this world, this time, this place?" But his hand running up her thigh made her gasp.

"Trust me," was all he answered. Her gown slid to the floor. She stared into his eyes, and raised her arms, knowing how he liked to see her breasts rise, tautly, as she freed her hair and let it cover both of them as she kissed him, again. He had said more than ever before, even if it was all poetry: he would say no more, she knew, concentrating now on playing with her on his lap, his tweeds rubbing against her skin, until he couldn't stand the tension any more and led her into the bedroom. There he was a James Hornwell Otis none of his associates could guess: patient, yes, but finally impassioned, demandingly masculine, overtly dominating.

They said no more, then. And now? He only smiled at her as she walked back out.

This gray morning James Hornwell Otis was examining his world. For a long time he had successfully ignored the incontestable facts of life; although he practiced moderation, he consciously closed certain doors in his own mind. Behind those doors lay questions that tore at his peace, questions that had empty silences for answers. He would not accept any recognition of sterility in his mind, of impotency in his life stream. He refused to visualize himself stripped of power, prestige, and a place that commanded respect. Long ago he knew how he would protect himself, long before Ted Wayne, William Hopper and Barton Hills had their first open talk of the need for change. Long ago he'd won over the formidable Tony Gordon, given him his sphere of authority. Gordon had accepted the arrangement and would never challenge Otis. Wayne was different. He'd known Wayne was the real threat. He'd known Hop was expendable. And now he would deal with Bart.

As Bart entered the office the older man waved him to a chair in his familiar, easy way. Both men seemed to sense that the end of the waiting was at hand. Mr. Otis believed in moving rapidly to the point when his own directions were clearly etched in his mind.

"Bart, in three months—a day or two shy of three months—I'll be sixty-five."

Bart nodded thoughtfully. He would try not to make any comment until Mr. Otis had made his final statement. His fingers were moist, though, and he did not like experiencing a clammy sensation, and he was surprised, too, by his inner nervousness.

"I believe you're forty-six, Bart."

"Forty-five, sir."

Mr. Otis smiled. "A nice age. And a lot of time ahead to do things. All kinds of things."

Bart shifted uneasily. He hoped Mr. Otis wasn't going to reminisce; he detested conversations in which older men were constantly parading their memories, each one seeming to precipitate other incidents of men and events long since forgotten—anecdotes of meaningless purpose.

"Now that I'm approaching sixty-five, I've come to an important decision, Bart, and I think you should know about it. I dictated a memorandum this morning to Miss West and it will be sent to the organization tonight."

Bart measured Mr. Otis carefully. He recalled seeing Florence earlier in the day. He recalled that he had complimented her on her dress. He recalled her looking at him and his saying, "You have the enigmatic look of the Mona Lisa," and her reply, "That is the secret weapon all women try to acquire." She had just stepped out of Mr. Otis's office and had been moving swiftly to her computer. Now that he recalled her, there was a note of urgency in her manner. Bart stared straight ahead into Mr. Otis's eyes, trying to fathom his words before they escaped his lips.

"To run this company, a man must have three assets: judgment, courage and a sense of team importance. These three are the pillars and the roof of the whole structure. Take one away and the whole structure disintegrates." He paused. "Bart," he said, stabbing out each word, "you have two of these pillars. Two only."

Bart felt the harsh blow of the words; in that instant he saw the collapse of all of his efforts, perhaps the futility of the effort in the first place. Now his eyes continued to stare straight ahead at Mr. Otis, but they were suddenly lifeless, as though all vision had abruptly ceased.

He heard Mr. Otis talking. "You're only forty-five and you've got years of good living ahead. I've taken careful consideration of your future into the announcement now going to the office and to the press. I'm your friend—you know that—and I'm going to help you in every way I can."

In every way but one, Bart knew. He had a sudden impulse to topple Mr. Otis out of his chair, but he knew he wouldn't. He was no Ted Wayne. He wouldn't toady either. He was no Hop. He was like them only in one way. He was out. It was all too clear now; Barton Hills wouldn't fight it; he *couldn't* fight it. Mr. Otis had beaten the three of them.

If he had backed Ted, it wouldn't have happened. But it was over. The old man had figured it out himself. He must have known Ted would quit; he must have known Hop was useless; he must have known Bart could be handled.

"Take a vacation," he heard Mr. Otis saying, "it will all work out fine. You have a lot to offer. I'll have to stay on here until I find I'm not truly needed." He offered his hand to Bart.

Bart automatically took Mr. Otis's hand. His own felt weak in the grip of the other. "Just one question, Mr. Otis."

"Of course."

"Did you know Ted Wayne would quit?"

Mr. Otis smiled. In that smile Bart saw the pitiless and pitiful human that summed up James Hornwell Otis. "There was never any doubt of it. But I don't think speculation on the past is helpful in matters of this kind."

Mr. Otis watched Bart shuffle out. He thought perhaps Bart could see it clearly now, but that was always a vision of the victim—to see it all very clearly when it was too late.

He buzzed for Miss West. "Florence," he said, "I want to set things right for the future. I've been watching three men who could contribute a lot to the company during the next five years. I think it's time to promote Benson, Chase, and Farrington. Three young men with good records. Three new senior vice presidents."

Florence smiled and her smile seemed to say, "And again, there were three."

FAIR-WEATHER FRIENDS

HENDRIK TAYLOR, WHO'D BEEN THE coxswain of a championship crew at Harvard, and who'd come from a wealthy Newport family, was someone destined to move into the lofty offices of Otis & Meade. In a special business course at Harvard where top industrial and corporate leaders posed questions to the class, Hendrik Taylor had impressed James Hornwell Otis, who'd been a guest lecturer at the university and who'd presented an advertising problem to which Taylor responded on paper with unusual insights. Otis had always liked Ivy Leaguers and his immediate impression was that Taylor would be an excellent recruit.

Taylor was rather short, with slicked-down black hair and piercing blue eyes. Everyone knew he was a feisty opponent, but he was shrewd enough never to arouse hostility; this attitude of unswerving loyalty to O&M was adopted by those who worked with him and above him, because it was felt very early on that he was an Otis favorite.

Taylor had style, not only in the manner in which he conducted himself, for he spoke with authority backed up with facts. He compensated for his shortness by being the best-dressed man in the department; some would say he was even dapper. He came to the office sporting a derby and a tan tailored military overcoat which fitted him perfectly. The fact that no one else in all of Manhattan was wearing derbies never deterred him; in fact, he knew that people would talk about his expensive and eclectic wardrobe. He had a determined manner, but was always courteous to the losers who later found it profitable to become part of the Taylor team.

Taylor's bulldog manner, jaw jutting out, his capacity to marshal facts on programs and media—for he had a remarkable photographic memory—made him an instant success within the agency and with its top clients. Those colleagues who would not accommodate themselves to his manners, courtly but devastating in debates, gifted him with a small Boston bulldog, whose face bore a curious, even an amusing, resemblance to Taylor's. Taylor, ever courteous, accepted the gift as sincere, not by expressing his thanks, but by petting the dog with what turned out to be quickly enough, mock affection. Those who had given him the dog told him its name was Major. Taylor nodded with a smile, well aware of the not too subtle reference to his own love for things of a military nature, including his great coat, but also the sword of his great grandfather which was conspicuously displayed in a glass case on the ledge of an office window. His rise in the TV department, headed by longtime vice president in charge, Jack Hasting, a tall and lean onetime Ivy Leaguer from Dartmouth, and a favorite as well with James Hornwell Otis, had resulted in a new symbolic status: an office with two windows looking down on Madison Avenue. He thanked the small group who'd made the presentation; his response the next day was to lead a French poodle, standard size, into his office. Major was gone; General was the poodle's name.

Young Steven Lane, who'd worked on a show which Taylor supervised, gradually became a Taylor favorite. Lane himself, with his own formidable talent—for he, too, had a prodigious memory—impressed Taylor. When a word or two of praise escaped Taylor's lips—and that did not occur with frequent regularity—words such as, "Well done, Lane," or "You attacked the problem very well," the praise almost always conveyed in a brisk military fashion, the recipient felt high praise from a man who in fact rivaled Jack Hasting himself; Taylor had quickly become Hasting's second in command, a decision enthusiastically approved by Mr. Otis.

Lane, who'd handled a demanding client with quiet persuasion was commended by Taylor and invited for cocktails at Taylor's well decorated upper East Side apartment, Taylor's way of rewarding supporters who exhibited real accomplishments. An elderly Japanese butler opened the door to admit Lane, leading him into Taylor's study. Steve studied its ornate bookcase, its wooden edges decorated with superbly carved Union battle flags and various types of Union cannons. His eyes were drawn to a glass-enclosed box placed on top of the bookcase which contained a hand-carved wooden frieze depicting a hurtling horse-drawn caisson: the horse, nostrils flaring, a Union soldier leaning forward on the caisson whipping him, the caisson followed by a column of racing soldiers charging a distant hill. There were also two pedestals on which authentic Rodin bronzes rested, and a mix of paintings on one wall ranging from a

Lee clown, to a small Hopper with its theme of loneliness and detachment, to a glowing colorful Cortez depicting a nineteenth-century Parisian street scene.

Entering the room, Taylor observed Steve Lane with pleasure as he watched him touching the glass case as though he could finger the spirited horse. Taylor said, "Steve, that's an authentic scene of a battle in which my great-grandfather led a charge against a Confederate strong point. It's been in the family for years. The old man is there," Taylor said, pointing to a soldier at the forefront beckoning his troops to follow. The butler, who'd followed a few steps behind Taylor, served drinks. In a few moments Steve saw a side of Taylor, the imperturbable television leader, which was never visible at the O&M offices. Taylor simply could not hold his liquor, and in a few minutes his speech was characterized by a slurring of his words. He approached Lane, one hand already slightly trembling from the effect of the drink, and placed a finger under Steve's stiff white collar. "No one at O&M wears this kind of collar except Mr. Otis and me." He poured himself another drink, then beckoned Steve to follow him. Taylor led Steve Lane into his bedroom past a four-poster bed and opened a closet. He pointed to a row of neatly hung suits . "And you don't wear blue striped suits, gray striped flannel suits, grays and blues, and blazers and slacks. "Got it?" he said, jaw jutting out, eyes riveted on Steve.

Steve was disconcerted by the strange demands made by Taylor, but he managed a conciliatory smile. "Hendrik, I've worn this kind of collar ever since I went to Penn."

"Not anymore you do."

Steve Lane shrugged his shoulders in a manner that Taylor construed as compliance. "Just remember, one day

I'll be in charge of the whole department, soon as Hasting departs."

Steve was surprised when Hasting had fallen from favor with Otis. "How soon is soon?" Lane ventured.

"Soon?" Taylor replied with an enigmatic smile, "Soon could be tomorrow, the week after, a year from now. Got it?"

He did now. He would be careful around Taylor.

● ● ●

But Taylor's prediction failed to materialize the next day, the next week, or the next year. Otis had, in fact, promoted Hasting to a permanent seat on the agency's prestigious plans board, a goal to which Taylor had always aspired. That promotion prompted Taylor, by now considered to be one of the sharpest of program executives, to seek another post, the top programming at Continental Broadcasting which had just opened up. Its program chief had resigned abruptly, although the trade knew that Charles Connally, the urbane chairman of Continental, had actually forced some of the shows on his program chief and had then, as was common practice with all network CEOs, boldly announced the latter as a failed executive. Steve realized it would be a move into a precarious realm for Taylor, as far as job security went, but also that it would make him one of the handful of gatekeepers in the industry, a man with the power to shape the taste and fantasies of a nation.

Taylor made an appointment to see James Otis. "I owe you a lot, Mr. Otis," Taylor said, "but I've come to the conclusion that it's time for me to make a change."

"Oh?" Otis replied, trying to conceal his surprise. "Are you certain, Hendrik? Are you unhappy?"

Taylor repeated with his familiar quick way of smiling, baring his teeth for an instant, giving him a moment to set forth his reason for leaving O&M. "Perhaps. But not in my association with you."

Otis nodded, "Then what is it?"

"Jack Hasting's done a brilliant job in the television department and I'd thought, some time ago, from conversations I'd had with him as his chief lieutenant, that he would become a partner in some other agency."

"What makes you think he'd do that?"

"It's common knowledge that he wants to be an owner, not a hired hand, as generous as you've been in promoting him to the plans board, new title and so on."

"And so you feel you have to resign," Otis said.

"Regrettably, yes. I think the trade has been wrong about Jack's goals and, as I see it, I've reached the ceiling of the job I hold."

"You're not being impatient?"

Taylor studied Otis's disarming face. "Not at all. Realistic is what it boils down to. I've had an offer from Continental—Charles Connally, its president."

"I see," Otis replied, and then, eyes focusing on his coffered ceiling, added, "you don't want to wait on whether Mr. Hasting might want to leave us one day. Is that it?"

Taylor nodded. "That's it, to use your words. I know that Charles Connally is no James Hornwell Otis, but he comes as close as any top officer I know."

Otis smiled pleasantly. "Hendrik, you've done a fine job here, brought up some bright talented men, Steve Lane for example."

"I've always thought of him as one of my protégés, very smart, very knowledgeable."

"Well," Otis said, reaching out a hand across the desk as Taylor took it, "we'll be sorry to see you leave. And you're right about your protégé, you've trained him very well." Otis stood up and walked Taylor to the door. "Good luck, Hendrik," he said, patting Taylor on the back.

Taylor, seated in his resplendent study, was shocked the next day when he discovered that Jack Hasting had already resigned to take a partnership in another agency. What shocked Taylor even more was his sickening awareness that Mr. Otis had known Hasting was leaving, but had chosen not to reveal it, never really giving Taylor a final choice. Hasting was gone and Steve Lane, Taylor's onetime protégé, was in his place. He liked Steve, but he recoiled at the unpleasant thoughts he now nurtured about Mr. Otis. Would Otis have given him Hasting's job if he, Taylor, had not resigned? Or would he have jumped Lane over him?

Taylor's butler appeared on schedule handing Taylor his usual drink and then quickly shuffling off. Taylor drank it and set the glass on a marble-topped table, focusing his eyes on his great grandfather leading his soldiers to battle. There was a winner, he mused, and he was a loser outsmarted, even humiliated by a man whom he'd come not only to respect, but to love. "Otis, you damned confederate," he muttered to himself as he rang for another drink. He looked again at the frieze. "You didn't really want me, you just let me go," he mumbled to himself tossing down the drink. "Bastard. You bastard. Bastard!" he said, shouting out the derisive word louder each time as his head slumped to his chest, tears suddenly flooding his eyes. "Bastard," he repeated softly, shaking his head in disbelief as he reviewed every nuance of his final fateful conversation with Mr. Otis.

His butler appeared with another drink. Taylor gnashed

his teeth and lifted the glass toward the butler. "Sumo," he said, "you know what?" The butler stood at attention, Taylor's words now beginning to slur. "We'll show them. All of them. Mr. Otis, Steve Lane—got it?" he said looking at Sumo. The butler nodded in his familiar, docile manner.

"Bastards, all of them," Taylor repeated, his eyes closed, "We'll show them. Wait and see."

Taylor's success at Continental was a foregone conclusion; he knew every nuance of the business, was comfortable dealing with creative people, and pleased that they, in turn, felt the same for him, since he had a penchant for writing and selling short stories from time to time to top magazines. Most importantly, he felt certain that he had Charles Connally's confidence; Connally did, indeed, like Taylor and Taylor was a frequent guest at Connally's sprawling Darien estate.

When the opportunity arose—and it did with some regularity—Taylor very carefully gave preference to some of O&M's Madison Avenue rivals. Tony Gordon, one of O&M's most senior executives in charge of all media and next to Otis in actual power, bristled at some of Taylor's decisions which clearly placed O&M at a disadvantage with important clients.

Gordon called him and pushed directly to his point. "Mr. Taylor," Tony said, a smile in his voice that concealed the real anger in his heart, an attribute which Taylor, on the other end of the line, could easily visualize, having experienced Gordon's sharp temper more than once. "Mr. Taylor," Tony repeated, a touch of sarcasm creeping into his tone, "am I getting a message that you're pulling a tent down over O&M? We wanted Thursday at nine as a time franchise and you damn well know it."

Taylor was a bit pleased at Gordon's discomfiture; he knew how clients at O&M counted on the agency's toughness, as well as its enormous power to deliver on its recommendations. "Tony, this was just one decision, and it had to be made. In fact, Mr. Connally was very supportive."

"It just so happens, Mr. Taylor," Tony replied coldly, "that this agency was very instrumental in backing Charlie for the job he's holding today. That's a friendly tip. Remember it the next time O&M comes calling. Calling, I repeat. Not crawling. And frankly, with you there after your stint here all of us, from Mr. Otis down, thought we could count on you."

"I appreciate that, Tony. But there are times when choices have to be made." Then he added, "The fact that I worked at O&M shouldn't imply that I still work for them."

"Balls!" Tony roared. "I've given you our position. There are times when we expect you to deliver."

"Tony," Taylor replied, after a pause, his voice also beginning to harden. "Like I just said, you seem to forget that I don't work at O&M anymore. Sorry about that. If I didn't give the same degree of loyalty to Charles Connally that I gave to Mr. Otis, I wouldn't be here. I've won his trust. I hope I'm not losing yours." Taylor heard the phone on the other end of the line slam down.That was Tony's answer. Taylor could picture Tony holding the phone. He'd seen it many times, Gordon clutching it as though it were a living thing. And killing it as he slammed it down. It wasn't that he rejoiced in Gordon's anger, he knew only too well O&M's power, but the networks were now in control and no one exercised it more vigorously than Connally himself. Hendrik Taylor had even had the instinct to clear his decision with Connally before transmitting it to Tony

Gordon and O&M. Times were changing; the agencies, all of them, small ones and the behemoths like O&M, would have to recognize their power was ebbing in some media areas. Especially network television.

A few nights later Taylor had cocktails with Jerry Moss, an agent who represented the fastest growing TV production company on the coast, United Productions Entertainment, thanks to its special relationship with Joe Gratton at Federal Broadcasting. Moss, a genial gray-haired man, who now only drank Perrier, was making his familiar pitch to Taylor. "You should have an agent, Hendrik. Think of it—shall we call it protection?"

"Protection?" Taylor asked with some surprise.

"Exactly. Guys in your position—I don't care how much they think the big man loves them—guys like you are on the varsity." Moss sipped some more of his water. "You're visible. Very."

"Varsity? You trying to remind me I was once a coxswain at Harvard?"

"A damned good one, too. But what I'm telling you is that once you make the varsity—you get another V letter. That one spells vulnerable, capital V."

Taylor, too, sipped his own drink slowly, well aware of his inability to remain sober if he gulped it down. "Jerry, are you trying to tell me something? I'm vulnerable—expendable—that it?"

Moss grinned. "What I'm telling you is that you need us. United Productions Entertainment. Look, it's no secret, we represented Joe Gratton in his deal at Federal. Paid off for him, too, sonny. We're still a talent agency, too. A complete package."

Taylor shook his head. "I don't think executives need

agents—they have lawyers. I have a lawyer who guides me. Roger Rubin."

"Good man. I know him. But lawyers, Hendrik, lawyers know the rules, terms, they can protect you legally." Moss waved to a waiter. "Let's eat something, Hendrik, okay?" Then turning without looking at the oncoming waiter, Moss said, "Menus, please."

"Right away, Mr. Moss," the waiter replied. Moss glanced up and smiled, "Well, if it isn't Little Joe Scibetta. How go things?"

The waiter, passing out the menus, bent down over Moss. "Great, well maybe not great, but good, very good. And thanks for the introduction, Mr. Moss."

Moss waved him away. "Wants to be a writer," he said turning back to Taylor. "Kid has some talent; he got me to read a script. And getting me to do that proves he has talent."

"Will he make it?"

Moss shrugged. "How in the hell do I know? Costs me nothing to be a nice guy, but if he gets on first base, well, then, who's to say? Sure, he could be a client. Hey, even hairdressers learn to produce, cab drivers become stand-up comics, the barber with a gift of gab becomes a radio host—I've seen it happen. That's why I get them on the way up. Always be nice to the juniors, that's what Sam Colman says. And he's the smartest man in the business."

"Next time he comes east, tell him to drop by."

"He'll tell you what I'm telling you. Get yourself an agent. If not us, then William Morris."

Taylor smiled. "Jerry, why are you so nice to me?"

Moss spread his arms. "Business, Hendrik, business. We keep in touch with everybody, the top, the bottom pressing to move up there. Everybody."

"And when we slip?" Taylor asked.

"You slip," Moss replied with a smile, "and the next day we're dealing with your successor. So what else is new?"

"The king is dead, that it?"

"That's why I'm giving you good advice. Get an agent; he has to protect you. That's a legal obligation."

"I'll remember that," Taylor said.

● ● ●

Two years passed and Taylor felt comfortable: his program selections were working; his relationship with Charles Connally was closer. Then Herb Seward, Connally's next in line, suddenly resigned because of poor health. Immediately, the trade papers began to speculate on who would succeed him as president of Continental.

Taylor's natural ambitions, however, outweighed his talent for survival in the executive jungle, for when it came time to find a new president for Continental, Mr. Connally brought in a new man he'd enticed from a rival network, Jim Bentley.

Taylor was astonished and angered. He felt his record as program chief, his building an array of successful shows, warranted his being elevated to the presidency. When the news broke, Jerry Moss happened to he in the building touching base with lots of juniors. He popped into Taylor's office. Taylor was seated at his desk, his head cupped in his hands.

"You heard the news, Jerry," Taylor said, his voice no longer vibrant with authority.

Moss sat down. "Like I told you, Hendrik, some time back—you remember?" Taylor nodded. "An agent, you should have had an agent. Agents pick up the scent; we might have stopped Bentley cold in his tracks."

Suddenly suspicious, Taylor asked, "Is Bentley one of your clients?"

"No, but it wasn't for lack of trying. Sam Colman made the pitch."

"He got the job without you or any other agent, that it?" Taylor countered.

"You hit it on target, sonny. But, you got to remember one thing. Your Mr. Connally always liked Bentley. You know he once worked here."

"I know."

"Old man Connally doesn't like to see his rivals clip him. He knew when Herb Seward suddenly resigned he had the right carrot."

Taylor sat up erect. "I'm going in to see Mr. Connally."

Moss raised a warning hand. "Don't fight it, Hendrik. Remember, Bentley's there. He's got the job you wanted and I'll agree one you deserved with your record. Trouble is you didn't see it coming, right?"

Taylor shrugged. "I knew Seward was ill. I'd heard it at a meeting, the big C."

"That's when you should have made your move, Hendrik," Moss said with his genial smile, "it's the way of the world. When there's a vacuum and you want to fill it, you go to bat, all at once, you lift he boss's arm and make him knight you."

"Merit doesn't count?" Taylor replied, sarcastically.

"Well, sure it counts. But that's a given. Understand? You want a bigger job, okay. What did you do to get it? And don't tell me your terrific Nielsen ratings."

"From what I hear, Bentley was only doing administrative work on the coast."

Moss nodded his head. "He was and that's because his boss wanted him to find out what it means to be a top executive, not just a program chief. Bentley was being groomed for bigger things, and that's when Connally played his ace. Connally had the offer that would work."

"Okay, Jerry, I get your point. Now, if you'll excuse me I'm going down the hall to see Mr. Connally."

Moss shook his head. "Like I said, you shouldn't do that, Hendrik, Connally's the man who made the decision. He's not going to change it."

"Maybe not, but I'm still going to see him. I can't sit here and say nothing."

"I'm telling you, I wouldn't do that. It's a lose-lose situation."

Taylor brushed past him. "Fuck you, Mr. Moss."

Moss grinned. "Okay, sonny, have it your way."

Taylor stood at Connally's open door. "You're here to see me, Hendrik? Come on in." Connally pointed to a chair. "What's on your mind?"

"Bentley."

"Oh?"

"Why?" Taylor bit his lower lip. "Why?" he repeated.

Connally shook his head and smiled. "How old are you, Hendrik?"

Taylor flushed. "What in hell does my age have to do with it."

"A lot, Hendrik," Connally replied softly. "I know your age. You've done a great job here, great. And you've got some good years ahead at Continental. Plus you have me as your friend." Connally leaned forward on his desk. "Like I say, years ahead of you. But Bentley has more."

"Age? That was the reason?"

"Only part of it. You know Jim Bentley worked here. We had quite an investment in him; we saw him as prime executive talent. But when we delayed, GBS made him a deal. They saw in him what we saw in him. And now I was able to get him back."

"Making him president."

"Making him president," Connally repeated. Then taking a more conciliatory view, he added, "Hendrik, you know how very much I like you. You'll be able to work very well with Bentley. He knows how close we are." Connally reached out to touch Taylor's arm. "I've already told him."

But Taylor's enormous pride got in the way of his judgment. He called Moss. "You said you wanted to be my agent. You've got the assignment. If you want it."

"Sure we want it," Moss said easily. "What do you want us to get you, a crack at another network? You call the shot."

"No network."

Moss sat back in his own of office, feet on his desk. "You got a lot of credentials, and there may be an opportunity. Joe Gratton's on the prowl, that's what I hear."

"Gratton's a son of a bitch" Taylor replied contemptuously.

"So?"

Taylor gritted his teeth. "So—like I just said, if I wanted to stay in the network business I'd stay here."

Moss shook his head. "Okay, no Gratton."

"What I want, Jerry, is a setup at your company, an independent production company with UPE as an umbrella, to handle deficits, to deal with the networks when they come at you with their suggestions."

Jerry Moss took a moment to respond and then he said, "I'll take it up with Sam Colman, okay?"

Moss's remark irritated Taylor. "You said you wanted to be my agent—and your company's handling production and representation, I don't know for how long—"

"We'll settle that when the time comes."

"I thought you had a lot of authority, Jerry."

"I do, but in coming through with your idea I'd like to run it by Sam. It's routine. Sam likes to make the final deal when it comes to this company. You know how he operates."

Taylor concealed his vexation. "Run it by him."

"Done," Moss said. But he never ran it by Colman. He was using Colman's name and setting him up as a future heavy if a Taylor deal didn't work out. He already knew it would work out; he'd given his word to Charles Connally that very day—Connally had called and said he'd had a feeling that Taylor would make a move because of the Bentley appointment. "You can take care of Hendrik," Connally had said only an hour before Taylor had made his decision to leave, "and you know I like him. In fact, I'll be sorry to lose him if that's what he wants."

"We can handle it, Mr. Connally," Moss replied.

"It won't be forgotten, Mr. Moss. Pass that on to Sam Colman."

"Figure it's a done deal." Moss smiled as he heard the phone click on the other end. He knew that Sam would be pleased. There would be at least a couple of deals coming their way—one or two shows on the air, a couple in development. "Not bad," he whispered to himself.

And so Hendrik Taylor moved out to the coast, felt the welcome mat was sincere at UPE. Sam Colman, the urbane but taciturn CEO, had even gone out of his way to escort Taylor to his private table in the studio commissary; he wanted Taylor to have the feeling that he was really wanted, in fact, needed. And to prove it Taylor was set up in a fancy bungalow, the kind of premises reserved for UPE's inside coterie of top producers.

Taylor was impatient to demonstrate to his onetime boss, Charles Connally, that aside from being an expert program chief, skilled at selecting the right shows for the right time spots, he could also come up with his own ideas, saleable ideas that could turn up on Connally's rival networks. Colman had been helpful, providing Taylor with a group of talented aides. Taylor worked with the group on a number of ideas, polishing them with his own touch: after a few weeks of careful preparation he submitted two shows he thought would work at one of the key networks. He waited patiently for word from the front office—Sam Colman's—but the shows were put on hold. Taylor had gotten the word, not from Colman, but from Irv Levine, one of Colman's closest associates. "And just what does Sam Colman mean when he tells you to tell me put the first two shows I submit on hold?" Taylor pointed to his phone. "Can't he just call me and explain?"

"That's just not his way, Hendrik," Levine said with a shrug.

"On hold. Does that mean, like it sounds, they're on ice?"

"No, no, no, Hendrik," Levine said, his cherubic face breaking out into a friendly smile. "Sam never gives anything a casual touch. He's hands on with everything that goes on at UPE. On the phone at 6:00 A.M. checking New York. Closing down here maybe twelve hours later. The man's a machine, you know that. When he's ready to talk about your ideas he'll have you in his office, never you mind. Never likes to break the news, good or bad, by phone. He's always judging people and he'll study your reactions even if you think you're not reacting. The man has what we call focus."

Taylor began to pace from one end of his office to the other, a steady rhythm of calculated movement. Then he stopped abruptly. "And how long do I wait? At the network I was used to making decisions all day. Tough ones. I made them fast."

"You're not at a network now, Hendrik," Levine replied gently, his eyes narrowing. "And you must never forget that. You made decisions about shows, lots of them, from a big group of suppliers. But with us, a single production house, there are angles that Sam Colman always weighs. It's just not your shows that matter, Hendrik."

"No?" Taylor shot back. "And just what is it that does matter?"

Levine stood his ground. "Like I said," he whispered, "angles."

"What in the hell does that mean? Angles!" Taylor retorted spitting out the word.

"I'll try to explain," Levine said as Taylor resumed his pacing without looking at him. "Sam's got us servicing all of the networks. He knows the schedules like you do. He knows what else is out there, too."

Taylor stopped in his tracks. "What are you trying to tell me?"

Irv Levine scratched his face. "I'm not sure you should know. I'm not sure you'll want to know." Levine walked over to one of the windows in Taylor's office.

"From here you can almost see two, maybe three, of our biggest competitors."

"So?"

"So?" Levine repeated, turning back to Taylor. "They're always trying to figure what we're offering, who we're offering, what the deals consist of."

"And you're doing the same," Taylor countered, "so what else is new?"

Levine stood his ground shaking his head. "Hendrik, I thought you'd have been able to dope it out."

"I just told you. Everybody's trying to learn what everyone else is doing. That's the nature of the business," Taylor replied.

"Missing one point, my friend."

Taylor bared his teeth, but not in a smile. It was his way of unsettling those who tried to outwit him. "All right, I'm waiting. What is the point"

"The point, Hendrik, the point—" Levine stopped and suddenly his whole manner changed. "If you don't get it, I'm not here to spell it out. Sam would have my head. You're going to have to tell me!"

"You're beginning to speak in circles, Irv. Why don't you come to the point?"

Irv Levine shook his head as he brushed past Taylor. He stopped at the door. "I always thought you were the one topper at the one network who had a natural instinct, who could have figured out how come UPE stays on top, too."

"Sure, while the other fellows just move out of your way, that it?"

Levine put his hand on the knob of the door. He glanced up and down the aisle outside. "I like you, Hendrik, always have. This is it—the final tip. Okay?"

"Okay. So?"

"The point, Mr. Taylor, is this. We *know*," he said, emphasizing the word. Then he took a step forward and tapped Taylor's chest. "No more questions. Okay? They're trying to find out. We know that. But—we don't try. Because, Mr. Taylor, we know. We *know,*" he emphasized again. "Now do you understand?"

Hendrik Taylor looked across at Irv Levine's crafty smile. Suddenly, he nodded. "I think I know what you're saying."

"I'm not saying anything, Hendrik. You're doing the saying. You're doing the figuring. I'm only like a sign, pointing a direction."

"Intelligence," Taylor said as he saw a smile cross Levine's face. "That's it! Am I right?" Levine continued to smile. Taylor began to pace his office again, thoughts flooding through his head. Sometimes Taylor turned to look directly at Levine, sometimes whispering to himself. "Sure, sure. It figures. I've heard a lot about Korn's beginnings. St. Louis wasn't it? Working with some muscle men? Tough hombres? And Colman was Korn's right hand. . . ."

"Bright hombres," Levine said quietly as he left the room.

Hendrik Taylor continued his pacing, his thoughts racing through his mind. Intelligence, of course, UPE had their own corps of moles. He reflected on how when he was back at the network he'd occasionally been surprised to find a UPE show suddenly turning up on the market bearing similarities to one that had just been presented, or a UPE show that surprisingly turned up ahead of a competitor's version.

It was a week later that Taylor got a call to drop by Sam Colman's office, but only after he'd finished reading a story called "The Incident" that Colman had sent down the day before. Taylor raced through the material and showed up on time at Colman's office located atop a thirty-story building on the studio lot. When he got off the elevator he was surprised to find the entire floor housed Colman's office; he was struck by the wide expanse of the corridors, space that could have held other of offices, but devoted instead to some of Colman's art acquisitions, impressive Rodins, large Matisse and Picasso paintings, his own private dining room, a conference room, a large screening room, plus the boardroom. A prim and efficient secretary, Carla Rittenhouse, ushered Taylor into the inner sanctuary. Colman sat behind an immense desk, nothing on it except an old-fashioned bronze and glass inkwell—Colman never used a ball point pen. Behind him was a special Swedish credenza on which were placed autographed photos of distinguished Americans, two of them former presidents of the United States, a number of cabinet officers, other recognizable political leaders of the current Congress, and famous figures in the past ranging from Churchill to Eisenhower to Einstein.

Colman waved Taylor to a seat across from him; Taylor was aware of the fact that his chair placed him at a somewhat lower level than Colman's, a psychological Colman ploy. He instantly resolved that he'd say nothing about the works of art he'd seen, the autographed photos, or the elaborate hand-painted ceiling like something out of a Renaissance palace. The two sat in silence for a few moments as Ms. Rittenhouse left the office.

"She worked at the White House for some years in the protocol area," Colman said. "Crackerjack executive in her own right. Runs my office." Abruptly, Colman changed the subject. "What'd you think of the material I sent you?"

Taylor took a moment before answering; what he really wanted to know was what Colman thought of it, and why was it sent to him.

"Interesting," he said, deciding to be noncommittal.

"Meaning?"

Taylor shrugged. "Interesting. Nicely done, in fact well written. Very well written."

"Meaning?" Colman repeated.

"What'd you have in mind for it? Television? Pay? Theatrical?"

A half smile crossed Colman's face. "That's what I want you to tell me."

"Written by a very fine writer," Taylor responded. "I know his work."

Colman sat back in his high-backed chair. "Interested in doing it?"

"In what capacity? For what medium?" Taylor countered.

"I want you to tell me."

Taylor felt even more annoyed. He was certain he was being tested and he didn't like it. He also knew that he didn't like the material even if it was sent by Colman himself. "If it's meant to be a feature film," Taylor started and then stopped wanting to probe it a bit further, "I'd have to step aside. Feature films. That's not my department."

"Features, pay, television, Hendrik, it's all one basket here. A producer measures it according to the market." Colman smiled. "I don't have to tell you what you already know."

"I've never produced a feature film for theaters if that's what you intend. I'm television."

"Hendrik, here you're a producer. You decide what direction material takes you."

Taylor shook his head. "I always thought it was the other way. The material, more or less, dictates the medium."

"Okay. Then what medium is this," Colman pointed to the manuscript in Taylor's hand, "best suited for? Let's say initially."

Hendrik Taylor knew now that he *was* being measured. "Frankly, Sam, I would hesitate—despite the writer's fine track record—to do anything with it." He placed the material on the edge of Colman's desk. "I have a feeling it came out of his trunk."

Colman's jaws tightened. "I happen to think it's an excellent premise."

Taylor shrugged. "Then I'd guess I'm not the man for it."

"Hendrik," Colman said softly, "I learned one thing long ago when I was strictly a talent agent. One thing. That's not to judge, but to sell."

"Well, Sam, you're not a talent agent any longer. You're the head of a studio. Now you know that before you sell you *have* to judge. Just the reverse of your former role."

"The same goes for you, Hendrik."

"How do you mean?"

"At a network you had the luxury of dealing with lots of submissions. You could choose one. And you could choose a couple of backups just in case you were wrong. Here, as a producer, you have to zero in on the right show because you may not have that second chance." Colman pointed to the manuscript lying on the edge of his desk. "Mr. Connally likes this project. Jim Bentley's approved it. I thought this might be one that would work for you, as well as for us. But, okay. We'll do one of the two you sent up the other day. Jerry Moss has a pilot deal set."

"With which one?"

"Whichever you want to do. Joe Gratton at Federal likes them both."

Taylor was puzzled. "Gratton? What's he have to do with my shows? What about George Cates out here?"

Colman waved the question aside. "Jerry Moss has a direct line to Gratton, Cates understands that. We put Gratton into that office—Jerry handled that deal. So?" A half smile crossed Colman's face.

Taylor nodded. "Nice deal." Taylor stood up; he was ready to leave. One thing he knew—never wait for the other fellow to look at his watch.

"Nice deal. Right. For us, for Gratton. Now for you. You pick the one you want to do—" The smile vanished from Colman's face. "You be the judge, Hendrik," he said as he reached across the desk to retrieve the manuscript Taylor had turned down. He held up the script as Taylor edged toward the door. "Every producer on the lot's been wanting to do this one."

Taylor stood by the door, hesitating. He wondered if Colman was giving him one last chance. He wondered, too, how, if he abruptly changed his mind, Colman would judge him. And he wondered why Colman hadn't told him right from the start that the property was hot at the studio. He concluded he had to hold his position. He wouldn't give an explanation now that he had the facts. He'd been measured for his judgment on one property. He wanted Colman to realize that he was a man of conviction—with principles. He would not take the bait, if bait was being offered. "I hope it works, Sam," he finally said.

"It will, Hendrik," Colman replied as he pressed down a key on his telephone bank. "Miss Rittenhouse," he said, talking into the speaker, "tell Alan Porter he has the 'Incident' script. Mr. Taylor has passed."

Hendrik Taylor closed the door quietly behind him as

he headed out of the office. He'd disappointed Colman, he knew. Now he'd have to deliver one of his own projects for a man whom he'd always despised, the formidable head of Federal Broadcasting, Joe Gratton. As he sat at his desk looking out at the large elephant-ear plants that shielded his office from the curious, he knew he'd have to make the project a winner for Gratton.

That wasn't going to happen. One week after he'd finished production on the pilot he received a call to drop by Sam's office. When he entered he was surprised to find Jerry Moss waiting. He was even more surprised to find Alan Porter there as well. Sam Colman walked in, glanced at the group, took a seat in the back row and without a word to anyone signaled to the projectionist to play the film.

When the screening ended, there was silence broken finally by Colman's terse request, "Jerry?"

Jerry Moss had seated himself beside Taylor. Porter had sat alone up front. "Lot of good things there," Moss said as he patted Taylor on the back, "nice touches." He turned around to look at Colman. "Only one problem. Gratton was disappointed. Didn't explain why—he's no expert on production. But," Jerry Moss shrugged, "he is the buyer."

Hendrik Taylor sat facing the screen. He wouldn't turn around to debate with Colman and he wouldn't toady to anyone. Then he heard Colman's voice. "Hendrik?"

At that moment a wave of nausea struck Taylor. He was being asked to defend his pilot. What was even worse, he was being asked in front of Alan Porter, the current favorite producer of Sam Colman's. He detested the way Colman had elected to present his film. He knew that Jerry's words were meant to be less than a compliment and more of a writing off of the pilot. He was certain that he was about to be operated on, not only without the benefit of any advance warning but without anesthesia. But he would stand his ground.

Without turning to look at Colman, Taylor said, "Joe Gratton doesn't know shit about programming." He smiled inwardly; he felt Jerry Moss edge a bit away from him. He thought he could smell his corporate fear; after all, it had been Moss who had engineered Taylor's deal. He felt a touch of confidence.

Colman reacted with a terse, "Alan?"

Porter turned around to look at the group, all eyes focused on him. "Like Jerry put it. Nice touches, some very nice." Porter, a younger man who wore rimless glasses, was practically bald, his sideburns clipped precisely on a parallel line with the top of his large ears. His eyes showed a lot of white under the pupils, his whole appearance suggesting the image of an old owl. "I don't know about Gratton. Maybe he knows, maybe he doesn't. Doesn't matter. One little problem for me." He focused his colorless eyes on Taylor. "Maybe a question of style. Maybe Gratton missed a sense of pace, a change of scene. You know what I mean?" he added as he looked directly at Colman.

"Go on," Colman said.

"Well, it's just this. We're in the midst of the MTV generation. They like things to move. They get restless looking at the same people in the same place, just talking. They don't like too much talking."

Taylor suddenly blurted out, "There's no room for a car chase or for shooting things up if that's what you're trying to suggest."

"Movement. That's what I'm saying, Hendrik. I haven't said a word about car chases or bullets. Movement."

"Porter's right," Colman said, sharply. "The film is too static. We don't want to try a revival of *Studio One*, where everything was talk, where everything was interior, people talking to people in the same room."

"That's what gives the film its focus," Taylor insisted. "These people have something to say and the audience will stay with them."

"The audience will stay with them saying the same things exactly as you have them, but they can say it on a street, in a car, on an escalator; same dialogue, but shift the setting. Get away from the same stodgy compressed atmosphere of a single room."

"That's where the action takes place," Taylor interjected.

"There is no action, and that's the problem," Sam Colman said, speaking with a sharpness new to Taylor. Taylor was surprised to find that Colman seemed to have every frame of the film in his mind's eye. He proceeded to reshape the film as he spoke, quoting actual lines of the dialogue, placing the characters in one new setting after another—in short, preserving the thrust of Taylor's approach, but giving the pilot a new, more energized look.

When he finished Jerry Moss said, "Gratton will like that."

Sam Colman stood up. "It'll cost, but that's secondary. If necessary we'll restage half of the pilot."

Taylor continued to stare ahead, but he wouldn't kowtow to anyone. "I should have been told about Gratton screening the film. This was my concept. I think I know something about programming."

Colman was at the door. "Hendrik, that's not the issue," Colman replied coldly. "Alan can fix it." And with that he was gone. Jerry Moss patted Taylor on the shoulder and quickly followed Sam Colman out of the room.

Taylor glanced up at Porter. "So, that's the way they do business here. Take a man's work. Don't let him take it to New York to screen it. Everything behind his back." Taylor stared into Alan Porter's lifeless eyes. "That's it?"

"In a nutshell, yes. Colman's way."

"He's a no-good goddamn bastard and you can quote me," Taylor said, his anger breaking through.

An unpleasant smile crossed Alan Porter's face. "Not necessary. He knows what he is. And me? I know who I am, Hendrik, you might as well know it. I'm a prick. The pilot'll be redone, but the series has been picked up. I'm telling you. I know the score here. That's the Moss-Gratton connection. You'll still have your title, your office, the works. Come to the roughcuts, the dailies, your option. I'll be calling the shots. Like I said. I'm the new fair-haired prick. Me." And with that he was gone.

Taylor sat alone for a few minutes damning the day he had ever met Jerry Moss. He sighed in relief as he finally stood up, the projectionist holding the door for him. Taylor knew what he'd have to do. Crawl back to Charles Connally, work things out, find a way to deal with Jim Bentley. Anything would be better than to prowl alone in his sumptuous bungalow sitting out a contract, having to play second fiddle to an Alan Porter. Once he was back at the network he'd know how to deal with the likes of a Jerry Moss and a Sam Colman. Give them the deep six, the Taylor way—he'd play the game, lead them on, encourage them, wine them and dine them. And never buy anything from them.

Connally was receptive to Taylor's return, or so it

seemed. They discussed a high-level post where Taylor would function as Connally's chief administrative aide. Bentley had been away on a short skiing vacation in Switzerland and when he arrived at his office he immediately voiced objections. It wasn't that he objected to Taylor's return, he felt that Taylor's real talent was in programming and he, Bentley, wanted to take advantage of it. At least that was the way he made his argument. "I need him," Bentley insisted to Connally, "the network needs him. Jamie Vogel's a good program man but he doesn't have Taylor's depth of experience."

When Connally explained the move to Taylor in his office, Taylor was instantly discomfited. "I'd much rather be working closer to you. I'd get the chance, finally, to pick up the administrative background you once said I lacked."

"Well, you were preoccupied with the heart of the business, programming. The rest, well—" Connally shrugged, "it's all part of the support system."

"That's true, but getting the chance to work closely with station relations, research, sales, the legal department, the international areas—"

"Hendrik, you're missing the point."

"The point?" Taylor repeated.

"Jim Bentley wants you. He said he needs you. Jamie Vogel's a good man, but nowhere near as seasoned as you." Connally saw the look of disappointment in Taylor's face. "It's not forever. You give the new chap a hand. And Jamie will be grateful." Connally reached out to pat Taylor's arm resting across his desk. "Try it." "It's not what I want. Not really," Taylor said.

"Jim's president. He operates the company. Programming is the heart of the Company. I don't have to explain that, do I, Hendrik?"

Taylor recognized the pointlessness of resisting. As he sat in his new office close to Connally's he knew in his heart that Bentley had simply made a better case. Bentley was smart, too smart to let a man have a vague title—something of an executive assistant to the chairman—simply marking time, holding down a staff assignment and waiting for the moment when Bentley's own good fortune might ebb. No, Bentley would put him under his wing.

For the next year Taylor spent half his time on the coast doing his best to be helpful to Jamie Vogel, the other half in New York at Bentley's request, taking meetings with agents, producers and studio chiefs when Bentley was tied up. While on the coast he dutifully attended Jamie Vogel's weekly staff meetings, read material that Vogel sent on to him for comment, and participated occasionally in meetings dealing with program scheduling.

Gradually, it dawned on him that while papers were crossing his desk on either coast, while he met with a wide variety of talented people, nothing that he suggested had been implemented and the people with whom he met were not the people on Bentley's 'A' list or, for that matter, on the 'A' list of the other networks. The truth was driven home one day when he found himself in an elevator in the network's New York headquarters with none other than Jerry Moss.

Moss had a ready smile and reached out a hand. "Hey, Hendrik, long time no see."

Taylor's tongue ran across his teeth. "If you wanted to see me you knew where to find me. On either coast."

Moss grinned. "Right, right, sure."

"So?"

Moss watched the floor lights slip by. "Look, Hendrik,

we're alone, right here. Right in the bowels of your great network. You're a buyer. I'm a seller." He sidled up closer. "No hard feelings, but I'm a fair weather friend. And I figure you're no longer a great friend of UPE. So? Why waste your time, right?" He tapped Taylor on the shoulder as the elevator door opened. "Why waste my time."

"At least you're honest," Taylor replied.

"Honest? Who the fuck's honest? I got my job. Sell UPE programs. To you? Not a chance. And you? You're in a well, dear boy, at the bottom. Nice offices, both coasts. A word of advice." Both men stepped out of the elevator. Moss looked up and down the first-floor foyer. "Look, I made you a deal once. It didn't play. Now you've got yourself a niche. I don't know why I'm bothering telling you this. Maybe there's a grain of sentiment still alive in me, who knows. But Hendrik, it's not Bentley who's put you in the pigeon coop. Bentley can take care of himself. A second-class jerk, but I'll deny I ever said it. You keep flying one coast one week, the other coast the next week. But, I'm telling you, sonny, you lost your balls on the way. And the fellow who finally cut them off, giving you a nice job with no authority—that fellow's the real shit, first class. I'll deny that I ever told you that, too. Ranks up there with Gratton." Moss took a deep breath and then whispered, "That's your old pal, sonny. Charles Connally."

Hendrik Taylor watched Jerry Moss scurry down the foyer as he reached the door leading out of the building. Moss turned and saluted and then vanished. Hendrik Taylor hurried back to his Park Avenue apartment as fast as he could. When he closed the door behind him he sat down in his favorite chair. He saw now with utter clarity how too full of himself he had been, how he had made it too easy for others to get him. Jerry Moss was right. Fair weather friends. But Moss didn't know the half of it.

There were worse.

AN AMBUSH OR TWO

TONY GORDON, PUSHING A PUDGY hand through his thick shiny, black hair, turned to the younger man seated next to him, "Steven, my boy, what time do you have?"

Steve Lane, Otis & Meade's new television chief and newest shareholder, whispered, "Almost noon."

Gordon chuckled. "Two empty seats at the head table," and then he added, as he looked about the unostentatious room, "maybe two, maybe three seats empty among us fifty-eight or so bourgeois."

The fifty-eight or so weren't bourgeois. They were the shareholders of Otis & Meade, the leaders in their field. Tony Gordon was the acknowledged smartest man of the agency, smarter than either James Hornwell Otis, his roots set firmly in midwest soil despite his patrician appearance, or the lanky and aging John Longworth, the agreeable and judicious agency compromiser, who held the title of agency president. Longworth had earned the title for his years of dedicated service to O&M, and especially to Mr. Otis, but everyone knew that the real operating head of O&M was its senior executive vice president, volatile Tony Gordon.

"Watch that door, Steven. At any moment, Mr. Nicholas J. Craven, he of elephant ear fame, Mr. Nicholas J. Craven the third, will stalk in, look east, west and south and then seat himself right next to Mr. Otis. There he is now," Gordon said, a touch of sarcasm in his voice, "you watch." Craven, the tallest man in the agency, head of its marketing division, glanced quickly about the room and settled next to Mr. Otis. A few moments later, sandy-haired Curtis Coster, the agency's copy chief, stood at the entrance to the shareholders' dining room. Coster, brushing an errant strand of hair from his forehead, took in the room at a glance and unhesitatingly took the chair next to the agency president.

"Mr. Lane, these two smart-ass bastards," Gordon whispered, "are always—emphasis on always—the last two to arrive. The only question is, which one will outmaneuver the other to get the chair next to Mr. Otis. Today's winner, Nick, the craven brown-noser. He's outsmarted Coster two months in a row. Look at the way he's casing the room. He's so uptight he hasn't even bothered to greet Otis or Longworth. An asshole of the first rank."

Steve Lane was momentarily surprised, and yet not too surprised by Gordon's frankness. Gordon had been one of the first to congratulate him when it was announced that he would head up all television operations; Gordon had summoned Lane to his office. "Steve, my boy, first thing I did was congratulate Mr. Otis. Made a smart move. Hendrik Taylor could have gotten the job, smart as hell, the little son of a bitch, but lacking one essential ingredient. Know what that is, kid?" Gordon said, as he leaned forward and placed both hands on his large, cluttered mahogany leather-topped desk. "Judgment," Gordon added, without waiting for Lane's response, eyes squinting through his heavy glasses; "judgment," he repeated. "The key quality to real leadership. I hate to admit it, but James Hornwell Otis has it. And if he didn't think you had it you wouldn't have gotten the nod."

Gordon eased back into his chair. "We'll be working together, my boy. With your new title, you're already automatically on the agency's plans board. Now, as chairman, one word of advice. Be prepared. Do your homework. Stick to your position. Don't be pushed by the likes of Mr. Otis, who rarely attends, Mr. Longworth who always attends, or any of the other ten members including yours truly. I'll eat you alive if I have to, cut off your balls if you vacillate. There's only one guiding principle. The clients' interest. Just never forget that—that's what makes O&M the greatest agency on the street. The client comes first, his interests first, his money first."

Steve Lane knew quite a bit about Tony Gordon, his penchant for never taking meetings outside of his office except with major clients. Top members of the media, publishers and editors of fame, even the top brass of the networks, they respected Tony Gordon not only for his winning personality, but because he had power enough to make and break powerful media interests.

Gordon's zeal for being prepared was legendary. There were many in the agency who'd experienced this characteristic. Gordon's way was to meet with a new account executive prior to any plans board meeting. He would finger the fat book the account executive had prepared for the forthcoming session. Gordon would fix his eyes on his visitor and ask, "I have only one question," as he stroked the richly bound copy of the presentation to be made before his board. Gordon would then abruptly stop, his eyes narrowing as they bore into his visitor's.

"What's that?" the visitor, somewhat shaken, would ask after a moment or two had passed.

"This!" Tony barked. "Is this the best you can do?" he demanded as he lifted the presentation and then dropped it on his desk. The startling demand always had predictable results—an executive squirming in his chair trying to deal with the squinty-eyed terror seated opposite him. And almost always the executive would reach out, timidly, for the presentation.

"Let me take another crack at it, Tony. Okay?"

"Twenty-four hours," Tony would snap.

The whole process might be repeated again, the account executive even more ill at ease. "I asked you before," Gordon would sneer, "is this the best you can do, the very best?" After one or two such encounters, the visitor might pull himself up straight in his chair and answer respectfully but firmly, "It is, Tony."

And Tony's response? A quick smile, a reaching out for the presentation, and a terse, "Okay, now I'll read it." It was a game that Tony Gordon liked to play on the uninitiated, and those who experienced the exchange knew better than to alert new officers to the Gordon routine.

Steve used his newfound status to get to know the top brass and even to forge closer relationships. On one occasion he stood at Otis's door; although the agency had an open-door policy no one barged into the chairman's office. Otis at the moment was cleaning his reading glasses when he looked up and spotted Lane.

"Come in, come in, Steve," he said, affably, "what's on your mind?"

Steve took a seat opposite Otis. "Well, not anything, to be perfectly honest. I was just in with Tony and passing by—" Steve smiled and shrugged, the rest of his statement hanging in the air. Steve pointed to Otis's clean desk. "I know all of the big decisions that aren't resolved below have to come up to you. How is it that Tony's desk is, well, so different from yours?"

Otis chuckled. "That's Tony's way. Clutter. Clutter everywhere, but," he added, a finger touching his forehead, "not upstairs. If he needs a paper, believe me, he can pull it out from the jumble. People have told me that was Einstein's way—a messy study—but Albert Einstein had a pretty good set of marbles. And so does Tony Gordon."

"But your desk—I never see any papers on it," Steve persisted.

"A different style, that's all. Tony thrives in the midst of crises. He loves it, the action, handling two calls at once, an office filled with people, lots of meetings, he loves challenges, and the give and take of debates. It's all fireworks with him—but, remember, that's just on the surface. Tony Gordon is very cool where it counts." Again, Otis put a hand to his forehead. "His whole operandi is a facade. He loves tumult. Fireworks. I handle matters a bit differently. I know that when I arrive in the morning there'll be a crisis waiting for me, a decision to be made. I know when I'm about to leave for lunch there'll be another, and maybe one when I come back. My style? Handle them expeditiously, never allow something to hang over an extra day if possible. Handle all memoranda at once. And I never take anything home. No papers, no calendar of the next day's events.

Once I'm out of here I concentrate with Mrs. Otis on where we're going to dine. We like to try new places. And Tony—you'll always find him in one of two restaurants: 'Twenty-One' or the 'Oak Room.' I may appear to be a creature of set routines and habit, but it's really Tony Gordon who lives a disciplined precise life. I leave the business behind when I'm out of here. Tony lives with it day and night."

"Quite a difference," Steve said. "I guess appearances often are deceptive."

"Know who said that?" Otis asked with a twinkle in his eye.

"Shakespeare?" Steve ventured.

"Aesop. Worth reading because a lot of folks think they're quoting Shakespeare when they're really quoting Aesop. And it wasn't deceptive what he said, it was deceiving. But close enough, Steve." Otis rose from his chair, indicating that the meeting was over. As he walked Steve to the door he said, "Remember your Shakespeare, but don't overlook Aesop. He came first."

As Steve left Otis's office he saw the drooping angular figure of John Longworth entering Gordon's office. He heard Gordon's hearty welcome and then saw Tony close the door to his office, something Tony rarely did, something all of O&M top officers seldom did.

Inside his office Tony pointed to his brown leather couch. "Take a seat, John."

Longworth, his few hairs touched up to conceal their whiteness, his long face stretching out from too large a collar like some ancient turtle's from his craggy lined neck, settled into the deep comfort of the sofa. Tony wedged himself into a corner. "And what brings Long John to my quarters." Tony asked, a big open smile crossing his face.

Longworth nodded his head and emitted a throaty grunt. "Short John these days, Tony," Longworth said. "Long John," he repeated, "yes, once upon a time. A long time ago to tell the truth. Today, shrinking Long John is more like it." It had been a nickname given to him many years before when, as a young basketball player for Yale, his height, his straight muscular back and long arms made him a star player. Now, age had struck him down, but the agency had always refrained from establishing an automatic retirement age. "Tony," Longworth began in a solemn voice, "they're pushing. Both of them. They're trying to push me out."

Tony needed no further identification. "Brothers Craven and Coster, right?"

A small smile crept across Longworth's face. "You're always right, Tony."

"Two bastards, first class," Tony said.

"Bastards, yes. Well, maybe. A man's got the right to be ambitious. And they're both full of it."

"I've noticed," Tony replied, dryly.

"If I didn't feel I can still make a contribution, Tony—"

"Hell's bells," Tony snorted, "Who says you have to prove anything. You're Long John—you're John Longworth. You've made your contributions."

"Yesterday," Longworth murmured.

"That's part of why we're here. You and others like you. Old man Grimes in accounting. Herm Grimes. How long's he been here?" Longworth looked at the ceiling trying to figure out the years. "Don't give it a second thought. Herm was here before you. Before Otis. Long before honorable James Hornwell inserted his name in the company logo."

"No one's trying to ease Herm out, Tony. It's me they're after."

A cagey look crossed Tony's face. "Do you think our Mr. Otis is getting ready to anoint three more potential agency leaders, John?"

"It wouldn't surprise me," Longworth replied laconically. He pulled out a slender cigar. As he began to cut it he looked across at Tony. "Mind?"

Gordon grinned. "Mind?" he repeated. "Mr. Longworth, you've been pulling out a cigar maybe a thousand times since we first met. Have I ever objected?"

Longworth struck a match and carefully lit the end without touching flame to tobacco. He drew in deeply. "Always a first time, Tony."

"Three," Tony said as he pushed back his thick hair. "Two of them we know. Craven and Coster. I don't think there's a third yet."

"Mr. Otis might not want to wait this time."

"Maybe." A quick smile creased Tony's face. "Maybe our Mr. Otis is feeling a little bit of the pressure you're feeling, John. Ever think of that?"

Longworth pulled on his cigar, even as the large pouches under his eyes seemed to sag. "No, I haven't, Tony." Longworth took another puff. "Never entered my mind."

"Well, don't think it hasn't entered his."

Longworth frowned. "You think they'd go that far?"

"Why not?" Tony replied.

"You mean it's not just me?" Longworth asked, his brow furrowing.

"Time marches on, they say. But there is one good sign."

"And what's that?"

"These two smart-asses haven't got the brains to work together. They're competing with each other and that's their joint Achilles' heel."

Longworth scratched at one of his drooping ears. "You're really saying that it's not me, it's Jim Otis they're after?"

"You're a roadblock, okay. But now that I think of it, like I said, it's been some time since our Mr. Otis anointed three prospects for bigger things." Tony reached over and slapped Longworth's bony knee. "Brother Longworth, you got me to thinking."

Longworth smiled. "I like doing that, Tony."

Gordon leaned back and bared his teeth with a sudden smile. "I got an idea. Just so happens that I've got two plans board meetings coming up. They'll both be there. You'll be there."

"I'll be there."

"Right. And this time I'll make sure brother Otis is also there. "

Steve Lane took a seat at the rear of the spartan conference room where the O&M plans board met. He watched as the group began to assemble, ten of whom were heads of major departments at O&M, plus a smaller group representing the agency's key personnel assigned to a particular account. A plans board session always created an atmosphere of tension, and this was perceptibly visible when James Hornwell Otis made an unexpected appearance walking arm and arm with John Longworth.

Otis and Longworth, despite their superior titles, took seats toward the rear, the better to observe the presentations made by the special group assigned to the account, a giant food-processing company. The account executive

Harry Adams and his group, who had gathered earlier to prepare for the presentation of the advertising campaign for the company's cereal division, were busy setting up easels on which the campaign's major elements would be exhibited; gold-bound copies of the official account presentation which had passed muster with Tony Gordon were placed around the board table. Gordon arrived and took the seat reserved for the board's chairman. In a brief opening statement he welcomed the participation of Mr. Otis and Mr. Longworth and commented on Steve Lane's appearance at his first plans board meeting. The amenities concluded, Gordon nodded to Harry Adams to proceed.

As Adams stepped in front of the first easel to begin his presentation, Curtis Coster hurriedly entered the room. Coster glanced at the assembled group and, spotting a vacant chair near Otis and Longworth, started toward it. But before he reached it, Tony Gordon spoke in a crisp voice, "You're late, Mr. Coster." Coster, now halfway to his targeted seat, flushed and turned to look back at Gordon.

"I'm sorry about that," he muttered taking a step toward the empty chair.

"There's a seat right up here, Mr. Coster, near me," Tony shot back pointing to it. "You'll see better."

Coster was taken aback, plainly discomfited, but he nodded affirmatively as he made his way back toward Gordon. Gordon waited until Coster had taken his seat, a half smile crossing his face as he exchanged a swift look with Longworth, whose raised eyebrows and pursed lips indicated his approval. "Are we ready, Mr. Coster?" Gordon inquired.

"Sorry, I apologize for being late," Coster murmured, Gordon nodded to Adams to commence his presentation.

It was de rigueur at the agency for all members of the plans board and its accompanying product group to be punctual for plans board meetings. As Adams, a slender, well-groomed middle-aged executive, began his presentation all those in the room followed it by consulting their goldbound presentation copies, except for Tony Gordon. It was a well known fact that Gordon's prodigious photographic memory had already absorbed the entire presentation before he'd entered the room. Adams proceeded methodically in outlining the print and television campaigns that the product group had developed. Storyboards for the campaign's commercials were displayed on a second easel as Adams called on a young woman responsible for the creative work to explain the commercials, an assistant cuing in the new music that accompanied the art work.

Adams went through his presentation, taking care to call upon all members of the product group to participate with him in their specialties. Artwork for supplementary outdoor and subway/bus campaigns was exhibited; Steve Lane's deputy outlined the media plan for a spot buying plan coupled with selected network time buys.

As the presentation proceeded, Tony Gordon continued to exchange fleeting glances with John Longworth; in his own way, although he had not discussed the board meeting in advance, he wanted Longworth to enjoy the direction the meeting was shortly to take. Gordon also observed Nicholas Craven, who'd been an early arrival; Craven sat slumped in his chair directly opposite Coster. Gordon waited for Adams to sum up the group's recommendations, inwardly amused at the plans he'd made for the board's participation. The common practice at these meetings was for the chair to thank the product group for its work and then to open the proceedings for questions. This time it would be different.

Harry Adams clasped his hands before him. "Mr. Chairman, ladies and gentlemen, those are our recommendations. We'd be pleased to have your comments."

Tony Gordon thanked Adams and then abruptly turned to Curtis Coster. "Mr. Coster? Your thoughts?"

Coster flushed. He was stunned by the direct question. "My thoughts?" he repeated.

"Yes," Gordon repeated, "your thoughts."

Coster felt a sudden outpouring of venom toward Tony Gordon. He looked into Tony's sharp squinting eyes and he knew instantly that he'd been put on the spot deliberately with not only Longworth present, but James Hornwell Otis.

"We're waiting, Mr. Coster," Tony said pleasantly, his white teeth bared and bright, dark eyes flashing an amused glance toward Longworth.

Coster felt a dryness in his throat. This wasn't the way a plans board operated, at least not while Coster had become a member. His stock in the company had risen precisely because he'd learned how to play these meetings—he would wait until everyone else had made his or her comment and then, as the last speaker to participate, he would be able to commend all sides, to weigh one option against another, to have time to assess the reactions of those people whose opinions counted most, namely, Gordon's and Otis's. And now he'd been suddenly, without warning, put on the spot, not as a volunteer who'd had time to weigh matters, but as Gordon's sacrificial goat. He was being forced to take sides, to express a judgment before he'd had the opportunity to assess everyone else's opinions.

Coster wiped the hairs off his forehead and stared into

Tony Gordon's penetrating black eyes. He felt as though he were facing a firing squad and he knew that everyone else in the room had to be aware, too, of how singular was Tony Gordon's abrupt demand. "Well," he began, trying to formulate a response, "this was an impressive job and Harry," he said, happy to turn his eyes away from Gordon's, "you and your team have examined the challenges, all of them." Coster stopped and once again brushed his forehead, noting as he did, the supercilious smile on Nicholas Craven's face.

"That's not exactly a judgment, Mr. Coster," Tony rasped.

Coster glanced toward the end of the room at James Hornwell Otis's impassive face. This was the one man who had to be pleased even above Gordon. Coster continued to look directly at Otis. He knew he could speak of his department's work. "I think Harry's team has done a very fine job particularly with respect to the commercials and the copy, all of them are targeted within the copy policy we set in my department." Abruptly Coster ceased speaking; he felt a gnawing uncertainty; he hated to find himself out on a limb.

Suddenly the limb was cut off from under him. Gordon spoke sharply. "This is a lousy job, Mr. Coster, pure, simple lousy. And some of the worst parts of the plan are the commercials you're championing."

Coster was suddenly adrift. "Tony, I'm not saying they're the best ever, what I'm trying to say is—"

But Coster never got to say more; Gordon's powerful voice simply overrode his mild protest. "Mr. Adams, when you brought me your presentation I asked you one question, do you remember that?"

"Yes, sir," came the timid response.

"And what was that question?" Gordon demanded.

"Was that the best we could do. After I'd submitted it twice," Adams added softly.

"Right. And what did I say?"

"You'd read it."

"You never came back to question me, did you?"

Adams was flustered. "Tony, I just assumed it would be okay—you'd read two previous ones; I'd made changes and then you said you'd read it."

"You just assumed that everything would be fine after you'd done your work—you and your team."

Adams nodded. "I'm afraid we were overconfident."

Gordon rose. "The whole campaign needs rethinking. The copy policy. The media buys." Then glancing toward Craven, he added, "The marketing plan as well. We'll meet again in two weeks unless someone has something else to say." Gordon's eyes swept the room. No one spoke. "This meeting's adjourned."

Curtis Coster sat in his chair as the others filed out, Longworth being the last to pass. "John," Coster said reaching out a hand. "Where'd I go wrong? This is the first time Tony's ever run a meeting this way. Where'd I go wrong?"

Longworth looked down at Coster. "Curtis," he said, puffing on his cigar, "you were unprepared."

"I'd read the presentation," Coster protested. "I've marked my copy, here, look," he said lifting the presentation toward Longworth.

"Read it, yes. But you had no opinion. You were waiting for others to express theirs."

"So? I've done that dozens of times, what does that prove?"

Longworth coughed. He knew he didn't want to have

this conversation, but Coster pressed on. "What does that prove?"

"Perhaps a lack of judgment," Longworth said, noting how the words pierced Coster.

"But," Coster continued, "I've always rendered judgment. Haven't I?"

Longworth tapped the dangerously long ash of his cigar against an ashtray. "Yes. After everyone else has spoken."

Tony Gordon sat in his office reviewing the meeting with Steve Lane. "Your first plans board, Mr. Lane, and I've a feeling you won't forget it."

"It was pretty short," Steve ventured.

Tony grunted. "Oh yes, short it was. Shortest one we've ever had. What we did there today, kid, was to unmask Mr. Curtis Coster. We unmasked his game, finally. I don't think you'll be seeing him play sycophant to Mr. Otis for some time. Unmasking is humbling, kid. Did you see his face, hear his whimpering when I asked him straight out for his opinion?"

At that moment John Longworth poked his head into Gordon's office. "You did it, Tony. In style."

"That's number one, John," Tony replied raising an index finger.

"My thanks," Longworth said, as he headed toward his own office.

"Great guy, Long John—that's what we used to call him in the old days: smart, cagey, the diplomat. But diplomats are always targets for the ambitious, especially the overambitious. Like our Mr. Coster. But don't get me wrong, kid, Coster's got talent, lots of it. I respect talent. He'll settle down for a while and concentrate on using that talent, putting aside his newly discovered lack of talent for pushing his way up the ladder. If he comes in and says he learned a lesson I'll be supporting him, but that'll take a lot of introspection and something else."

"What would that be?" Steve asked.

"Guts," Tony replied, and then tapping the side of his head, he added, "guts and judgment." Gordon stood up and stretched. "We nailed the son of a bitch, all right. The perfect ambush."

It would be different with Craven at the next plans board meeting a week later. Steve noted that Curtis Coster had been an early arrival and had taken a seat quite apart from Gordon as well as from Otis. The routine of the plans board meeting reverted to its past manner: those wishing to speak simply volunteered after the presentation of the campaign had been completed. Curtis Coster was one of the early volunteers; Steve observed Gordon smiling at John Longworth. Coster, it now appeared, would perform like the others.

At a critical moment during Nicholas Craven's defense of the marketing plan which he had hinted he had personally authored, the subject of the dollars needed to implement the plan was on the table.

"This plan of yours, Mr. Craven," Tony began, and then paused, as he pointed directly at Craven, "this is your plan, right?"

"Right," Craven replied. "Approved by our group. Unanimously, I might add."

"And it would cost eight million dollars, right?"

"In that neighborhood, yes," Craven responded.

"A pretty hefty chunk of a client's dollars, right?"

"They have the money," Craven replied easily.

"That's not the point, Nicholas."

"What is the point, Mr. Gordon?" Craven demanded tartly.

"The point is that this client was a little concerned last year at the budgets we recommended."

"We're only talking about a million more, maybe a million and a quarter," Craven said.

"Last year's sales didn't quite measure up to our prognostications. Am I right?"

Craven went to an easel. He pulled out a card from the back of the stack and pointed to it. "You're right, Tony, but O&M did well if you look at this chart showing how this account has grown and how we've grown with it."

"At their expense," Tony growled.

Craven shook his head in disbelief. "They approved every recommendation we made, every penny we spent."

"And now we're recommending—after last year didn't measure up—that they spend more, a million plus more, is that it?"

Craven smiled. "That's it, right."

"A million more?"

"A million plus," Craven insisted.

"And in spite of our failure last year, you want them to spend a million more, am I hearing you correctly."

Cravens tood his ground. "I'd roll the million. Yes."

Gordon leaned forward in his chair. "Roll the million? Is that what I heard you say?"

"That's right," Craven said. "A million, plus a hundred thousand, maybe two hundred more."

"Are you rolling that with your money, Mr. Craven?"

"My money?" Craven asked puzzled.

"Your money, that's what I said," Tony repeated.

"Not my money, of course not."

"The client's money," Gordon said, "right?"

"Well, of course. This campaign will do them a lot of good."

"We don't roll their money, Mr. Craven. We husband their money. We plan very careful advertising campaigns. We don't take chances. We aren't part of Vegas."

"That was just a figure of speech, Tony."

"A poor one," Gordon retorted. "Mr. Craven," Tony said, his eyes riveted on James Hornwell Otis, "this agency is very fussy about its reputation, about its way of doing business. We don't profit from a client's resources. They profit from ours. There is a difference. Do you understand?"

For the first time the overconfident manner so characteristic of Craven had vanished. He resented Tony Gordon's pummeling particularly in the presence of Otis.

Gordon's eyes narrowed. "Mr. Craven, I've been told that you recently had a meeting—yesterday in fact—where you called all of your senior people into your office and that the meeting lasted less than a minute, is that correct?"

Craven flushed and felt a sickening desire to leave the room. He recognized that Tony Gordon had elected to pillory him and that there was no escape.

"Am I correct," Tony went on, "that you had your key members in and that you told them that from now on you would do the 'think'—whatever that is—and that they would do the 'work'? And that was all that was said?"

Craven winced as he heard the exact words. "I just wanted them to get on their toes, anything wrong about that?" he retorted, determined to hold the line in front of Otis. "If you wanted to humiliate me, may I ask why? Why here? Why with Mr. Otis and Mr. Longworth present?"

"That's easy, Mr. Craven. For the very simple reason

you chose to humiliate thirty executives—your department, you say—but they're Otis & Meade personnel, real people. Our people. We don't do that sort of thing here."

"And isn't this all a bit irrelevant? Aren't we discussing an advertising campaign and isn't how I run my department my concern? Not yours?" Craven replied defiantly.

"At O&M we all think and we all work, Mr. Craven. And we do not roll the client's money. We protect it. We make every dollar of it work. Not for our bottom line. But for our clients'. There is a difference, Mr. Craven." Tony stood up. "This meeting is adjourned."

One week later Steve Lane accompanied Tony Gordon to the shareholders' monthly meeting. Otis and Longworth were seated in their usual places. Standing at the door Steve scanned the room and saw Craven and Coster already seated, huddled together in the back.

Tony whispered to Steve. "Remember the lesson of the week. 'Self-conceit may lead to self-destruction.' Know who said that?"

"Was it, maybe, Aesop?" Steve replied.

Gordon grinned. "One for you, Steve." Then a quizzical look in his eyes, Tony asked, "Could you maybe have picked up something from our Mr. Otis?"

Steve nodded. "Bingo. But I'm still learning, Tony."

"Never stop and you'll never self-destruct."

Gordon took a step into the room and said, with a soft chuckle, "Mr. Lane, I see two empty seats at the head table. You take the seat next to Aesop while I sit beside Long John."

THE LOVERS

THERE WAS SOMETHING ABOUT ROY Pearson that separated him from every television producer Steve Lane had ever known. Pearson was a perfectionist always in pursuit of the innovative and the provocative. Steve Lane had brought Pearson's first success to Otis & Meade before he joined the firm, and now as head of TV he was able to satisfy friendship and business by helping Pearson develop and market additional shows that brought added luster to him and O&M. Lane knew any Pearson show, even if it failed to become a major hit, would always be produced with the touch of Pearson quality. That was because Pearson supervised each of his shows as if each were the actual premiere.

But despite his success both artistically and financially, Roy Pearson had a surprisingly low self-esteem. While he managed to keep this a secret from many, Steve Lane had been in his confidence since their early days in Philadelphia. His present success had not changed his attitude. "I know," Pearson would say to Lane, "that most people think that because I've been successful I must have arrogance in my makeup to get as far as I have in this cutthroat business. But the truth is I have enormous fears, which is why I've never made a movie or produced for Broadway. Television is something I know—whether it's a comedy, a game show, or a movie of the week. And, most conspicuously, I've been a failure with women as well as with my kids."

Pearson's first wife, a young woman who'd been a classmate of his at Penn, had died in childbirth, leaving him the responsibility of raising their two children. But Pearson scarcely knew them, having hired a live-in nanny to care for them. Both children were growing distant—the absence of a mother and his preoccupation with his career were creating an unbridgeable chasm. That, plus Pearson's marriage to Veronica Grant, a beautiful patrician woman from Philadelphia's Main Line, daughter of a family that could trace its history to colonial Virginia. What Pearson didn't know at the time of his marriage was that the Grant family was in financial straits and that Veronica had been the bait that would ease their financial burden.

Pearson's children detested Veronica and Veronica snubbed them as people with no family lineage to match that of the Grants. And from her point of view she was right: what had Pearson's father been except the foreman of a steel plant in Bethlehem? What claim to 'blood' did Pearson, or his children, have? What claim even to be Philadelphians? No psychiatrist could alter the facts—his second wife detested his children with the same enthusiasm with which they detested her. She stunned her husband when she let him know—as he made an effort to bridge the gap between his wife and his children—"Why should I waste my time doing something you never bothered with until I came into your life?"

To which Roy had replied, "Because you're my wife, Veronica, and they're my children."

"Yours, yes, mine, no," was her blunt response. "I'll see them when it's absolutely necessary, but socially not at all. They wouldn't know one end of a horse from the other."

Snobbish as that attitude might be, there is no doubt Pearson saw possession of Veronica as attainment of a status he perhaps told himself he despised, yet desired. Life for Roy Pearson was always an emotional and psychological roller coaster.

There was something about Veronica that had always remained an enigma to Pearson; it started with their first encounter. He had been a guest of the Grants; he enjoyed the luxury of dining in the select quarters of the turf club, but the business of racing, the studying of charts and past performances, the pageantry of horses, jockeys, trainers, and judges bored him. Still, there was a snob appeal in going to the races that he couldn't resist, and there was the comforting thought that association with people like the Grants could help his business. He could invite important people like Steve Lane; even a Joe Gratton was susceptible to an invitation to the Grant's track club. The association with the Grants led not only to important business contacts, but to romance with Veronica.

Pearson had almost not met Veronica; it was only at the quiet insistence of old, elegant, white-haired Chet Grant, an executive of a major advertiser whose company bought spots on Pearson shows, that Pearson visited the track. Grant had taken him down to the paddocks ostensibly to get a closeup view of his favorite horse due to race in a few more days. But the real reason was to bring about a meeting with Grant's daughter. It baffled Pearson that well-groomed people like the Grants could be so indifferent to the dirt that swirled up in the stable area no matter how often it was wetted down; somehow he could never quite accept horses —particularly race horses—as animals to be fussed over and petted like favorite dogs. He loathed the dust, the horses sometimes frightened him, and though he had learned that it was more secure to stay close to them and to move slowly, his instincts bade him stay clear of their unpredictable movements and withdraw swiftly whenever they came near.

Thanks to old Grant, Pearson had spotted Veronica that first time wearing tight blue jeans and a blue silk blouse, which was tailored to accentuate the lines of her figure. She was standing just outside a stable, talking softly to a beautiful race horse prancing about on its four slender legs. The girl's long hair fluttered in a light breeze, glistening in the sunlight; what made her even more dazzling was that this luxurious crown of flaxen-colored hair was of the same subtle tone as the mane of the horse. Later, Pearson was to discover this striking combination of horse and girl was no mere accident: Veronica had bought the horse not only because of its proven ancestry but partly because its majestic mane matched her own.

"There's a beauty," old Grant had murmured, as they approached Veronica and her horse. Pearson, already familiar with Grant's fanaticism about horses, was certain Grant was directing his attention to the horses, when the old man added, "both of them."

Roy Pearson could hear the girl's soft voice as the big horse continued to prance about, his large eyes flashing red darts of flame, and he wondered how the girl could stand so fearlessly before the nervous animal. When the horse suddenly reared up, Pearson had a sickening thought that its sharp forelegs would strike the beautiful girl standing so near to him. He marveled at her coolness, how she stood her ground, and how the horse finally settled down at the sound of her reassuring voice.

Then, suddenly, the girl struck the horse forcefully across its nose. The horse's eyes seemed to roll in its head and to be lost in a red anger that surged up at the sudden violence. Its great nostrils flared, its whole body quivered, but still the girl held onto the halter, still she continued to talk in that soft purring-like manner and then suddenly the horse relaxed and nuzzled close to her. There was no doubt that she was in command.

It was then she spotted Pearson with her father. "You've got to know just when to show them if you want to control them," she said simply.

"Men or horses," Roy Pearson asked.

"Both," she said with a laugh. "I'm Veronica Grant," she added, extending a small, gloved hand.

From the moment he had first seen her standing in the sunlight at that stable, taming her horse, Roy Pearson had wanted her. And her surrender—if it could be called that—had come as much of a surprise as anything that had ever happened to him. He'd often wondered about that, how and why it happened, for their romance hadn't been just one of those quick summer things. In fact, she had made matters plain any number of times when he had pressed too hard. "Nothing will come of this," she had said once as he tried to subdue her in her apartment one night after the theater.

"Really?" Pearson replied, holding her in his arms.

"Even if you win," she'd said, looking at him in that enigmatic way of hers.

And so their courtship, if one could call it that, had progressed. Pearson, the successful but inwardly insecure producer, was determined to win: to elevate his place in the world, to win the girl of his choice, and to win at any price. Veronica had treated him with an amused superiority, confident of her poise and command, secure in her estimation of her own person. Pearson knew that she could have married any one of that group, they were all part of her world—the Lawrenceville men who went on to Princeton because their fathers had taken the same route, the Groton boys who had gone to Harvard, the Choate men who had followed their family tradition at Dartmouth, Yale, and Harvard. Meanwhile, he had had to work his way through school while his own father hung on as a minor clerk in a small hardware company in Allentown, Pennsylvania.

And then came the decisive night. Pearson had finally persuaded Veronica to came over to his apartment and he had hired help to serve them a lavish dinner, while he himself mixed the drinks and mixed them strong, clumsily urging her to drink up. "Do you have lots of other girls up here, Mr. Pearson?" she asked, sipping her drink, her eyes seeming to laugh at him.

Pearson hated her at that moment. The truth was that he had already given up dating other women and he knew Veronica was sure of it. "Why do you ask?" he replied defensively.

"You've been trying to get me up here for so long, and now I'm here." She stood near him holding her glass out. "More ice, please."

He reached down and dropped two cubes into her glass. "You are trying to get me drunk, aren't you?" she asked in her soft voice.

"Do I have to?" he said, filling up her glass.

"You have had other women here, haven't you?" she persisted. "Lots of them? Pushovers?" she added.

There was something in her eyes, a look of mild contempt, something in the sound of her voice, a subtle kind of mockery that began to anger Pearson. She began circling him as though he were a yearling about to be auctioned off. "And you've had your own little plan all worked out. Just the way a successful producer would," she said. "You arrange a perfectly lovely dinner, and send the help packing. Then on come the soft lights and sweet music. Continue with the attentive manner. Serve more drinks. Bigger drinks. And pow! You're all set to take your ticket to the cashier and cash it in—win, place, and show! That is," she said looking at him quizzically, "provided you have the winning ticket."

Pearson said quietly. "And do I?" He moved a bit closer to her.

For a moment they stood quietly staring at each other. "At the track you never waste good money on a long shot," she replied coolly as she picked up her wrap.

"Why you . . . you . . . damn!" he felt his face flush as the words choked in his mouth and he saw her hand strike out toward him and in that single moment he remembered how she had reached out to strike her horse suddenly, without warning. He blocked her blow, heard the stinging slap of his own palm across her cheek, saw her hair fly back as her head was jolted to the side, watched the crimson stain rise on her cheek. In the next instant she started to strike again, but he seized her and crushed her violently in his arms. She struggled and clawed at him, but he growled in his throat "I'm no damned animal you can abuse, no damned gelding, either!" He silenced her with a long, hard kiss.

She fought him at first, and then, as suddenly as she had struck out, tightened her arms around his neck and responded hotly. The dinner went uneaten, the ice melted in their drinks. He bent her back against the couch and then they tore at each other in a paroxysm of passion, clothes flying. He let her have no pause, no time to push him away and take stock, however briefly. He didn't think much of his body, but perhaps the stocky, male hairiness of it inflamed her. She was all sleek curves, with perfect pink nipples on milky breasts accentuated by her dark tan that he took into his mouth hungrily. After that he stopped thinking, and she stopped thinking, and if what followed was as much a fight as lovemaking, there was no doubt she responded to a strong hand. He was so carried away he almost didn't hear how her cries finally filled the room—almost. But he did, and that was his greatest pleasure. And then she did hit him. . . .

Both lay spent and bruised.

They were fated to marry, he thought: doomed to love and to hate, to bring pain and pleasure, and not to understand each other.

And throughout the early years of their marriage that had been a constant thorn—Veronica's absorption with horses, hunts, shows that took her away from their home in Beverly Hills and their New York condo—a world foreign to Roy and in which he had no interest. To make matters more difficult, after their marriage Veronica lost all interest in his own creative activities. Their life together became a series of escalating arguments that blackened eyes and inflamed skin, artfully concealed by clever makeup.

The climax came one night when Pearson, in from Beverly Hills, and Veronica, in from a Virginia hunt, had agreed to have a quiet dinner with Steve Lane at "21." Lane had brought good news from his agency—their clients would purchase all of the available time on Pearson shows carried by Federal Broadcasting. Joe Gratton stopped by to help celebrate the deal. Gratton was vital to Pearson's visibility on Federal's day and night schedule.

The celebration didn't last. Veronica felt Joe Gratton's pudgy fingers caressing her thigh beneath the tablecloth and she flared up in instant. No amount of backpedaling could stop her flood of angry contempt. Gratton, stunned by the bluntness of Veronica's reaction, and somewhat in his cups, tried lamely to minimize his behavior, but his excuses only provoked her scorn. Pearson, alarmed at his wife's rising temper in the quiet of the restaurant, as all eyes turned in their direction—and concerned, too, about anything that would threaten his close relationship with Gratton—tried to defend him. Perhaps, he said apologetically, it was all a misunderstanding. Veronica then turned her scorn upon her husband. Steve Lane tried to intercede, but Veronica abruptly rose from her chair suddenly striking a bewildered Gratton across his face, blood quickly flowing from his nose as his glasses flew across the table. Then, lifting her cordial glass filled with creme de cacao, she flung its contents into her astonished husband's face as he reached out for Gratton's glasses.

Veronica looked down at the bleeding Joe Gratton triumphantly, and at her husband's light gray suit stained with her drink, his embarrassment showing in his flushed cheeks, the stillness rudely broken by the sound of her laughter and the applause of other diners in the room. Veronica, chin held high, joined in the laughter as she looked down at Pearson dabbing at his stained lapels and at Gratton holding a napkin and trying to stem his flow of blood. A moment later she turned from the table and left the room.

Pearson and Gratton sat still, the former still mechanically stroking his stained lapels, Gratton muttering "bitch" as Steve Lane tried to replace Gratton's glasses on his face. Gratton picked up his drink, stumbling across to the bar. Pearson knew that his wife would have commandeered their limousine, and that Jeffrey, the chauffeur, would in due time send in a signal that he'd returned to "21"—this breach by no means being the first Jeffrey had encountered.

Pearson and Lane watched as Gratton, squaring his shoulders, ignored them both as he quietly left the room. Pearson continued to sit, letting his suit dry, confessing to Steve Lane his private concern, his fears that the escalating violence of some of his quarrels with Veronica could lead to a climax that no one could foresee.

After his suit had sufficiently dried Pearson prepared to take leave of Steve Lane, who counseled him to let matters calm down. Pearson strained to hold back his anger and frustration as he reassured Lane that everything would be all right, that he knew Gratton had overstepped his bounds, but that everyone also knew the man could be boorish. He would tell Veronica that he regretted not speaking up more manfully; the whole affair, when analyzed, was just another example of his own low self-esteem—his passivity in the face of another's insulting behavior toward his wife as though the purchase of his shows included access to her, too. Pearson knew as well that he would make the effort to try to win back Veronica's trust and respect by this confession. Perhaps, this would be the final episode of their senseless arguments; indeed, it had been Gratton's arrogant presumption that as a network official he could take advantage of his position to extract favors from a producer's wife. Perhaps it was this very act that might restore something that had been lost between Veronica and himself: mutual respect and trust.

Jeffrey had returned and Pearson left "21." He sat in the car quietly brooding. He remembered how he wanted to teach Veronica to use a gun, but when he'd presented her with a dainty, pearl-handled twenty-two designed to be carried in a woman's purse, she'd thrown it across the room. She spurned his anxiety that in these times of crime she might need a weapon for protection.

Their kind of violence baffled him, frightened him, for it was violence which so often surprised them both. It seemed to come out of very little, almost nothing. And he fretted over where it might one day lead. His concern for her had been genuine, and that was why he'd given her the twenty-two. Not all of their relationship was like tonight; there were good experiences and warm recollections, and yet there was an awareness, too, of lost time which should have been spent in gathering more memories of things to be treasured and savored.

As the limousine moved across town Pearson found himself shaking off images he'd long tried to forget, images of discovering how artful Veronica had been in concealing her addiction to alcohol. He remembered how he had come across her one night at home after he'd spent a long time at a studio run-through of a new game show. She had declined to attend the rehearsal and greeted him in his study wearing a flimsy negligee and waving a bottle of Drambuie over her head. "We're out of scotch so this will have to do," she exclaimed as she poured herself a full glass.

Pearson raised his hands in a futile protest, "Veronica, it's liqueur. You don't drink that by the glassful, for God's sake!"

Veronica snickered. "You don't," she laughed at him, "I do!"

"Please," Pearson entreated as he moved to grasp the bottle, twisting it from her.

"Let go!" she screamed as she held on to her drink with one hand and the bottle with the other.

"No!" Pearson shot back, fiercely twisting the bottle out of her hand and hurrying with it to the kitchen sink, Veronica clinging to his suitcoat as he drained it.

"Bastard!" she shouted. "You leave me here alone all night and expect me to do what? Play solitaire?"

"I wanted you to come to the run-through," he said.

"What? To watch one of your crummy little game shows?"

"They pay the rent," Pearson replied quietly, then pointing to her half-filled glass. "They pay for that, too."

Veronica turned her back on him and rushed down a hall to their bar. There she extracted another battle of Drambuie and held it high over her head. "You make sure there's no real scotch in this place, but at least I know this is a liqueur made from scotch." She then raced past him down another long hall to their bedroom, slamming the door and locking it. Pearson stood behind it, listening to her laughter. He knew it would be twenty-four hours before he'd see her again.

Other images floated through his mind as the car headed to their East Side home. He remembered a day during a Southampton vacation, barely twilight, when he'd left the spacious summer house they'd rented angered by inflammatory remarks she'd leveled at his children. He'd stalked out of the front door and turned down a bush-lined street to cool off his anger when suddenly Veronica, barefoot and wearing a short silk nightgown, caught up with him and began hammering away at him with both fists.

Pearson raised his hands to fend off the attack, pleading with her to go back home, "Calm down, please. We'll talk about it later, go on home, Veronica, please. You can't be seen like this!"

"We won't, you gutless little nothing, we'll talk about it now!" She grabbed an arm, and as he tried to stave off her attack she whirled him about and threw him into the sharp pointed branches of the bushes. Pearson, taken aback, his face scratched, lay as Veronica pointed to him with contempt. "Little nothing-asshole!" she whispered. "You talk about those children who you don't love and who don't give a whit about you except for your money! You compare them to me?" She lifted a bare foot and pushed it against his face as she left him struggling to rise.

And then there had been another incident he'd never forget. Veronica had been at home in their exercise room; she'd studied dancing earlier in her life and continued to stay in shape.

Pearson, who hated arguments, had backed away from one and retreated into his bathroom, but Veronica had followed demanding that he open the door. When he was convinced from the tone of her voice that she was, indeed, trying to placate him, he gingerly opened it, but the moment he did so Veronica pushed in and then with a tremendous sudden thrust she lashed out at him, raising her right foot, crashing it with great force against his chest, sending him reeling against a wall where he collapsed on the floor. A moment later Veronica hurled a heavy cut glass decanter at his head, the edge nicking his forehead as it splintered against the tile walls.

As the car approached his street, Pearson fretted about his own weakness, his actual brush with real injury, reviewing a montage of memories, too few pleasant, too many colored with hateful passions that seemed to be escalating into more and more violent confrontations. He knew he'd been the victim of spousal abuse, but what of it? He could never acknowledge it to others; it would be too demeaning, too repugnant to publicize his own low self-esteem. He simply knew that they could not continue any longer in such a pattern of constant emotional upheavals. He would make the gesture to be conciliatory because, like it or not, he still loved Veronica, but he knew it would be futile now.

As Roy entered their condominium he heard the distant sound of music, his favorite songs, the music he'd given Veronica as one of last year's many anniversary presents. The strain of "As Time Goes By" floated toward him. He knew Veronica would be in her bed waiting for him—her way of making up for their bad moments, wearing her newest lingerie as she'd so often done before, surrendering to *his* apologies. But as he pushed open the door, he saw her seated on the bed—still, strangely, in the same clothes she'd worn at "21"—and then he heard the little sound as though a champagne cork had popped in the distance. In that split second he noted the smile on Veronica's face, heard the second popping sound. And then he felt the sting, the sudden surge of fire within his body, the heat and the roaring of blood in his throbbing temples. He looked down at his chest and saw the tiny red marks and then their sudden swift and widening surge.

Now he saw the tiny, toy-like, delicate little mechanism that he had given to her. His head slumped down, and he noticed the red stain spreading across his shirt, and to the left he saw the frayed tear in his suit. The tailor would have to send it out for weaving, but it embarrassed him to think he'd have to face up to the question of how the tear got there, and there was a new sense of humiliation. The red stain kept growing and it was hot and he saw Veronica's eyes—that enigmatic, superior look that made him wonder if she ever could have loved him.

Then he knew, as only a man could know when only a split moment was left and nothing mattered, that she must never have loved him but must have hungered, instead, in dream after dream for a moment like this. He remembered in that same flash how her father had singled her out when he first saw her, and realized how profoundly misused he had been. It was unbearable, unbearable!

His left arm quivered as he sought to raise it to slow down the hot sliver of steel that was driving into him, breaking apart a thousand processes, but there was no holding it back. He felt his eyes rolling back in his head. A moment of rage enveloped him. Could Veronica sit there so calmly as he, Roy Pearson, drowned alone in a roaring red surf? He would always remember later how, as total darkness enveloped him, he heard her laughing.

● ● ●

Sometime later, Pearson would tell Steve Lane of the feelings that swept over him as he recognized the small revolver he'd given Veronica for her safety, her protection in case an emergency ever arose that threatened her—an intruder who might have sought entry into the sanctity of their bedroom. That turned out to be her defense, and Pearson had not challenged it. He preferred it rather than acknowledge the truth of their relationship.

The divorce did not surprise Roy Pearson; he had to admit that "irreconcilable differences" was a modest, though maddening, euphemism for a cold, premeditated attempted murder.

Perhaps, Steve Lane had pointed out, as Cynthia Warner approached their table at "21" some six months later, things would be different, particularly as she had told Lane she simply marveled at Roy Pearson's creativity. Perhaps, Lane insisted, she would restore his self-esteem.

Pearson shrugged his shoulders, a flicker of a smile crossing his face. "Restore?" Roy had replied. "Restore?" he repeated. "Doesn't that imply that my self-esteem had been there—before?" Pearson stood up to greet Cynthia, and then looked down at Steve Lane. "Nothing has changed, Steve, nothing."

THE LAST PERFECT BEST

THERE WAS ALWAYS SOMETHING TANTALIZINGLY elusive about Rob Sanford, his sometimes contradictory manner: one day easygoing and approachable, the next, aloof and preoccupied. These were attitudes—combined with his at times excessive exuberance and the penetrating way in which his eyes darted from one person to another at agency meetings—that aroused curiosity, even hostility, among some of the men with whom he worked, and admiration and fascination among most of the women. It wasn't that Rob ever boasted about his experiences; to the contrary, his references to place and time and famous names, which peppered his conversations, were dropped in almost as throwaways. And most of that came into the open in the midst of arguments which he always seemed to enjoy provoking.

Sanford, although he dutifully reported, at least on paper, to Steve Lane at Otis & Meade, nevertheless became Steve's chief rival, at least in the eyes of James Hornwell

Otis. Just as disconcerting to Steve was Rob's sudden winning of the favor of Laura Kent, one of New York's most beautiful models.

The irony was that it was Steve Lane who had discovered Laura and had helped lift her to prominence by recommending her on one of O&M's most important accounts, but it was Rob who went overboard in his enthusiasm for her by signing her to an exclusive deal for all O&M clients, an action that won the applause of Mr. Otis.

The truth is no one at the agency ever quite figured out who the real Rob Sanford was. He had the natural gifts of a born storyteller. But while his stories about his own experiences prior to joining O&M charmed some, there were others who wrote them off as the mark of an insecure man simply bent on enlarging his own standing at the agency. Once he claimed that he could have made the pro circuit with the best golfers, but he shrugged off insistent invitations from his associates to play a round. It was Steve Lane who finally confided to an associate that he suspected Sanford didn't know one golf club from another. To everyone's surprise, however, and to Steve's discomfiture, it was Otis who, at the monthly O&M shareholders' luncheon, startled Steve and the others by reporting that Rob had recently joined him in a foursome at Otis's Greenwich country club, and that Rob's outstanding playing had astounded the club's pro and the state champion who'd been the pro's partner.

Still, other stories persisted that Sanford wasn't the figure he made himself out to be. People in his circle were never quite certain whether Rob Sanford was merely a gifted liar in the Baron Munchausen tradition, or whether, as he claimed, he really had run up a heroic record serving in a secret special elite force in Vietnam, or had actually participated in bull fights in Madrid or accomplished a dozen or more of his other claims to fame. If these were all true, then being at O&M seemed too tame for him. He should be living the life of a contemporary Hemingway.

But one accomplishment was beyond question. Rob Sanford carried off the beautiful Laura and that alone left a gaping wound in Steve Lane's life. Steve had never forgotten how his affair with Laura had happened. It had begun at a most inappropriate time. She had agreed to come up to Steve's apartment for cocktails some two weeks after they'd met to celebrate her initial contract. Steve hadn't told her that he was exhausted, that he'd been up half the night before working against an Otis deadline to complete a presentation for a new campaign that he had to bring in the next morning. And Laura hadn't told Steve that she had a fever and that she was carrying her small overnight bag because she had to catch a train at Penn Station in about an hour—that she was visiting a brother who was a naval officer, whose ship had docked at the Philadelphia Navy Yard en route to the Panama Canal. That night Steve didn't finish the presentation and Laura didn't reach Philadelphia. Steve did come down with a raging fever and a worse case of being in love. But the affair was to be short lived.

When Steve finally finished the presentation he felt that he'd earned a special treat; he'd called Laura and left a message for her to meet him at "21" for drinks and dinner. When he got there he found Rob Sanford at the bar. There was another thing about Rob that singled him apart from others. He was direct and to the point. "She isn't coming, buddy," he said abruptly to Steve.

"Oh?" Steve was plainly jarred. "You're here to tell me that?" was all he could say.

"Give the man a double bourbon," Rob said to the bartender as he turned to Steve. "It was a couple of nights ago. I was getting ready to meet a couple of clowns who'd covered Vietnam with me when there was a knock on the door. When I opened it there was the lady." He sipped his drink and watched Steve. "She was wearing a white moire coat trimmed in mink and she was holding a tiny bouquet of roses. Buds they were, really. She looked absolutely splendid."

"She always looks splendid," Steve said realizing that he must have looked as foolish as he sounded. "I think I know the end of the story."

"You don't. There is no ending. There probably never will be an ending." He put down his glass. "I just thought you ought to know."

"I never had a woman bring me flowers," Steve said lamely.

Rob picked up the check and patted Steve's cheek as he leaned in close. "There's always a first time." Then he added, "You don't mind, do you?"

"Would it make any difference?"

"Not really."

Even more surprising than Rob's winning Laura was his sudden departure some months later from O&M.

Sanford had sought the meeting with Steve and made known the startling decision. Steve, sitting in his elegant corner office, could only blurt out, "But why? Why now?"

"Because it's the right time, that's why," Rob replied.

"Is there something here that's bothering you?" Steve asked and then added, "something about us, maybe you and I . . . ?" concern etched on his face.

"Not at all, not at all," Rob countered. "It's just what I said: it's the right time."

Steve, shifting uneasily in his chair, ran the events of the last few days through his mind. They had just made a General Foods presentation—or Sanford had, as Steve watched, impressed by his brilliance as usual. Why wasn't he writing novels? Making movies? Going to strange places and making electrifying documentaries? Afterward he had complimented Sanford on his creative powers, even suggested they were more than an agency could use. Had Sanford taken that amiss? Steve stared at his open, happy face, the untroubled blue eyes: no, that couldn't have been it. And if Sanford had, he wouldn't have resigned in a huff and given Steve such an easy triumph, if triumph it was. After all, he wondered, how would Mr. Otis take the departure of Rob Sanford, someone whom he plainly liked? Would he, Steve Lane, be thought of as the real reason for Sanford's sudden decision? Or, as Lane struggled to find a specific reason, meanwhile studying the charming man seated before him, was this just a Sanford ploy, maybe a way to persuade Otis to move Sanford up, even over him?

Sanford lifted both hands toward Steve. "Steve," he said, his eyes dancing with laughter—or so it seemed at the moment to Lane, "it's just how I said it. No games here, no making a move to get anyone bothered—"

"Mr. Otis thinks the world of you," Steve cut in.

"I think the world of him," Rob promptly responded, "and, if the truth be known the same goes for you. I've had a helluva good time here and if," he added with a smile, "I ever gave you any contrary feelings, consider them dead."

"I still don't get it."

"I've said it straight out—that's the only way I deal, you know that, Steve."

It was the one thing Steve Lane did not know, not for sure.

As though he were reading Steve's mind, Rob said with some finality, "Take it from me, Steve, it's just the right time."

The two men sat quietly for some moments and then Rob abruptly rose from his chair and edged toward the door.

"You don't want to say anything—anything more?" Steve asked, adding, "I think Mr. Otis would do a lot to encourage you to stay."

"That's the whole story, Steve. And I'll leave it to you to tell Mr. Otis and anyone else you think it might interest."

"You're giving up a lot, Rob," Steve said as Rob opened the door.

"Could be. But I have Laura." And with that he was gone.

Steve sat in his office puzzled. When the word got out it was plain that Mr. Otis missed Sanford, and while he didn't precisely blame Steve for losing him, he'd made a point of telling Steve how he saw matters. "A good man," Otis had said as Steve advised him of the sudden resignation. "A good man," he'd repeated, adding, "good men are hard to find, even harder to keep." As he walked Steve to the door, Otis tapped him lightly on the shoulder. "There's a lesson there for you, Steve, in fact a lesson for every man who exercises responsibility. A company is built by special men and women and those men and women must have one key element that sets them apart from others—and that's judgment." As he and Steve stood outside his ornate office, Otis went on, "I wouldn't trade our group of shareholders for any of the top leadership of any of our clients. Sanford had the right stuff as the saying goes." Again, he patted Steve on the shoulder. "He'll be missed."

When Steve returned to his office he closed the door behind him and glumly slouched in his chair. He glanced at the phone and wondered if he should try to reach Sanford. He was fully aware that he had been reprimanded in Mr. Otis's own cool style. With that he instantly knew he had to make an honest effort to persuade Sanford to change his mind.

Steve buzzed his secretary. "Ring Rob Sanford at his apartment, please."

While Steve Lane waited to discuss the Otis meeting with Rob he pondered every word of that meeting. The rebuke had been verbalized in that evenhanded manner that defined Otis and set him apart from all the others at the agency, particularly from Steve's mentor, the firebrand Tony Gordon. Steve's uneasiness about the meeting was abruptly ended by the appearance of his secretary, Anne Koyce. She stood at the open doorway, surprise showing on her face.

"His phone doesn't answer," Anne said.

"So you'll try later."

"No," Anne replied. "The phone's been disconnected."

"Disconnected?" Steve said, startled.

"I had it checked," Anne said. "Then I spoke with the doorman. And he said the most surprising thing."

"Which was?"

"That the Sanfords had put all of their furniture in storage and had left in a cab a few moments before I'd called. No forwarding address either."

As Steve was outlining to Tony Gordon the sudden

events that had transpired in his office and in Otis's, Gordon sat still except for the occasional familiar gesture of his, his running his hand through his thick black hair.

"Okay, I understand it all. Sanford just ups and goes. Never liked the lying son of a bitch. Then you get dressed down by that Scandinavian icicle down there in the corner office. Makes no sense, unless—" Gordon stopped and looked quizzically at Steve.

"Unless what, Tony?"

"Unless he's got some goddamn new job. What else?"

"I don't know about a job. All he kept saying was that this was the right time."

"The right time for what?" Gordon snorted. "He's a smart son of a bitch, I'll give him that. Probably be making an announcement in a couple of weeks—maybe sooner. And you, my friend," he added, smiling at Steve, "don't you give a day's thought to—" he pointed toward Otis's office—"Mr. Big and his lecture on judgment. You sit quiet and make him reach out for you. He needs you and with Sanford gone he'll need you even more. Remember, you don't do anything except send the old bastard a note on how Mr. Rob Sanford prepares his exit—moves out, cuts off his phone, probably figured it all out to see how far Otis will go to try to reach him." Tony chuckled. "That's where that smart-ass Sanford figured Otis wrong. A man does that, our Mr. Otis takes it personal, real personal. Remember, no one ever gets invited to play at his golf club unless Mr. Otis has plans." Gordon's eyes narrowed. "We'll probably never know. But, you, Steve," Gordon said, his dark eyes narrowing, "remember, he'll forget Sanford. And you make Mr. Otis reach out for you."

● ● ●

Three years passed and where Rob Sanford had been, what he'd been doing, had continued to be a mystery until his first novel suddenly appeared. It was highly praised, but like J. D. Salinger of *Catcher in the Rye* fame, Sanford had shunned the limelight, avoiding all interviews.

And then, one day, Lane got a call at his office: Rob and Laura were in town and wanted to see him. He agreed to meet them at the Oak Room of the Plaza, Rob's choice.

Arriving first, Steve selected a table where he could easily spot them as they approached the maitre d's desk. A few minutes later Rob entered the room a step ahead of Laura; Steve saw that Rob was all movement, scanning the room like an up periscope searching and spotting everything and everyone all at once, the periscope finally seeming to focus on Steve Lane.

Steve instantly sensed the man's old flamboyance as Rob pounded the maitre d's shoulder, greeting him with the camaraderie of bygone days. Laura, standing beside him, a bit in a shadow, looked beautiful and radiant at first glance, still wearing the mark of one who lived by her own standards, slim and elegant, but even from that distance Steve slowly detected a change. It was the color of her skin, the shape of her face, no longer a pure oval. Then as Laura and Rob moved further into Lane's line of vision—the two of them simultaneously saw Steve's upraised hand—he saw, to his instant shock, that Laura had really changed. With each step she took Steve had the sensation of observing a fast moving series of snapshots, watching an aging process that had destroyed that Hepburn-like image and left in its place an emaciated caricature of past glory. Her hair no longer had that lustrous shine, and that chic, tawny mass that swung away like a race horse's mane was shorter, too, brittle in tone and texture, limp instead of alive; the gray green eyes were there, but deeper in their sockets, as were the once barely perceptible dimples under her high cheek bones, now larger, appearing as sunken hollows. She was thinner, pale, and seemed, in fact, more like a wraith than the fullbodied woman Steve remembered.

They greeted Steve with affection. Steve listened to Laura's husky voice, as she offered a hand to his. She pressed it and there was that special warmth in her touch. Her voice still had that peculiar hypnotic sound that formed itself into words, a sensuous, throaty sound, enveloping, no less embracing as he remembered for a moment the curl of her arms sliding soundlessly about him when they'd first met.

Laura took a seat across from Steve, her eyes fixed on his. When she spoke Steve kept feeling the magnetic sound of that extraordinary voice, its compulsive attention-getting quality. For a moment they sat in silence and Steve thought it was a curious scene, frozen, like something from a Hopper painting, the three of them, each with his own thoughts, Laura's eyes riveted to Steve's, Rob's fastened on her, admiringly. It was Rob, his blue eyes suddenly darting about the wood-paneled room, who broke the silence and who began to tell Steve that it was he, Steve, who had been his inspiration. "Do you remember the moment?" he asked Steve.

"Not exactly."

Rob chuckled. "Think, my friend. It'll come to you. One day after a presentation we'd made you said to me that my creative powers, or juices or whatever, were far greater than an agency could ever use in its work. Remember that?"

"The General Foods presentation?" Steve ventured. The incident flashed back into mind, and the left-handed praise he had offered Sanford, afraid at the time that Rob had taken it amiss.

Rob turned to Laura. "Told you, honey, he'd remember that moment with a little prod." Then turning his attention back to Lane, he went on, "That was the exact moment I knew the time had come to turn the key on the old front door and set sail for bigger things. That first novel," he added, beaming.

"A very impressive job, I must admit." Steve hoped he was hiding his surprise. He knew, of course, the impact chance remarks could have on people who, for reasons unknown to the speaker, were in a particularly receptive frame of mind, but he had never guessed his own had had such an impact! Rob Sanford must have been thinking all the time he was at O&M that life had cut him out for a far different purpose, too: Steve had just said the right thing at the right moment in supreme ignorance.

"You started it, Steve." Sanford leaned down and retrieved a briefcase he'd set beside him. "Brought this along. Has some notes, private things I thought might interest you whenever you get a chance." He pushed the briefcase toward Steve.

Laura stood up and glanced down at Steve as she excused herself before he could think of anything to say. Steve noticed her teeth had lost their brilliance and their whiteness, and her smile creased her features in a thousand fractured lines. He almost felt compelled to glance away. "Laura was always one of a kind," he heard Rob say, Rob's eyes following her until she left the room. Then, turning back to Steve, he whispered, "She's still the most beautiful thing in the world, right?" moving in closer to Steve and continuing in a confidential tone. "You might say the last perfect best. Agreed?"

Steve was at once relieved, at this turn of the conversation, and embarrassed, since to him Laura had so plainly lost that freshness and sunshine-clear look that had set her apart from the other top models. Nevertheless, Rob continued with his excessive, or so it seemed to Steve, praise of Laura, placing her on some kind of pedestal, likening her to the legendary beauties of literature and history. His voice fell almost to a whisper. "What I'm trying to tell you, Steve, and I may not have the words for it, but Laura's simply the best, the most perfect of all the people I ever met. Plain and simple." He edged in closer to Steve. "Like I said, the last perfect best. Agreed?"

Steve was uncomfortable. He concluded that Rob, the gifted author of so many wild-eyed experiences he'd claimed were his, might well he speaking from his heart. How else could one explain his ravings—or so they seemed to Steve—about a beauty that had so obviously faded. And he wondered if this could simply be a protective affection to bolster Rob's own desire to be proven right especially when Rob kept moving in closer and closer again to remind Steve that it was he, Rob, who had been the winner and that Steve had been the loser. "Like I said, old man," Rob repeated, "she's simply the best that ever was, the most perfect. Right?" He reached over to touch Steve's arm.

Steve found the final answer to this puzzling recitation several weeks later when he opened his morning paper and read of the sudden death of Laura Sanford, the onetime, fabulous beauty whose last wish, according to a statement written by her husband, was to return to Manhattan where she had been the idol of so many and to die there from an untreatable cancer. And with the tragic account was the even more startling news that her husband, the noted novelist, Rob Sanford, who'd been somewhat of a recluse since the publication of his first book, had made his wife—whom he termed, in a final note left on the bed where his body had been found next to hers, "the last perfect best, the most perfect of all the beings he'd ever known"—his special concern, caring for her to the very end, for Rob was found next to her with a small bullet wound in his right temple.

Steve Lane thought of Rob's reason for leaving O&M, and the colorful stories he had doubted. He thumbed through the briefcase Rob had left with him the night before; in it were citations and medals Rob had won in his service in special forces in Vietnam, plus colorful posters of bullfights staged in Madrid and Mexico, the matadors' names, with the banderillaros—all Spanish names except for his, Rob Sanford.

Steve stayed home that day reading the rest of the contents of Rob's briefcase, finally aware that in the end it was Rob Sanford who was, in fact, the true last perfect best.

THE NICE GUY

As Steve Lane reached for his salad, he spotted Mike Harris conferring with Emile, Sardi's maitre d'. There was Mike's same old captivating manner, mixed with his special blend of belonging everywhere. Emile looked half protestingly at his reservation book and shook his head politely, but in the end Emile was escorting Mike to a table.

Steve's wife saw him coming. "Good Lord," Susan said, "here comes that—man." It was funny, Steve thought, how often he had heard women label Mike "that—man," and how often they continued to succumb to his blandishments.

"Can't stay, kids," Mike said, sitting down and reaching both hands toward Steve and Susan. "Got a dish coming that could thaw the North Pole. Still, she can't touch you, Susie," he added gallantly. "Made up your mind, genius?" he said to Steve; he made a move to playfully and ingratiatingly nuzzle his nose against Susan's, but at that moment she reached for a compact from her purse and forestalled him. Susan was not one to succumb to unwanted blandishments.

For a moment Steve studied Mike Harris. Mike had the vigorous bounce of a man not yet forty, and he posed—preposterously, it seemed to everyone—as someone old enough to be everyone else's father. This, he boasted, gave him the right to take little personal liberties women would tolerate from no one else. Mike was probably in his mid-fifties, Steve guessed, but it didn't matter. No one cared, because Mike was a little beyond time.

"Still thinking," Steve said, in response to Mike's question.

"Well, come on, kid, get a move on," Mike replied, smiling. "Papa can't wait forever. Ah," he added softly, nodding toward the entrance of the Oak Room, "the dish has arrived. How's that for keeping all the chromosomes hopping?"

Steve saw the overdressed, overbuilt girl standing at the door. So did everyone in the room.

Mike chuckled softly. "Never failed yet, kid. Walk into a place with a million dollars sticking out of your handkerchief pocket, nobody cares. Get yourself a tightly dressed, twenty-year-old female, and the whole place comes alive. If I had come in with her, nobody'd have noticed me, but now they're just as curious to find out who she's with as who she is. It's guys like you, Steve, who drive me to dames like her," he said laughingly. "I just gotta be kept busy. Oh, sure, and one more thing," he said, going to lift Susan's chin with a finger, but failing as she leaned back gracefully, "business." Mike never missed a beat. "Strictly business. She's a new bit of talent, just waiting to be discovered."

"And you're Columbus," Susan replied.

Mike chuckled, and hurried to the girl.

"What is he waiting for you to decide on?" Susan asked.

"It's very simple, Sue. Mike's out of the network."

"Fired?"

"Fired, resigned, what's the difference? He's out, and he wants a job."

She started to laugh. "Why is he talking to you about a job, of all people?"

Steve lifted his drink. He was bothered by a strange, sensuous odor.

"It's Mike's afterglow," Susan said, "he still bathes in some oriental mixture."

The soft, tantalizing fragrance seemed to echo in the past. Steve knew how ridiculous it would seem to Susan that he could even consider hiring Mike. Experience is supposed to be a great teacher, and Steve had had his lesson.

Mike had been a publicity man, one of the best. He had invited Steve to meet him at Sardi's: Mike had a faded Hollywood star to sell. "Look, kid," he said, "I'll give it to you straight. This dame's had it, as far as the big time. Still, she's got something. Fay Lester, that's still a name," he emphasized.

"Television doesn't pay her kind of money," Steve said.

"Who's talking money?" Mike replied. "This dame's loaded. She owns half of Sunset Boulevard. But she wants to hear that old music. You know, kid, you advertising guys still have a lot of influence in shows, but you don't understand show people. Loaded or busted, they gotta hear music, their kind. Applause. Attention. Name in the paper. Interviews with columnists. Now I'll level with you. This dame's my bread and butter. Her agent's given up, but Uncle Mike's gotta pay the food bill you just ran up on me, and I gotta get her publicity and guest shots on TV."

Steve had to laugh. Mike's candor was disarming. "Would Fay Lester be willing to work in commercials, for example, sell soap?" he asked.

"Soap?" Mike grinned at Steve. "Look, kid, she'll even do your laundry. When do we start?"

It was at that moment Steve got the wild idea. "Mike," he said, "I've got a notion. Instead of just selling Fay Lester—"

"Anything she wants to do after the show, she's a big girl and on her own time." Mike folded his hands as if he'd just delivered a sermon. "But, kid," he whispered, leaning toward Steve, "if it's the sine qua non of the deal—"

Steve cut him off. "No, no, Mike. It's not that at all. I want both of you."

For a moment Mike sat in silence. Then he chuckled. "I come high," he said.

"We can pay."

"Then let's forget Fay and talk about Mike."

So Mike Harris joined Otis & Meade as Steve's chief lieutenant; but there were times when Steve felt he'd made a serious error in judgment in hiring him. "You've got to conform, believe me," he once told him. "You can't just tell a client to roll the dice and shoot a million on some whim. Television is a business, not Las Vegas."

Mike stood before Steve's desk, patiently listening. Finally, he gave some advice of his own. "What you say is true, kid," he said, "but you've got a missionary job to do, too. Teach the big wheels that the television business is a lot closer to Las Vegas than it is to Detroit, or Tokyo. Grinding out cars is a lot easier than grinding out shows. Especially when models last for years now! In show business a bunch of pastrami-eating geniuses sit down to build a new situation comedy. They get a good idea. Then they get the best writers, the best talent. They make a pilot. It's new. It's funny. But the same schnooks that loved Bill Cosby's last show yawn the first night. You're dead. Worse than dead—because you have an ulcer that keeps you alive and a pink slip to go with your hot-water bottle."

Steve had to laugh. That was one of Mike's characteristics—making a man laugh even when the man was trying to correct him. And men laughed even when Mike showed another of his talents—the talent to push ahead. Steve had seen it within six months. Fay Lester had been willing to sell soap, but the American housewife wouldn't buy it. Mike was the one to recommend that she be dropped.

"I thought you wanted Fay to succeed," Steve said.

"I did. I do," Mike replied.

"Then why not work with her?"

"You're a nice guy, Steve. Me? I'm Mike Harris. I hear signals. Like Mr. Otis doesn't like her. That's enough for me. But you'll give it the schoolboy try. I give her a double Martini, tell her she's wasting her time. Did Bette Davis sell soap? Hepburn? Look, every day she's here she's a personal reminder to Mr. Otis and to Commodore Soap that Mike Harris can't pick a winner any better than an office boy can, and costs ten times as much." Mike smiled. "It's simple. Fay walks the plank. But you wait—she'll be in to thank you."

It was true. Two weeks later, Fay Lester visited Steve and asked to be released from her contract because she felt it was an impediment to her return to the screen. Mr. Otis complimented Mike on having effected the change; he had already forgotten that Mike had sold her to the agency.

As the months rolled on, Mike followed some of Steve's

advice; he learned that to conform was the pattern for steady progress. One morning Steve found a new name on the office door next to his.

Mike appeared suddenly, studying the gold lettering.

"How about that, kid?" he said, poking Steve cheerfully. "Happened last night. Met old man Otis at '21.' Had a drink, and the next thing I knew, I was promoted to your floor. The works."

"New title?" Steve asked hesitantly.

"Associate something or other. Kid, we're going to have a ball."

Steve went home disturbed. Susan put it tersely. "Watch your back."

"Nobody's been hurt, Susan," Steve said, trying to put the best face on Mike's rise.

She laughed. "You are so naive sometimes!"

"Me?" he was too startled to control his response. She laughed again.

"If you could just see your face! What could you be thinking, hiring Mike Harris? He's so slick bodies keep moving around even after he's taken their heads off. You said Fay Lester actually *thanked* you. You'll be next."

"Mike's not after me, Susan. I brought him in, coached him, taught him our side of the business. He owes me some kind of loyalty," he said.

"You didn't have to teach him everything you knew!" She leaned over and kissed him to take the sting out her words. "I love you because under the business veneer you have such decent impulses," she murmured. "It's so unexpected. Usually someone who comes across hard, even ruthless, is the opposite in private, weak and whining. Not you. You try to be a good man. So just be careful you don't let your brilliant ideas and instinctive trust in others blind you to someone who could hurt you." She put her arms around him. He was still a little stiff from being caught up short, but there was no way to resist this mix of asperity and sweetness.

Susan had created an atmosphere of domestic security for him, and if his career had been at times a source of concern, he was realistic enough to appreciate not just the necessity of competition between home and work, but the need sometimes to see things from an entirely different perspective. Susan seemed so conventional: a lady, somehow, in a time when ladies seemed history. Yet there were unexpected facets in her, a strength, an astuteness, an unshakable balance that startled him. He had no idea what their source was in her. Ultimately, she was his greatest mystery.

As for Mike: his promotion was just a "business change," one of Mr. Otis's favorite sayings, and Mike was the quickest bee in the O&M hive, buzzing about this show, lighting on another, and building up a vast reservoir of honey. To no one's great surprise, when the head of the television department was promoted to supervise media operations, Mr. Otis narrowed his choice as successor to Steve and Mike and he chose Mike.

Mr. Otis explained his decision to Steve, going out of his way to make the point that Mike had never discussed the job with him. He had made the decision on a simple premise. "Mike is a showman," he said.

"So am I," Steve insisted.

"Of course you are," Mr. Otis said graciously. "But it's a matter of emphasis. You're also a thoughtful, purposeful man with managerial talent; but Mike has a peculiar flair." Mr. Otis went on to describe clients' reactions to Mike's roster of friends in the entertainment world. "He makes important impressions for us."

"How about contributions?" Steve asked sharply. Mr. Otis breathed wearily. It was irritating to him to have a decision of his become a matter of further discussion.

Otis liked Steve and Steve liked Otis; in truth Steve couldn't blame him for liking Mike. "The question is only a rhetorical one, Mr. Otis. I accept the decision, and I understand it." They shook hands, and Steve returned to his office.

Mike was waiting for him. "I didn't ask for the job, kid." That was true, and in Mike's code, Mike had won the job. Steve realized that most of all he couldn't have won against Mike's newness—newness had a powerful fascination in the world in which he labored. "Let's celebrate tonight, kid," Mike said, "you, me, and Susan. We're a one-two combination, and we're shooting for the stars."

One and two, Steve thought, but he knew that in Mike's world there could be no number two. He himself could hire a Mike, train him, and work with him. Mike was different. He would worry because number two was next to number one. He would promote other men—three or four, so that their chief personal preoccupation would be not which of them would rise to number one, but which would hold number two.

Steve's premonitions proved correct. In a few weeks, two new men were brought in; like Steve, each was made an associate director of the television department. "You need relief," Mike had said, explaining the new setup to Steve, "and one thing's for sure—you can't get good men without moving them right to the top. But you and I are still the team," he said.

But the newness of two new men was an intrusion on the old way of life. Steve stopped frowning in front of Mike, but Susan was harder to fool. At home one night, he stood staring at the crowded street below.

Susan never said anything remotely like, "I told you so." She only fretted about his own unhappiness. Steve didn't take his eyes off the street. "Do you think, Sue," he said, faltering, "do you think I'm wrong if I give it up?"

"Do you mean you're giving up Mike or he's giving you up?"

"Pretty shrewd way of putting it," he said ruefully. She went toward him, and he pulled her into his arms. "I don't know that he's giving me up, honey. I only know that I don't want to find out."

She kissed him lightly. "Write. I'll bet anything you have some good novels in you." Steve stared at her. Susan was way ahead of him. "Produce television shows independently. It's ironic," she murmured.

"What is?" He was still taking in how far ahead of him she had been.

"That you like Mike. But you've never liked playing games."

"Everybody likes Mike," he said. "Even the ones who hate him." Then, "How long have you known?"

"How deep is my understanding? How much further have I seen, than you?" He nodded, ruefully, but she laughed. "I've only had to watch *you*. That told me everything. And you were caught in the middle of it. Who sees things clearly then?"

Mike was genuinely surprised when Steve dropped into his office and told him he had resigned. Steve tried to explain; but the more he elaborated, the more puzzled Mike became. "I always thought you were a nice guy," Mike finally said.

"What's that supposed to mean?" Steve asked.

"You sell me on coming here. Then, as soon as I hire two new faces, poof! there goes Steve Lane. I counted on you, kid, and you're walking out on me." Steve watched Mike as he shuffled from one end of his office to the other. "Let's face it, kid. I don't really know which end's pointed in this business. Nice guys don't run out, that's what I mean. Now maybe it's the other way round." Mike tapped Steve on the chest. "Maybe," he said, "maybe I'm the nice guy. I try to get a couple of schnooks in so you can train them and we can do the matinee circuit together, and you go resign to Otis without giving me any reasons."

"I've told you why, Mike."

"And I don't think so," Mike said, pushing his face close to Steve's. "You afraid of me? You afraid I was going to push—all the way?"

Steve looked into Mike's eyes. He was troubled by what he saw. He couldn't recall ever having been as close to Mike as he was right then. Mike's eyes were a dark brown with an almost black inner ring, and they seemed to be surrounded by bony armor; the lids lay heavily in folds, giving him the appearance of an ancient armadillo. "You never had to push, Mike," he said softly. "When a man starts pushing in this business sometimes he sets off a chain reaction."

"Nobody pushes Uncle Mike. Nobody," Mike replied sharply.

Three months after Steve left Otis & Meade, Mike himself abruptly resigned and took over as vice president in charge of programming at Federal for Joe Gratton. Steve sent him a congratulatory note, and Mike replied, "Greetings, and Uncle Mike requests the pleasure of your company at four o'clock, high tea, my office, next Wednesday."

Steve remembered now, as he sat together with Susan in the Oak Room, that he had shown Susan the note at breakfast. "Maybe we misjudged him."

"Maybe he's just curious," she said.

"Could be," Steve said. "I haven't set the world afire, yet. Who knows, maybe Mike wants me to do something at the network. As Machiavelli said, Mike Harris can be a lion one day and a fox the next."

"And did he add that when he starts the lion-fox bit, he winds up being a louse all the time?" she asked.

"You're just cynical in the morning," he said, kissing her lightly. "Even if you're probably right." She was mollified.

At four o'clock, Mike came out to the reception room, escorting a visitor. "Good to see you, kid," he heard Mike say to the man as the elevator door opened. Steve watched as they shook hands and he heard Mike call out, "See you Friday at noon." Then he walked over and pumped Steve's hand. "Hi, kid. How are you and Susan?"

"Couldn't be better, Mike. Does everyone get the royal treatment? Personal escort all the way to the elevator?"

Mike chuckled. "Royal treatment, my foot. It's an old trick to walk them out, see them going down—just to make sure they don't come back."

"Well, this one's going to come back. I heard you invite him."

"Doesn't mean a thing, kiddo. In this door," he said, leading the way to a highly modernized office. "You gotta see some guys a couple of times. Appearances. I wouldn't hire him if he was the last man on earth, but I'll see him one more time. Three times altogether. He'll figure I treated him nice. Nice guy, that's me." He walked around the desk and sat on its edge looking down at Steve. "Want to come here with me?"

"Now, why would I want to do that?"

"Simple. Unless you're well heeled, and you're not, you haven't the time to write the great American novel. What's more, you and Susan like your creature comforts too much. What's even more, you haven't been in print, on television, or on the back of the New York, New Haven, and Hartford Railroad timetable with a by-line. So why shouldn't you want to come here?"

"I resigned to write," Steve insisted.

"Okay. And you'd have resigned if old man Otis had tapped you to run his TV department? Your ego resigned for you. You should have stayed."

Steve looked up at Mike, now pacing the floor in his familiar shuffling manner. "Are you trying to tell me that if I had stayed, I'd have been in charge—that you would have left?"

Mike shrugged. "I don't speculate on might-have-beens. I'm not there. You're not there. All I know is you can't run a big beast like this one all alone. You gotta be an octopus with eight eyes instead of arms; you need to watch around you, back of you, under you, over you. I report to Joe Gratton, the meanest son of a bitch alive. Secretive. Jealous. An alcoholic to boot. I need someone I can trust."

"The way I can trust you?" Steve asked.

"Now, what kind of an answer is that?' Mike said angrily. "Am I interviewing you or are you interviewing me?"

"Neither," Steve said. "You asked me to come in. I didn't know you wanted me to work for you."

Mike stopped walking and sat down. Then, very carefully, he said, "All I want to know, kid, is what's on your mind."

"I've already told you, Mike. Writing. I've got to give it a chance. If you want to look at something I've done—I brought a script." He tossed it over.

"Okay, I'll read it." Mike's familiar grin creased his face. "I'm edgy, kid. Gratton offered me so much loot—a car, a New York apartment, a house in Beverly Hills—who could turn it down?" He fumbled with Steve's script. "Good title. Come on in next week, same time. If you won't do something for me, maybe I can do something for you. I'll walk you to the elevator." Steve looked at him quizzically. Mike chuckled. "You I want to see."

In the weeks that passed, nothing developed with Mike. He complimented Steve on his script and passed it on to a producer at the network. The producer returned the script to Steve with a terse—almost a form—letter. It so angered Steve that he called Mike, and Mike vowed he'd take care of anyone who didn't treat his good friend Steve as someone very special. "Trouble is," he said to Steve on the phone, "a kid attaches himself to someone who's had a little show business experience. Pretty soon the kid moves up, and overnight he's a producer. Everybody's a producer now! The industry is in the hands of children. I'll talk to him." But in the end the kid continued to be a producer, and Steve's script finally went into his files, unsold.

Not that all Steve's scripts were failures—if selling them was the criterion for success. Occasionally he had a piece in the slick magazines, sometimes fiction, sometimes an article, and occasionally a script was produced on television. He wrote a good novel, but quality was one thing, a bestseller too often something else. He realized then how long the road might be to financial success as a good novelist, and how isolated. Whether he would achieve distinction or not would be long in being determined: realistically, most likely not, if only because he would have to write so many commercial scripts to make ends meet. Then a job turned up, head of the television department of Kane & Shaw, as important as Otis & Meade.

Steve talked it over with Susan. "Might as well admit it," he said. "It's a lot better to face up to my limitations now than to have them catch up with me later."

"Right," she said crisply, "a living isn't enough." He stared at her: she had never breathed a word of criticism, until now.

"Let's just say I'm a better ad man than a writer. I'll accept the job."

"No, that's not it," she said, and took his hand. "You're a good writer, *now.* But you need to be in the mix. In the hunt, if you like. This is too quiet for you."

He knew that was true the moment she said it, and far more to the point than his own uncertainty over the prospects for his long-term financial success as an author.

"And you?"

"I liked the life," she said simply. "Too many of the people you have to work with aren't worth the time of day. But it's no good if you don't feel this way—there's too much of you that's the executive, the producer, the doer. . . ." She put her arms around him. "I can't be happy if you aren't."

That was that.

Letters by the dozen welcomed him back to the Madison Avenue fraternity. Network people, including Mike, sent glowing notes; so did film producers. Steve wasn't fooled by his new status. The trade was like that:

everyone respected a man who could buy into television programs for important sponsors. Many of these same people had treated him perfunctorily as a writer, even cavalierly; as television chieftain of a major ad agency, he had become someone again. Talent they could overlook; power they respected.

In the months that followed, Susan worried about Steve as she had before—worried about the way he drove himself, the pressures exerted on him, even about the way he thrived in that atmosphere. She told him repeatedly at least to get top, trustworthy help. Help, at least, was offered by numerous people—finally in the person of Mike Harris, who invited Steve to lunch in the network's private dining room.

"What'll you have, Steve?" Mike asked as he ushered him into the walnut-paneled room. He turned to the waiter. "I'll have my usual Martini, Walker."

"Nothing for me, thanks," Steve said. He looked at some elegant prints of early New York on the wall. "Pretty fancy layout. Is this for you personally?"

Mike shook his head. "Each vice president says it's his, but you book it with Joe Gratton's secretary. He's out of town, Uncle Mike has his own private dining room. Little fancier than Mr. Otis's, right?"

"Larger, too. We don't have anything like this at Kane and Shaw. Mr. Shaw doesn't believe in the big front."

"Mr. Shaw is in that wonderful and luxurious position where he can afford not to believe in it. What's your new setup like?"

Steve described his duties at the agency as Walker served a tasteful lunch. Mike paid elaborate attention. "Here I am boring you with a speech," Steve said, "when you must have something else on your mind."

Mike waved away the apology. He said, "In other words, kid, you're *it.*"

"I wouldn't have taken the job unless I was it," Steve replied. "Now, Mike, I know you didn't ask me here just for lunch. You're selling something, a package. Shoot."

Mike spread his arms wide across the table. "You know, kid," he said, "this is the turn of the wheel."

"Turn of the wheel?"

"Right back where we started from—except it isn't Sardi's and no Fay. You know me, kid, no fancy skating."

"I don't get it," Steve said.

Mike pursed his lips and shook his head. "I'll draw you a diagram. A blueprint. My lease runs out over here, and I'm looking for a new landlord."

Steve got the message. People always claimed they were being direct; but one subject was always arrived at after elaborate circumlocution—employment. It had taken Mike two hours to get to it.

Mike played with a pencil. "It's very simple," he said. "When you quit at O&M you left me alone. Old man Otis had to look to me for the answers. Every damn answer. Before you left, he had both of us. And I always had you. Steve, you were a nice guy up to the day you left. Then, I got news for you. You were a dirty son of a bitch." Mike chuckled in the friendly way that made his harshest epithets mere taunts, not insults. "I saw the deluge coming. That's what brought me here. Lots of people."

"Safety in numbers," Steve added.

"Right. Only one difference. There's an inside team here that watches the veeps duel with the pushers coming up. Remember the little punk that didn't like your script?"

"I remember."

"I should have fired him. I could have at that moment. This place is like a Roman amphitheater. With Joe Gratton as Caesar. The long-haired boys are the gladiators, and we veeps, we're the big game. We got an edge, to be sure; but they can afford so many of these pushers. And it gets to be a big pain. You finish off one, and there's a new one all set to take his shot. That's why I said, last time you were here, you gotta have eyes above you, under you, on either side of you. Listen," he said, "that's why I'm looking. You can have your safety in numbers."

"And you'd like to find a spot at a place like Kane & Shaw?"

"Not a spot, kid. A place. Big difference. A spot means a job somewhere in your department. A place means something with dimension, something next to you." Steve started to laugh. "Anything funny?" Mike asked.

"I'm just turning the wheel again. I hire you. Put you right next to me. Then the wheel begins to turn—and someone bottoms up. Could be Steve Lane."

Mike chuckled. "Not if you play it smart."

"And how do I play it smart with you, Mike?"

"Very simple. You fire me the day I step into Kane's office or Shaw's office."

"Kane is dead."

"That makes it simpler."

"I'll think it over."

"Be a nice guy, kid. Take twenty minutes. Twenty-four hours. Couple of days, if you need them. My price is your price."

Mike insisted on escorting Steve to the elevator. Then he saluted until the door clanged shut.

"All the way, sir?" the operator asked. Steve nodded.

"Now, there's a real guy for you, that Mike Harris. Always has the time of day for you. Knows the TV business. Picks good horses. And, brother! The dames he has. A real nice guy. And don't he smell good."

The twenty-four hours stretched to weeks. And now that same fragrance still seemed to hover about as Steve and Susan left the Oak Room at the Plaza and crossed Fifth Avenue. He felt her tugging at his arm.

"Thinking something special?" she asked.

"The turn of the wheel. That's the way he put it, Susan."

"Oh, Mike can turn phrases, heads, or wheels. Where were you when he was turning you out and himself up?"

"It wasn't quite that bald. Not if you analyze everything," he insisted.

"It ended up that way."

Steve smiled. Susan had a woman's sharp way of eliminating the subtleties of business life. He'd wrestled with the problem for days, analyzing all the events that had precipitated his resignation from Otis & Meade. Had Mike really pushed him out? Or had he, Steve, only anticipated that he would—if he could? Or, from another view, had he quit rather than tangle with Mike? He waited for Susan as she applied lipstick near a lamppost. "I love watching you."

"I love watching you shave."

"Really?"

"Got you!"

"Sue," he said, "do you think I'm a nice guy?"

"Everybody knows you are."

"How about Mike?"

"Oh, Steve," she said, "everyone knows Mike is a fashionable relic from another time! He's really passé, like a Hemingway novel; but he hangs on by coating his bravado with charm. And how can you say any man who claims every woman can be had at some price, is nice?"

He left that one alone. "He's never lied to me," was all he said. "And you like him—or did."

"What earthly difference does that make? I like these shoes, too!"

There it was, the utter heartlessness in a woman once she had made up her mind about someone threatening anyone in her world. Like himself. They walked along in silence for a block or two.

"Tired?" he asked. "Want to look in a few more windows before we taxi home?"

"You want to talk about Mike," she said. "You talk. I'll look."

He reviewed all that had gone before, from his first contact with Mike till their meeting tonight in the Oak Room. He told her how Mike had promised to stay out of Mr. Shaw's office. Sue found this difficult to believe.

"No, honey, you're wrong," Steve said. "He made that promise, but I wouldn't take him on that condition."

"He'd be ahead from the start." He nodded.

"Even if he promised."

"Didn't you say he never lied?" she needled.

"There'd be nothing to stop Mr. Shaw from visiting Mike, and if he asked Mike to his office and Mike declined, Mike would be obliged to explain." Steve shrugged.

"Then the turn of the wheel all over." But her gaze was caught by the jewelry in Tiffany's. "What are you going to do?" she asked.

"I have an opening. Mike would fit the job. So would another man I saw yesterday."

"What's *that* fellow like?" She was peering at the rings.

Steve smiled wryly. "A nice guy," he said. "A real nice guy. That wraps him up. Hire him, and he could last forever. He'd never get into trouble, never take a sharp stand, never be around to win a medal or feel the sharp end of your shoe. He could win out just by being very proper, very careful, very nice."

"And Mike?"

"He won't vegetate. He's very irreverent, very daring—and very rough. Last time we worked together, I wound up as just a member of the department. His department. This time I'm already head man. I start with a big lead. I also know Mike. He's bright, he's exciting. Mr. Shaw will love him. But Mike'll make mistakes. He always will. And he'll be expendable. He'll come expensive, because I won't take him cheap. I want his errors to be visible. An expensive man is always visible, always vulnerable. But Mike can also make contributions, big ones, because I won't let him make a mistake until he's done some good things. Then, because he'll be so expendable, he'll be careful—more careful than he ever dreamed he could be, like an old bomber pilot trying to complete his assigned missions. When each mission gets harder, each makes him more careful. Mike's getting on, and he won't be able to go the big wheel again after this."

Susan pointed to a diamond in the Tiffany window. "Isn't that lovely?"

"And when Mike goes conservative," he said, refusing to be distracted, "I'm going to have to fire him."

Susan gave Steve that half look, turning her head away from the display. "I'm beginning to feel sorry for Mike," she said. "Turns out he was a good teacher for you, after all. And I always thought you were the nice guy."

She smiled.

THE SKIRMISH

Steve Lane sat glumly staring out at his reflected image on a fourth floor window in the New York headquarters of Kane & Shaw. Life was different here than it had been at Otis & Meade. Most importantly Oliver Shaw, the onetime fullback of Yale's greatest team, and still an impressive giant of a man, was simply not in the same intellectual league as the trim James Hornwell Otis.

Otis measured assets in terms not of dollars, but of the quality of his officers as well as his clients. It was no secret that Otis had turned down major advertisers longing to be O&M clients because, in Otis's words, "They're not our kind of people."

It bothered Steve that some of those people were now Kane & Shaw clients. He remembered how Mr. Otis frowned on the big giveaway programs: "We don't want to lend our name to creating or recommending television programs that appeal to the people's avarice. It's not good for our clients and it's not good for America." Mr. Otis had also set a policy that O&M would never recommend the purchase of even a spot commercial on any program in which there was evidence of excessive violence: "It's just not in the public interest for our clients to be identified with such programming," Mr. Otis had proclaimed at the meeting of the agency's shareholders, all of whom were key employees of the agency.

This contrast in policy between O&M and K&S became more accentuated when advertisers no longer sponsored programs, but simply bought spots. "Sell, sell, sell," Mr. Shaw like to repeat. "We're not the custodian of the public interest. Hell's bells, we buy spots not programs. Let the networks worry about the public interest area if they choose to. Understand," he'd said in a confidential manner leaning toward Steve during a meeting in his own elegantly decorated office with a resplendent Matisse hanging on the wall opposite him, "we're not advocating junk on the air, but if it's the crap the public wants and if it brings in the right numbers. . . ." Oliver shrugged his broad shoulders and chuckled, adding, "well, then, it's got to be the right crap for our clients."

Shaw continued to smile. "Look, Steve, I know you don't buy all of that, and mind you, I'm not saying I prefer the kind of inanity I see on my television set nearly every night, but I'm not setting myself up to be the moral judge of what the people plainly want." As Steve edged forward to protest, Shaw continued, "I know where you're coming from, Steve. And I know how Jim Otis feels, but remember we can't afford to stand on a pulpit."

"He's done pretty well doing just that," Steve said.

"Sure, but he'll change. The way things are going with all of the sex and violence on television, the raunchy talk shows, and the creeping profanity, you have to move with the times. That's if you want to stay in business. It's that simple." Shaw's massive bulk slumped back against his red leather chair.

Steve stared at Oliver Shaw. "Yes," he said quietly, "moving down."

"If we have to move—your word—down, so be it," Shaw replied; then pointing a finger directly at Steve, he added, "Down, sure, but only if we have to. There are still plenty of acceptable shows on television and cable. Your job is to search them out, then sell, sell, sell! That's the name of the game."

"Is that the only way we should really look at it?" Steve asked.

Shaw chuckled. "You're a do-gooder, and that's no criticism. Jim Otis told me that one day—why he misses you. You let that smart-ass Mike Harris get an edge on you, quit, write a novel, then we get you. And then to top everything in this crazy business you bring that same Mike Harris over here to work with you."

"You approved him," Steve reminded Shaw.

"Sure, I did. I like him. Sort of. A top brown-noser if you know what I mean. But he understands people. You made a smart move."

Maybe too smart, Steve thought as he now sat at his own desk. He'd thought Mike Harris would make a real contribution when he'd brought him in to K&S, and that in due time he'd go conservative and outlive his usefulness. And Mike had kept his word—he hadn't tried to get close to Oliver Shaw; it was some of the clients who'd touted Harris's personality. And it was Oliver Shaw who had begun to cultivate Mike Harris even as Susan, Steve's wife, had predicted.

That was history. Now Steve Lane waited for his visitor from the coast, George Cates, head of television programming for Federal Broadcasting. Steve had wondered just why Cates wanted to see him. Since the big buying season for television was over, maybe Federal had some inventory of unsold spots that could be picked up at a bargain.

Cates, always a fashionable dresser, was ushered into Steve's office by pert Anne Koyce, Steve's longtime secretary. "You're maybe probably wondering why the program head of Federal wanted to see you, the buying season over and all that," Cates said, handing his topcoat to Anne, who placed it on a window sill. "No scattered spots to offer you, Steve. We've had a fairly good season, not as big as last year, but good enough." Cates settled into the easy chair across from Steve.

Steve knew George Cates's style. He'd made his opening statement. He'd sat down and placed his fingers in the familiar cathedral-like pattern. He'd paused for a moment, and then smiled at his own deliberate manner. "Federal likes you, Steve. We've liked you since your O&M days. Frankly, I should have acted with a bit more speed at the time you left; good manpower doesn't surface that often." Cates paused again and then, spreading out his fingers, said, "I'd like you to come out to the coast and be a top lieutenant. Run Federal's program development operations."

Steve was surprised. "Well, I didn't think that was to be the purpose of your visit, George, and I'm not prepared, frankly—"

Cates cut in. "Of course. I knew you'd be a bit surprised and I didn't expect you to say okay right off the bat—"

"I'm still fairly new here, George."

"Three years?"

Steve observed Cates and nodded appreciatively; Cates, as always, had done his homework. "I'm basically a New Yorker, George. Here, plus a bit of time finding out if I liked creative work, writing and so on."

"You're a good writer, Steve. Very good. I read that book of yours."

"Tough way to make a living unless you're a brand product like a Sidney Sheldon or a Danielle Steele. I mean a really good living."

"You can make a good living on the coast and doing what I know you like doing. Creative work. Working with producers, writers with ideas. Plus your own—"

"I'm not sure I should be jumping from one job to another. I was at O&M for a long time."

George Cates's fingers resumed their cathedral position. "I know it's a big decision, Steve. I wasn't expecting a decision on the spot. I'd like you to think about it."

"How soon do you have to know?"

"In a week or two. And we can talk more when you're ready." Cates stood up, crossed the office, and picked up his coat. "Salary, contract. You'd be reporting to Johnson, but that's only on a table of organization. He supervises operations, but creatively it would just be me you'd be dealing with. In the main, of course, plus the other people we have in the development area. You will think about it?"

"Of course," Steve said, "I know your job's a back breaker and I'm flattered at the prospect. You didn't come east just for this purpose did you, George?" Steve asked half jokingly.

Cates stood at the door. "Mainly," he said. "That's a fact." He put out his hand. "Call me, Steve, as soon as you've made a decision, want to talk." As he opened the door to leave, he added, "Reason I made this trip, Steve, is because I truly respect you. I know you can deliver the goods. I'm totally aware of your record. And, if I can be personal, I like you."

Steve took his hand. "That's mutual, George."

"We've done a lot of business together over the years. We know each other pretty well. I think we can really work together."

"No argument there, George, and like I said, the feeling's mutual."

"That's why I'd like you to come aboard. You know how it is in this business. The ups and downs. I feel I can trust you."

Steve studied Cates's eyes, certain that Cates had some inner worries. "I appreciate that, George. You've always been a straight shooter in all the deals we've made."

Cates smiled. "Why I made this trip." And with that he was gone. Steve sat at his desk tapping his fingers an his phone. He was sure now that Cates had come for another reason; Federal's ratings were down, the second year in a row. Joe Gratton had to be feeling some heat from the cold, patrician chairman of Federal, Robert S. Saunders.

It wouldn't be Gratton who'd fall if the pressure built; it would be some lesser executive, maybe Cates if necessary. And Cates, Steve figured, wise in the ways of television and wary of Gratton, close as they were, had come east with a solution—new blood to help him stay put. That was the way it was played on Madison Avenue and on the coast: set up a new echelon to take the heat. Be expendable. It was not a game Steve liked to participate in, even with the certain knowledge that Mike Harris was playing the same game in his own shrewd way once again. He would give

Cates time to make his stand with Gratton; he'd turn him down in a week or so. He speculated more about whether Gratton would actually nudge Cates out; they'd been friends for years, college classmates. But, Steve, concluded, that would not be enough, not if it were Gratton's turn to demonstrate that he could fix the blame for Federal's fall in ratings, not on himself, of course, although everyone knew he made all the key decisions at Federal, but on a chosen fall guy—and that could be Cates. Maybe.

All of this would be confirmed ten days after Steve had dropped off a note of thanks to Cates declining the offer. Shortly thereafter, there had been an invitation to lunch with Walter Sloan, technically Cates's boss, the head of the television network at Federal, another patrician by birth and schooling, but also the consummate salesman on Madison Avenue, master of the soft sell. Sloan was the top official Steve would sometimes have to see in order to make a deal for one of K&S's clients, especially when the solution rested with Sloan, a master of easing advertisers out of key buys another advertiser—more to be preferred—really wanted.

As Steve entered Sloan's private dining room at Federal's headquarters, its wallpaper containing memorable scenes of America's colonial history, he noted the doughnut-shaped rubber cushion on Sloan's chair. Sloan's courtly exterior manner, his soft and ingratiating voice gave no hint of the physical discomfort years of turbulent wheeling and dealing with fractious Madison Avenue buyers had obviously led to.

"So good to see you, Steve," Sloan said, waving Steve to a chair on one side of the large cloisonné coffee table. "I know how busy you are and I appreciate your willingness to come uptown to our offices. We'll have lunch here." Sloan waited until Steve was seated before taking his own place, the Sloan super-courtesy front with which Steve and all of Madison Avenue were familiar. Steve also knew that Sloan, never in a rush to settle matters, would make polite inquiries about family, work, business in general. And then he would come to the point.

Dabbing a napkin to his lips, Sloan, his ever present smile and kindly eyes beaming at Steve, pushed his chair slightly from the table. Lunch was over and Sloan would come to the point. "Steve, I know that our mutual friend, George Cates, told me of his idea and that he visited you recently. He'd hoped you would join him on the coast. I thought George really had a good idea."

Steve sat back quietly, confident that Sloan was not expecting a response to an offer he'd already turned down. Steve had been through the routine before; now was the moment Sloan would get to the issue.

"I've given this a lot of thought, Steve. You have a wonderful reputation on Madison Avenue; you're creative and very knowledgeable about this medium of television. Joe Gratton and I have been thinking of something that might have more appeal to you than George's offer, where you could remain here in New York and still make a major impact on our television programming needs. What I'm talking about is an operation, here, one that would actually put you on a par with Mr. Cates."

"Program decisions are made on the coast, Walter," Steve interjected.

"True. True in a way. But those, Steve," Sloan replied with an assured manner, "are, in fact, coast recommendations. Recommendations," he emphasized. "Final decisions are made here with me, Joe Gratton, one or two others.

George, of course. What we'd like is for you to be part of that executive group."

"Sounds a little superfluous, Walter, adding another voice to programming. Cates does a pretty good job considering the competition."

"Yes, he does. George is a wonderful executive. Very close to Joe Gratton as you must know—"

"College classmates, weren't they?"

"True, and associates; they've worked together elsewhere just fine. But times are changing, with cable, direct broadcasting, interactive TV: you're up to date, I know. Lots more competition. The only way to combat that is with more brain power, more experience, proven experience in your case."

"Is George aware of this?"

"Joe will handle him." And then Sloan added with a wave of his hand, "You know Joe, he has a knack of handling people."

Steve replied with an easy smile. "Nice way to put it, Walter. Dealing with Joe Gratton is no picnic."

"George understands Joe, maybe better than any of us, they've worked together so long and so well. Joe has great respect for George. I'd say even affection." Sloan stopped talking, his keen knowledge of Madison Avenue behavior signaling him that he shouldn't press. He stood up. "Just think it over, Steve. There's no big hurry, but we'd like you to be a part of Federal. What we're proposing is something new, but we hope that it will interest you." Steve rose, too, and as they continued toward the door to the executive hallway, Sloan went on, "Like I said, Steve, no big hurry. If you feel that this is a good move for you—we know it's a good move for us—we can get into the business details—

oh, and something new that might attract you even more. A bonus based on results."

"Nielsen ratings?"

Sloan smiled as he opened the door. "One part of an overall evaluation of contributions you're sure to make. We have a lot confidence in you, Steve."

"And in George," Steve added.

"Of course. He's family."

Steve would let ten days pass by as a courtesy to Sloan; the truth was that as soon as he left Federal's office he knew he wanted no part of the offer. It all sounded too contrived as he outlined the gist of the deal to Susan as they finished dinner at "21."

"The good part of it is that you'd be free of having to think of Mike Harris figuring out how to get past you. I tried to warn you."

"I remember, I remember," Steve countered, "but don't you forget what I told you: I'd ease him out the moment he went conservative."

Susan applied a touch of lipstick. Then looking over her case she said, "Mr. Shaw certainly seems to like him."

"Maybe you're right, Susan, but Sloan's offer really makes no great sense. Programming decisions, recommendations, call them what your will, are made on the coast, and—"

Susan interrupted: "And Mr. Joseph Gratton, he just takes other people's recommendations? Doesn't participate? He doesn't seem like that from everything you've told me in the past."

"Joe's the final word, everyone knows that," Steve said; "I've told you about that a million times. He loves programming, loves the stars when he gets out on the coast, likes having the big Hollywood talent agents and their counterparts here in New York kowtow to him. Gratton runs the show, not Sloan, not Cates, not even the chairman, Saunders."

"So?"

"So?" Steve echoed.

"What are you going to do? You turned down George Cates." She pondered for a moment, then smiled. "You're going to turn down Walter Sloan. Am I right?"

"You don't know the answer?" Steve said with a smile, reaching over to take her hand.

"I can never figure you out, Steve, which is what makes you so intriguing." He was surprised: after all, that was how she struck him. But he decided to keep that to himself.

"Yes, I'm turning him down," Steve said.

"I knew it."

"You just said you can never figure me out."

"I was teasing. I know you like a book."

"Except in the case of Mike Harris."

She smiled, conceding nothing.

"Shall we go?"

"I like the security of knowing where we fit, where you fit in. Networks, they're so mercurial." Susan stood up. "Yes, it's time."

"Do you think, maybe, this would be a good night to make a child?"

Susan turned to glance at Steve and with a smile, said, "You want to be that creative?" She laughed as she took his arm. "You can be such fun sometimes, Mr. Lane."

❁ ❁ ❁

Ten days later Steve dictated a friendly note to Anne Koyce, thanking Sloan for his splendid offer, but insisting that he couldn't step out of the world he knew, advertising, into the maelstrom of networking.

Sloan, after receiving Steve Lane's letter, placed it before Joe Gratton. Gratton, not touching the letter, glanced at it through his heavy silver-rimmed glasses, all the while slowly sipping at his early afternoon straight vodka. Gratton, shoving his glasses to the top of his crew cut iron-gray hair, muttered, "Son of a bitch. Cocksucker. Think he means it?" he growled looking up at Sloan.

"Steve Lane's not one to play games."

"Took his time getting back to you."

"Maybe to let us know he really gave it a lot of consideration," Sloan replied uneasily.

"Balls! He rejected it the moment you made the offer. Playing nice guy, that's his game. I know the type. Polite, careful, maybe even clever. Doesn't want people to think he's crafty. Not his style."

Sloan shrugged. "I think he really likes what he's doing."

"Sure he does. It's comfortable, secure." Gratton lifted his carafe and poured himself another ounce. "Needs a bit more freshening," he grumbled.

Sloan went to the sideboard, lifting up the sterling tongs, "Ice?"

"One," Gratton said holding out his drink. "Tell you what, Walter. You call that son of a bitch bastard and tell him to be at my place at seven tonight." He chuckled. "Remember what Brando said in that picture when he was the godfather?"

"We'll make him an offer—"

"Right. An offer he can't refuse, that's it. We need some new blood around here and by God we're going to get it whatever it costs."

Sloan shook his head. "His letter was pretty firm. I'd say, very firm. No go."

Gratton's eyes narrowed. "Mr. Sloan, that makes it all the more interesting." Gratton picked up some papers on his desk. "Goddamn it I have to do all the thinking around here. You set him up. Seven. Tonight. Tell him to bring his wife. It's a must, 'kay?" he said without glancing up.

"He'll be there, Joe," Sloan replied.

"With his wife."

"Right. With Susan Lane." As Sloan walked down the hall to his own office he analyzed every minute he'd spent with Gratton. He knew that the people at Federal always did that, trying to determine just what it was that was on Gratton's mind. A visit to Gratton's nondescript office with its worn-out furniture (Sloan knew that Gratton liked it that way) belied the power of the man who occupied it. Everyone knew he could have an ornate office right next to Saunders, but it was Gratton's way, a Spartan touch that set him apart from all his subordinates who would have to leave their luxurious setups to come to his shabby one. Despite its ordinariness, his was the office where the real power of the network lay. His, Gratton's.

As Sloan settled himself on his rubber tire, he worried that his initial failure to bring Lane aboard would be a mark Gratton would hold against him. He'd used all the authority Gratton had given him, hinted at the perks and the new bonus plan; he squirmed in his chair knowing that no matter what Lane's plans were Steve Lane would have to be at Gratton's apartment this very night, no matter what. When Steve came on the phone Sloan, true to his gentlemanly manner, made known his regrets at Steve's decision to turn the job down, but accepted it graciously.

Steve listened to Sloan, sensing that he was nearing the end of the obligatory statement of disappointment at Steve's rejection. Finally, Sloan came to the point. "I know that this is short notice, Steve, very short notice," he emphasized, "and I hope that you haven't any plans tonight—" and then in a rush to get to the point, "and if you do that they can be put off for a few minutes is what I'm really trying to say—"

"No plans, Walter," Steve replied. "What's up?"

There was a momentary pause as Sloan sighed, his relief evident to Steve at the other end. "It's just that Joe—Mr. Gratton—would like very much to see you."

"Tonight?" Steve interjected.

Sloan pressed on. "Yes, tonight. At seven at his place. You know his place?"

"On Park? I've had cocktails with him once or twice. What's the deal?"

Sloan settled back in his chair. "It's just that Joe wants to see you, just for a few minutes—with Susan if that's possible."

"Susan? He wants me to bring Susan?"

Sloan relaxed even more. He felt Steve's response was already in the affirmative. "His request, Steve," Sloan added.

"It's not about the letter I sent you, Walter, is it? He isn't going to try to talk me out of it is he, because it just won't work."

"No, no, I don't think so, Steve."

"Because if I didn't say yes to you I'm not about to say yes to him—I just want you to know that."

Sloan wanted to end the conversation. "He knows that, Steve. It was just his wish to speak to you personally." He paused for a moment to close the arrangement. "Then I can tell him that you will make it, at seven?"

There was a momentary pause, and then Steve said, "Seven. Okay."

"With Mrs. Lane."

"I'll ask her. Oh, by the way, will you be there?"

"I'm most grateful to you, Steve. And no, Joe wants to be with just you."

"I'd like it better if you were there, Walter."

Sloan smiled. "Thank you, Steve. But this is private—you know Joe . . . just you and Joe." And then he added to press the point, "Plus Mrs. Lane. The three of you."

"Mrs. Gratton? She won't be there?"

"She's in the Caribbean. With Sheila Moss. They're good friends."

"I'll be there," Steve said.

Sloan heard the click of the phone and sat back with relief. Then he buzzed Gratton's intercom.

"The Lanes will be there tonight at seven."

" 'Kay," Grotton rasped. The phone went dead. Sloan relaxed and wondered just what was on Gratton's mind.

Steve and Susan were ushered into Gratton's superbly appointed study by a courtly and elderly English butler, Henry. "Mr. Gratton will be with you in a few moments, sir. May I bring you a cocktail, wine?" Steve and Susan declined. Steve looked about the handsome room, aware of its sharp contract to the dingy surroundings of Gratton's

Federal office, its handsomely carved bookcases filled with fine leather-bound sets of books, its etchings of the White House and the Capitol, and the framed engraved portraits of all of the presidents of the United States, carefully positioned among a number of impressive documents signed by Lincoln, Jefferson, and Washington. Steve had to smile to himself: this room was much like the room of other powerful men, and underscored the affectation of simplicity in Gratton's Federal office.

"Wonder if he's read any of these books," Susan said as she stood by Steve.

"All of them," Gratton chuckled, entering from across the room, then moving toward them, his left hand holding his drink, extending his right hand toward Susan. "Only other man I know who can say the same is Steve's old colleague at O&M, Tony Gordon. Irish bastard's read everything." Susan placed her hand in his outstretched one. Gratton pointed to a leather loveseat. "Appreciate your coming by, both of you. Sit down, please."

"Tony's remarkable," Steve said. "Has the Koran, Mary Baker Eddy, the Bible, the words of Buddha, Confucius, all lined up on his desk. He's read them all."

"Something of an unsung genius if you want my personal opinion. Bastard's always quoting them when he's beating you down on a deal. Never been able to get him to my office, either. Or your onetime boss, Mr. Otis, for that matter. Buyers, real buyers, Tony says, deal on their own turf, that's his motto.

"They do that, provided of course, it's at one of their clubs or a restaurant of their choice. Rob Saunders and I humor them. Why not?" he added with a chuckle. "When they buy, they buy big."

"And you have the rest of us always available to meet you at your digs when we get the call," Steve replied with a smile.

"Yes, and I appreciate your dropping by on such short order."

Gratton moved over to a mahogany library table, and picked up an ice cube from a sterling bucket. He glanced across at the Lanes. "Henry must have asked you?" he said raising his glass.

"We passed, Joe. We have a dinner date at eight if that's enough time."

"Plenty. I'll get to the point. You turned down Mr. Cates's offer. You turned down Mr. Sloan's offer. Cates wanted you to report to him."

"To Johnson," Steve cut in.

"Same difference," Gratton said. "Walter suggested a new kind of setup. You turned him down. What you didn't know was that I sent them. It's me, Joe Gratton, who wants you. I thought you could get some indoctrination working with either of them—you've never been at a network, right?"

"Not as an employee, no." Steve responded.

"As a buyer, I know. And an important one." Gratton eyed Steve over the edge of his glass. "Mr. Lane, let's drop all the bullshit—you'll excuse me, Susan," Gratton said, bowing politely to her and then turning again to Steve, "I'm not going to play games with you—you don't work under Cates and you don't have a made-up kind of job that Walter offered. What I'm talking about is the whole shebang—they never knew my main objective—the whole program operation of Federal Broadcasting. Cates will report to you. Sloan will be your titular superior, but hell's bells, everyone knows the program chief of a network is right next to the president. That's me. That's what I'm offering you, Mr. Lane. The works, you understand?"

Steve tried to conceal his surprise. In a flash he realized that he'd missed out in deducing it was really Gratton who'd been talking through both aides, that it really was Gratton who'd wanted him to come aboard in a lesser capacity and that now Gratton was revealing a glimpse of how he operated, no doubt using his lieutenants and obviously not advising them of his real objective. Cates, Steve was certain, had clearly thought he was really asking Steve to be an assistant, albeit an important one, but it was Gratton who'd manipulated Cates—Cates the messenger inviting in a man Gratton had already decided would one day, and soon, be above Cates. He caught Susan's eye: there was the barest ripple of a brow to show she realized the dimension of Gratton's offer.

Steve decided to put the question directly to Gratton. "Did Cates have any idea of what was on your mind when you suggested he call on me?

"Who the hell cares whether he did or not. That's academic." Gratton rasped as he tipped his glass toward Steve. "Question. Do you want to be part of Federal. Yes, no."

Steve glanced at Susan. "It would be a big decision, Joe."

"And I'm waiting for it, Mr. Lane," Gratton replied, moving a step closer to Lane, tapping Steve on the chest with his drink.

This move gave Steve an opportunity to look closely into Gratton's eyes; they were sunken deep into their sockets, set in a fixed intransigent stare. Finally, Steve spoke. He wanted to be courteous. "I'll have to think about it, Joe. I appreciate your thoughts, but I have to think about Susan, what it could mean to her. The uprooting—"

Gratton bore in. "So, you'll move to the coast. That's why I wanted Susan here," he added, putting down his glass on a small marble stand and rubbing his pudgy fingers together. "So, what the hell's so hard about that? If you can stand New York what's so tough about sunny California? And you can still keep your place here in Manhattan—we'll take care of it. Deal, 'kay?"

"Let me think about it, Joe," Steve insisted.

Gratton's eyes narrowed. "What's to think?"

Steve Lane raised both hands as if to ward off Gratton. "Joe, I'm not a fellow who hops from one job to another. There are things to consider. Susan's friends are here—"

"She's not losing them," Gratton sneered. "She'll be making new ones to boot."

"I'm here," Susan said coolly, taking Gratton aback.

He smiled. "Of course. I know this is your decision, too. That's why I invited you."

"I'll have to think about it. Thank you." And she smiled at him. Nothing could have broken that smile. It made Gratton step back, and swirl his drink. He smiled back uncertainly.

Gratton's momentary distraction gave Steve time to think. He was a little surprised, even, at how easily Susan had made Gratton step back. Well, she had often enough startled him. He knew that his every move was being weighed carefully by Gratton, but he was determined not to be rushed—that would be too much a sign of weakness, of recognizing Gratton's overwhelmingly persuasive strength. "You'll have my decision. I want to think about this; I owe quite a bit to Kane & Shaw—"

"Mr. Shaw will be delighted knowing one of his best men's at a key post at Federal. He won't stand in your way, he's too smart."

Steve shrugged. "Could be, but have you thought of Hendrik Taylor? He's available with a great track record and I know he's looking—"

"We're not here to listen to you championing Taylor, Mr. Lane. If I'd wanted Taylor he'd be here, not you. For chrissake!" Gratton snarled, then again turning to Susan, he said, "Sorry, but I'm offering your husband the whole thing, not to be Cates assistant or Sloan's, but the whole thing! It's a stepping stone." He leaned down to Susan. "You want to know the whole truth? To my job!" Susan didn't quiver, but gave only a calm nod. Gratton turned back to Steve. "So? What's it going to be?"

Steve stood his ground. "Like I said, I'll have to think about it, Joe. I appreciate the offer, but Susan and I have to talk this out. I have to discuss it with Mr. Shaw, I owe him that. I've had some good years—"

"Know your record there," Gratton rasped. Then, his eyes narrowing again, he shot back, " 'Kay. Take your time. All the time you need. Get back to me, say by the end of the week, 'kay?"

On the way home Steve looked at Susan until her head tilted, quizzically. "I think Gratton expected to impress you more."

"He thinks too well of himself."

● ● ●

Steve Lane didn't get back that soon. He'd touched base with Oliver Shaw in the latter's office, and Shaw had let the matter rest. "It's your decision, Steve, yours alone." Shaw leaned back in his chair. "You've got a future here, no doubt about that and we'd hate to lose you. But I know Joe Gratton. We won't be able to compete with him—money, perks, and the good life a network can afford. And then there's that little thing called power. A program chief? He's one of the real gatekeepers; he can deal you in or freeze you out. Including major advertisers, including agencies like ours. That's power. You'd be a part of that at Federal. And, Steve, there's one more thing to consider." Shaw paused for a moment."Something for you, something for us.

"Which is?" Steve asked as Shaw stood up and glanced out a window at Madison Avenue below. After a few moments he slowly turned to face Steve. "It's how Gratton would react—especially if you turn him down. And this is important, too. How we would fare at Kane & Shaw. You understand?"

Steve looked at Shaw, nonplussed.

"Think, Steve, think how Gratton would react. He's not your typical network executive. He's more ruthless, more calculating. Mr. Gratton is someone you don't want to tangle with as long as the Saunders men want to keep him on and that looks like forever." He paused. "Mr. Gratton doesn't like to lose. You told me he dismissed the availability of Hendrik Taylor and Taylor's just about the best in his field, but he still prefers you." Shaw chuckled. "Oh for sure, Mr. Gratton would not take it too kindly if you said no."

"We take a hit, is that what you're saying?"

Shaw nodded his head. "But," he added, "and let me emphasize this, you stay with us, we'll survive the hit."

"Does it follow that if I go to Federal Kane & Shaw would benefit?"

Shaw smiled. "Wouldn't that be a natural—we make you available? That's the way the Joe Grattons of this world operate."

At dinner that night Steve discussed the Shaw meeting with Susan. "It's not an easy decision, is it?" she asked after Steve laid out the options.

Steve shrugged. "One of the problems with this business. The more visibility you achieve, the more complicated things get. Let's sleep on it."

It was Gratton who woke Steve up with a call at seven in the morning. "I'm in my office, Steve," Gratton growled. "I said a week. You're stalling. You've had enough time. I need your decision. Now!" he snapped.

Steve leaped to life the moment he heard Gratton's voice. No polite inquiries about himself and Susan, no easing into the subject matter. "I'm not stalling one bit," he countered. "I told you I had to think about this—"

"And I said what's to think? Remember? Now I've got Cates coming in today and I can't afford to wait. He's got to know our deal if we have a deal. We need help. And Mr. Lane," Gratton said sarcastically, "I do have other options."

Steve sat up in bed angered by Gratton's manner even as Susan slowly woke up beside him. He simply wouldn't be pushed. "Joe, I understand that. If you feel you're under some kind of pressure and you can't wait—"

"I have been waiting, Mr. Lane! For chrissake! Stop playing games!

"If you have someone else, you don't have to wait, Joe," Steve said tartly.

There was a pause. "Look, I'm on the phone with you, Steve, not anyone else," Gratton said in a more placating tone.

"There's so much we'd have to settle, Joe."

"Now that's got the sound of yes to it. Steve, Art Miller, our counsel, he knows the deal. You'll have no problem. You can meet him this afternoon. What I have to know is your intent. It's very simple. You're coming aboard. You're not coming aboard. Now, which is it? Yes. No. I'm waiting."

"Hold on, Joe, I'll be right back." Steve placed his hand across the phone and whispered to Susan. "It's Gratton. Demanding an answer. Right now."

Susan furrowed her brow. "He's calling this early?"

"He's in his office, Susan. And very demanding. It's yes or no. Right now."

"It's what you want to do, isn't it?" she asked, as if to say 'what could you possibly be hesitating about now?'

He stared at her. Yes, that was the question. Just as Shaw had said, it would mean being a gatekeeper. She was ahead of him again. He took a deep breath. In a quiet voice, he said, "Okay, Joe. Okay. We'll work it out." Susan turned lazily beside him and snuggled back into her pillow.

"Good!" Gratton snapped. "Be at my office at eleven." And with that Steve heard the phone slam down.

Steve immediately called him back. "There is one thing, Joe. I have to see Mr. Shaw. I don't want him to hear this from anyone else, you understand?"

"No problem this end. But remember, like I said, we can't wait."

"I've got to deal with some of our clients—"

"Understood. Take my advice. These kinds of things—best to be surgical. Make the break. Say your nice words. Show up here at eleven. We got work to do. Plenty." The line went dead.

Steve hung up and settled back in the pillows, his mind racing. The covers had fallen back on Susan, and the thin, crème peignoir dropped off a rounded shoulder. He pulled her hair back from the nape of her neck: she smelled sweet, like a barely wakened woman, and tasted better.

"Not now," she laughed, "don't you have to go?" And she shrugged him off. That was her way, he realized abruptly. He was always the importuner, not Susan: there was always another time, not necessarily now, not because she disliked him, or sex, but because it was her instinct to be private, and what was less so than sex? But he was suddenly inflamed, and pulled her toward him.

"Steve," she laughed, "it's bright outside! It's morning!"

That was typical too: she wanted romantic lead-ins, convincing, candlelight, more convincing. But now he had resolved his crisis with Gratton, resolved this crisis in his life, such a weight of distraction fell from his shoulders that the mere scent and sight of her ignited him.

"Think midnight," he said, muffling her laughter with kisses: "think candles burning low, think how many hours I have wanted you, how many years, and that this is the first time my hands have been on you."

"Ooh, that's sweet—"

"Think how happy I am this moment to have you in my arms like this—"

"Even better."

"In fact, don't think. Don't think at all, sweetheart," and he swept off her peignoir, reveled in her warm pink flesh. He could swear once Susan responded, now, anytime, her body began to change shape and weight. He wasn't being fanciful: he really felt her body lengthen to this touch, shorten to that, or her breasts swell, become heavy

—and the next moment become champagne-glass sized, almost ethereal to the touch. There were moments he could swear her arms lengthened, others, her neck: she was the river he stepped into that was never the same twice but, almost always, it seemed, virgin territory. He was beside himself with passion, he actually ached. It was an attack. And Susan had stopped laughing now: she was all pliancy, heavier, lighter, longer, shorter, he couldn't tell, he no longer cared, not when he couldn't tell himself apart from her, or whether his emptying was his filling or hers, whether he was the master or wholly overwhelmed, his mind a thing of darkness or brilliant light.

Later Susan curled into him, but only briefly. She was like no other woman he had known: she clung, with unnerving ardor, but briefly: then her back would turn to him, as now. Had he been tolerated, he wondered? Played with? Was her reticence a deliberate way to inflame him? He knew it wasn't, but it felt that way. And he knew beyond a shadow of a doubt the moment her back turned that way that if he was inflamed again he would have to wait, and after waiting, win her again.

He suddenly felt entirely at a loss. What did he understand about this woman, or women at all? He was very good in his chosen jungle, he knew, but between himself and Susan? That was another place, one where all men and women were when together, with few paths, and none that ran cleanly, but constantly opened and petered out, sometimes for good, sometimes opening against all hope when all seemed lost.

It was time to get up. To deal with the world he knew.

He made it to Gratton's office late in the afternoon after he had seen Shaw, who smiled all through lunch at the news, and had dealt with an urgent client later. Then he'd had to wait for twenty minutes before being ushered into Federal's ornate board room by one of Gratton's three secretaries. He was surprised to find that Gratton had assembled all the key executives of the network. Sloan was there beaming politely, the heads of sales, research, administration, personnel, and station relations. They were all there, plus George Cates, who, Steve learned sometime later, had been summoned from the coast the day before.

When Gratton made the announcement there was a hubbub of acceptance by everyone in the room, but Steve Lane noticed the visible shock on Cates's face; he was certain that Cates hadn't been told of the impending change. In a quick decision, after the obligatory handshaking, Steve made a gesture of reconciliation. He liked Cates and he walked over to him and put his arm around his shoulder. He wanted the assembled group to know that he was proud to be at Federal and proud, too, to be associated with a man of Cates's talent and that as far as he, Steve Lane, was concerned, he was coming to Federal to help Cates restore the network to a dominant position. As he pounded Cates on the back, Steve made a point of catching Gratton's eye. Gratton stared back, unperturbed, and then abruptly left the room. Art Miller, Federal's chief counsel, strode over to greet Steve. "Congratulations, Steve. If you're ready we can sit down and work out the details. Shouldn't take long."

Steve shook his head. "I'll do that when I return."

"Oh?" was all Miller could say before Steve began heading toward the elevators. He'd caught sight of Cates moving toward him and he didn't want to review the change at this moment. "Look," Steve said, "I told Joe I had to see Mr. Shaw and I've done that, but I can't just walk out without making certain the department I'm leaving is set up right, plus there are some clients who'll want to know, you know how these things are, I'm sure."

Miller clasped his hands. "I do. So, when do you think we can sit down?"

As the elevator door opened, Steve called back, "In a week."

"Joe knows this?" Miller replied, holding the elevator door.

"I told him I had to do this. It can't be done on the phone and it can't be done in a day. A week is pretty short to move out and move in. I'll be in next Monday."

Miller nodded, shrugged, and released the door.

● ● ●

When Steve returned to Federal one week later he went directly to Gratton's office. "Glad to see you," Gratton said coolly, "you work out your deal yet with Art Miller?"

"We're meeting late this afternoon, four o'clock."

"Good. Maybe we can all have a little celebration, by five? Shouldn't take more than an hour to get things settled. Rob Saunders wants to say hello. Time you met him."

"Be a pleasure."

"See your new office yet?"

"Not yet."

"Fix it up any way you want. Ted Coyne's the man to see, good decorator."

Steve looked about at Gratton's plainly furnished office. "No, he didn't do this one. I like it just the way it is. No frills, no fancy window drapes. In fact, nothing changed from the way it was when old Burton was here. I just moved in."

"Not exactly comparable to the study at your place"

"That's because Martha did that," Gratton chuckled. "I've never let her see this place."

"It doesn't really matter, does it? It's your office. That says it all."

Gratton nodded. "The seat of power, that what you mean?"

"Why not? You run the place. Right?"

"I report to Rob Saunders, Steve."

Steve shrugged. "Sure, but, like everyone knows, you run the place."

" 'Kay." Gratton picked up a carafe and filled his glass. "Too early for you?" he asked, raising a glass toward Steve, the latter declining. "Just remember, Mr. Saunders is special. He has the last call. And if he doesn't choose to exercise it, his old man's there. I have a free hand as long as we're winning. That simple." Gratton lit a cigarette. "Never been able to break the habit. Too late now anyway." He took a deep drag and then, his voice suddenly hardening, added, "First thing you should do is fire Cates and his assistant out there, Stuart."

"I don't know Stuart," Steve replied.

"A zero. Same as Cates."

"I thought you liked George Cates," Steve injected, taken aback by the harsh demand. "You were classmates, at Penn wasn't it? Worked together at CBS some years ago—"

"That's yesterday. My advice, get rid of him. Stuart, too."

Steve frowned. He didn't like the abrupt order. "Joe," he said quietly, "you remember me standing in the board room just a few days ago, my arm around George Cates's shoulder, telling everyone I was coming aboard to help him."

"Sure, I remember," Gratton said, coldly. "But now you're his boss, he's part of your department, and a weak part."

Steve instantly sensed that he was being measured and that he would have to hold his position if he was to deal as an equal with Gratton. "I can't fire him, Joe," he said, after a long pause.

Gratton's eyes narrowed. "You mean you won't, that it?"

Steve replied. "And I can't fire Stuart, either. I never met the man. I know nothing of his work."

"I do. He's a no-talent bastard."

"Then you fire him. You're the president of the company. The same goes for George Cates."

For a moment the two men measured each other. Gratton took a deep drag and snuffed out his cigarette. "You're rejecting my suggestion?"

Steve Lane observed Gratton. No James Hornwell Otis there. No Oliver Shaw. Gratton was not quite the same man he'd lunched with over the years with Tony Gordon, either. "Joe, you want them out. Okay. No problem." Steve paused and then continued. "I'll fire them in your name."

Gratton took a sharp breath, shoved his glasses to the top of his head, and began drumming his fingers on his desk top. Abruptly, he stopped, sliding forward in his chair stretching his arms across the desk. "Have it your way, Mr. Lane. We can wait." Gratton pulled back and deliberately reached over for some papers on his desk. Plainly the meeting was over. Each had explored the other's temperament for the moment. Steve stood up, fully conscious that he'd crossed Gratton on his first day. He wondered what might come next.

"I'll go up to see Art Miller," Steve said quietly.

" 'Kay," Gratton replied as he focused his attention on the papers before him.

● ● ●

The conference in Miller's large office, filled with legal folders piled neatly on an orderly looking desk, went slowly. Gratton had indicated that there would be no problems in working things out; but it was Miller's turf to make network deals and the negotiations had stretched out with minimum give and take. Miller, bald and thin, his lips pursed, closed his notebook. Steve studied Miller's dour look, his cold, faded hazel eyes. "That a signal?" he asked, "We're at an impasse?"

"Not yet," Miller replied. "But I don't see a deal either."

"Joe Gratton said the deal would be no problem."

Miller rubbed his bony hands together. "That's not his department."

Steve decided he'd have to push matters. "You report to Joe Gratton, right?"

"Sure. On a table of organization, sure. But on key deals that's Mr. Saunders's call."

Steve decided to play a little hard ball. "I've already given notice to Kane & Shaw. Mr. Gratton said the deal would be no problem. I suggest you get Joe Gratton to come up to your office or we go to his. And include Rob Saunders if, as you say, he has the final word."

Miller took a deep breath. "Mr. Lane," he began.

"Steve."

"Steve," Miller repeated. "It doesn't help matters to get them involved. This is my job. I make the deals. That's what I'm paid to do."

"So?"

"We have specific policies. We don't make five-year deals. No one has a five year deal. We don't—"

Steve cut in. "With all due respect, Art, you're saying 'we' and I'm saying bring the 'we' part down here." Then he added, "That's if you want to make a deal."

"I'm not holding it up, Steve. It's you. Your demands—"

"Requirements."

"Okay, requirements."

The four of them, Gratton, Saunders, Miller, and Steve, had been in Miller's book-lined office for thirty minutes with some minor issues being resolved. Two critical areas still remained on the table, the duration of Steve's contract and the definition of his responsibilities.

Miller sat back in his high judge's chair, a pencil clenched between his teeth. "Well, we still have the duration of the contract."

"Five years," Steve responded.

"We've offered three," Miller said, putting the pencil down.

"I hear you," Steve said quietly.

Gratton, who was huddled with Saunders, called out from across the office, "What kind of contract did you have at Kane & Shaw?"

"We don't have contracts there," Steve responded.

"So? So? What's so bad about three years?"

"Nothing, Joe. It's just not as good as five years. Agency life is a bit more secure than life at a network. That's why I've insisted on five years, not three."

Gratton walked across the room and stood behind Miller. "I want to get this settled, Mr. Lane. You've been demanding five years. 'Kay. Art, tell him how long my contract runs."

Miller glanced up at Gratton. "That's privileged information, Joe."

"Tell him."

Miller nodded. "Mr. Gratton's contract goes for four years.

"Four years, Steve," Gratton repeated.

Steve bit into his lower lip, evidence of his surprise. "In that case I'll settle for four."

Gratton grunted his acknowledgment as he walked back to join Saunders, who sat back, legs crossed, tamping tobacco into a Dunhill pipe. Miller pulled out a sheet of paper. "Now we're down to the final item. What you're being hired to do, which is to run the program operations of the network. But what happens if—and I emphasize the if," Miller added, "things just don't work out. You're here for four years and we have to find an area for you."

"I'm only interested in programming, Art," Steve said. "I've said that a dozen times since we met. I don't want any other job. I can't make it any clearer."

Saunders struck a match, took a quick puff, and rose from his chair. "Mr. Lane," he said glancing at his watch, "you and Miller have been debating this contract for over two hours—"

"Three," Miller interjected.

"Three," Saunders repeated. And then with some irritation showing in his voice, "It took me ten minutes to make my deal with Mr. Gratton. What's so special about this one? Why's it taking so long to get you aboard?"

Steve eyed the elegantly dressed chairman of the board. "It's very simple, Mr. Saunders—"

"Rob," Saunders said, with a tolerant smile. "Proceed."

"Rob. I'm not negotiating the terms of my coming in."

"Oh?" Saunders replied. "And just what is it that's—" Saunders paused for a moment glancing at his watch, "taking all this time and that requires Mr. Gratton and me to be in on what I thought would be a fifteen-minute negotiation at most?"

"To come aboard, yes," Steve replied. "But I'm not negotiating my employment, Rob, I'm dealing with my termination."

"Termination?" Saunders repeated, startled. "Termination?"

"That's what this is all about. I'm not interested in any other job except the one you've offered me. Programming chief. If you change that—and I accept the fact that if I failed in that area you would have the right to be disappointed—"

"But you'll succeed," Saunders insisted, "we're banking on that."

Steve smiled. "We all are. But network life is precarious. I'm sure George Cates has a contract, but I'd say judging from Mr. Gratton's first order to me, that Mr. Cates's future is more than precarious—"

Gratton called out from across the room. "Let's skip prognostications on Cates, if you don't mind, Steve. We're talking about you. We're talking about just in case. . . ." Gratton let the rest of his statement hang in the air.

Steve shook his head. "This is something Art and I have debated for some time. I'll repeat—I don't want any other job at Federal."

"But if you fail, Steve, and God knows we all hope you'll succeed," Rob interjected, "we have to be able to do something about that kind of event. Some other area," he said, groping.

"I don't want any other area," Steve insisted.

"What's wrong with being president," Gratton growled from his side of the room.

"Nothing, Joe, but you're not suggesting that if I failed as program head I'd be in line to succeed you?"

Rob Saunders put up his hand. "I think I have it. We'll give you the right to consider another position that has an equal policy-making function to that of being head of programming. Sales. Research. Station relations. There are a number of them. You have other qualifications beyond programming, so I've been told. That acceptable?"

"On one condition," Steve said.

The four men exchanged glances.

"And what is that?" Saunders asked.

"I have the option to decline that post and if I do you're required to pay off my contract."

"And do nothing, for Federal?" Saunders replied, somewhat bewildered. "Nothing in return?"

Steve took his time as the three waited. "That's it, Mr. Saunders. Nothing. I'll repeat, I do not want any other job at Federal. If you decide to terminate me, if you want the right to offer me another post with an equal policy-making function—and I'm telling you up front that there is no job that has an equal policy-making function—"

"Except president," Gratton sneered.

"That would be academic, Joe, as I said, in the case of failure."

Saunders beckoned to Gratton to retreat to a corner of Miller's office. The two men huddled together exchanging views. A few moments later Saunders, taking a moment to relight his pipe, quietly said. "You have your deal, Mr. Lane."

"There's one final matter," Art Miller said.

"And what's that," Saunders said, now plainly piqued.

"The penalty clause."

"Penalty clause? What penalty?" Saunders repeated.

"If Mr. Lane rejects your offer to accept another position with an equal policy-making function, he gets paid the remainder of his unexpired contract."

"We just agreed to that," Saunders said.

"Plus a $250,000 penalty."

"Two hundred—" Saunders gasped, then turning to Gratton, he asked, "You know about this, Joe?"

"That's his final demand."

Saunders turned an angry eye on Steve. "This isn't something you've just decided to add—"

Art raised a hand. "No, no. This has been part of his position from the beginning. From the moment we started talking employment contract."

"You mean termination agreement, Art," Saunders countered. "Well, I never—" he shook his head violently and tapped the bowl of his pipe into an ashtray on Miller's desk.

"The $64 question, Mr. Chairman," Art added, looking up at Saunders whose face had flushed.

Saunders turned angrily to Gratton. "It's your call, Joe. You operate the network."

Gratton thrust his hands into his coat jacket. He made eye contact with Steve Lane, who sat in his chair, arms across his chest, determined to return Gratton's intransigent expression.

Gratton finally spoke. "Done."

Miller reached out to shake Steve's hand. Steve stood up and moved across the room to take Gratton's hand. Then he approached Saunders.

"You've got your agreement to start here, Mr. Lane." Saunders said coolly. "Now, let's hope we never have to exercise the rest of the deal."

Steve took his hand. He'd won, for the moment. But he knew, too, as he studied Saunders's cold face and observed Gratton's stony look, that there probably would come a day when he would exercise his new contract. Television was like that. He'd won an initial skirmish, but the battle to survive had only just begun.

THE SURPRISE

Steve Lane stood in his elegant, newly furnished office and looked down at the sprawling but well-designed array of square smaller office buildings that made up Century City, a small enclave carved out of the old Twentieth Century Fox backlot, long ago derisively dismissed by a well-known Los Angeles architect as the boxes in which Disneyland had been packed.

For a short time it had bothered Steve that George K. Cates had had to vacate the office to make room for him, prompting a series of other moves by the network bureaucracy to accommodate Cates's own shift to a lesser post and a less prestigious office.

Steve made a special effort to minimize the shock to Cates in his diminished role at Federal, this despite Gratton's feelings. Now, a few weeks into the new job, Steve had a chance to observe Gratton's own manner of dealing with Cates. Gratton, on a quick visit to the coast, simply ignored him. In a review of program strategy in the coast boardroom, attended by all the coast program executives, Cates directed an idea to Gratton suggesting a time change of one program to another night. Gratton stared in silence at the ceiling. No one else spoke. Cates flushed and it was Steve who quietly said, "It's an interesting idea, George. Maybe we can get to it a bit later."

When the meeting ended, Gratton pushed back his chair, snuffed out his cigarette, and brushed the ashes off his lapel, nodding politely to those nearest him as he strode past Cates without a word. It was clear to everyone that George K. Cates had become Gratton's new invisible man. That was the standard Gratton treatment of those who fell out of favor, but no one had suspected that Cates would ever be subjected to a public Gratton snub.

What was even more difficult for Steve Lane to understand was Cates's own refusal to accept his new role as a Gratton target. "Joe has his moods," Cates said amiably to Steve as Gratton vanished down the hall to the senior guest office. "Unpredictable at times, isn't he? Right?" he persisted.

"You've seen him behave like this before?" Steve ventured.

"Oh, sure, sure. That's Joe. No way to explain it. You just learn to live with it. You'll find out in due time. Joe's simply Joe. Likes to play being the sphinx."

"What does that mean?"

"He stares into space. Sits like a hunk of stone. Says nothing. Gratton the inscrutable. It's an act; he loves it."

Steve looked into Cates's eyes. He was certain that behind the man's cheerfulness there was a small lump of fear clutching the back of his throat, a lump that would grow in intensity as Gratton played his cards.

The very next day Steve saw a trace of that fear emerging again on Cates's face. Gratton had returned to New York on the "red-eye" the previous night. Cates knocked politely on Steve's door and poked in his head.

"Got a minute, Steve?"

"Sure, come on in. Sit down."

Cates gritted his teeth. For a few seconds he paced in silence in front of Steve's desk and then said, "Damnedest day in my life, that's what." Abruptly, Cates sat down facing Steve. "Incredible," he murmured, shaking his head in disbelief.

"Want to spell it out?" Steve asked sympathetically.

"Sure. Sure. You won't believe it. You just won't believe it!"

"Try me."

"Okay," Cates said with a deep sigh. "You know how busy we are? You. Me. With everyone calling every day? Agents. Producers. Stars. Sometimes even Madison Avenue? Right?"

"Right. So?"

Cates took a deep breath. "All day, so far, my phone's been dead. Dead," he repeated. "No calls even from inside. No visitors either."

Steve studied Cates's eyes yet again. They seemed to have slowly sunk deeper into their sockets; he observed, too, his gray pallor. It was clear that Gratton had passed the word. Cates was not only to be invisible—he was to be ignored, forgotten, shunned.

"No one called you, all day?"

"No one on the outside, and no one here at Federal."

Steve Lane felt a surge of anger. "Nat Ford? Jay Cummings?"

Cates shrugged.

Steve sat in silence for a few moments. He could see the deep hurt in Cates's body language, his bloodshot eyes with their quiet look of defeat, his hands tightly clasped together. Lane picked up a sheet of paper. On it were listed all the calls of the day he'd been unable to return. Steve shoved the list toward Cates. "Take this list. Call every name on it. Tell them you're calling for me. Ask them what's on their mind."

Cates picked up the list and glanced at the names. He knew every caller. He stood up. "Maybe it'll work. I'll give it a try."

The moment Cates left, Steve buzzed his secretary and told her to summon Nat Ford and Jay Cummings to his office. While he waited for them he pulled out a memo from his top drawer. When they entered they were all smiles as Steve signaled them to be seated.

"What's up, pal?" Nat Ford asked, his eyes nervously darting from Cummings to Lane. Everyone at Federal knew that dour, thin Nat Ford, with his chalky complexion made even more striking by the jet black hair that hung low over his forehead, and his dangling arms, which gave him a peculiarly simian look, had been a longtime Gratton lackey. His role on the coast was to be Gratton's eyes and ears. Cummings, on the other hand, was tall, imposing and chubby. He was always the jovial member of the senior program executives and was responsible for overseeing all of Federal's television movies.

Steve took the memo he'd extracted from his desk and pushed it across to the two men. "This is a confidential memorandum that George Cates sent me when I took over the division. I think you should read it together."

Ford and Cummings pulled their chairs close to each other. As they read, Steve noticed Nat Ford's deepening frown; Cummings pursed his lips and Steve was aware of a slow sneer crossing his face. As they finished Nat Ford placed the document back on Steve's desk.

"Well?" Steve asked.

Nat shrugged. "Look, George's a right guy. Decent. And it's like him to say nice things."

"Then why have you ignored him all day?" Steve demanded.

Nat shifted in his chair, glanced at Cummings, then turned to Steve. "There's been nothing to talk about. That happens." Again he glanced over at Jay Cummings for support. "Nothing surprising about that," he added, "am I right, Jay?"

"Really?" Steve interjected. "Haven't you made it a practice to always drop by his office even when you had nothing to discuss?"

"Sure, but today, well, it's been so . . ." Nat stopped talking and extended his hands palms up as Cummings placed a hand on his shoulder.

"Steve," Jay said with a cold smile, "It's all very simple —the word's out. The man," he said pointing a finger to the ceiling, "iced him. We got the message, it's that simple."

"You were told to ignore Cates?"

Cummings smiled. "You don't have to be told at Federal. You know," he emphasized.

"Well, I have new instructions for you, both of you. When you leave my office you go to George Cates's. You find a reason to see him. Do you understand what I'm saying?"

Nat Ford cocked his head. "Pal, you call the shots. I hear you."

"Jay?"

"Sure, but what you're doing is inviting us to slide into the deep freeze with him. Gratton's not going to be doing cartwheels in celebration. But if you want us to put our necks on the block involuntarily—"

Steve slammed the top of his desk with a fist, startling his two visitors. "It's an order. Mine. You don't report to Mr. Gratton. You report to me and as long as George Cates is here you report to him. Do I make myself clear?"

"Sure, pal, sure. But aren't you telling the whole world that Gratton's wish is not yours?" Nat said, nervously, his brow furrowing in fear.

"I can tell George his time is up," Cummings said calmly, "if you want me to."

"He's right, Steve. Jay's always been Cates's hatchet man. George wanted somebody out, Jay handled it. Part of his job."

"I can do it for you, Steve. Say the word."

Steve Lane shook his head. He spoke quietly, deliberately. "When, and if," Steve emphasized, "I want George Cates to exit Federal I'll handle it myself." He fixed his eyes on Jay Cummings. He could see that Cummings was not intimated: he was the perfect organization man—whatever the top man wanted the top man could have. "I don't have any need for a hatchet man."

Ford raised his long arms. "Pal, you call the shots in this division. I'm your man."

"Jay?" Steve asked.

Cummings smiled. "No problem with me. You can live with it, I can live with it."

"Good enough. Now I suggest you both contact George Cates today, before he leaves."

An hour later Cates dropped by Steve's office. He returned the list Steve had given him. "I'm back in business, returned every one of your calls," he said.

"Any problems?"

"None. Everyone I reached was fine. Couple were out. Natural." Cates made his way back to the door.

"Nat Ford and Jay? They drop in?"

Cates nodded. "Both of them, together. They do that a lot. Both come in together. Something of a team. The three of us. We've been a team ever since I arrived at Federal."

"Survivors."

Cates smiled. "Experts at that." As he turned to leave he added, "Thanks, Steve," and then he was gone.

A few minutes later Steve's secretary poked her head into his office. "Mr. Gratton's calling. Line one."

As Steve picked up the phone he wondered if Nat Ford had already touched base with Joe Gratton. "Hello, Joe," he said.

"Want you back here for a nine A.M. meeting. A client problem. My office. you've got other plans I'd appreciate it if you changed them. 'Kay?"

"It's that important?" Steve responded.

"It's that important," Gratton said, and hung up. For a few moments Steve looked down at the phone, quickly reviewing the brief exchange. Gratton's raspy voice gave no indication that he was aware of the showdown with Ford and Cummings; the only facts that had been conveyed were that there was a client problem and that it was important. The Cates matter was a minor problem. Gratton's lack of a greeting and courteous ending to the brief telephone conversation was nothing out of the ordinary. It was par for Gratton who wasted no time on conventional niceties.

Steve brooded for a few moments as he tried to get some sleep on the plane to New York. He'd had relatively little contact with Federal's clients: Gratton and Federal's sales force together with Walter Sloan, the New York executive to whom Steve reported on the Federal organizational chart, handled Madison Avenue. For a few moments he'd considered contacting Sloan, but had rejected the notion, first because he never wanted to show concern about a Gratton order, and he knew, too, that if Gratton had wanted to give him any details he, Gratton, would have done so; second, he knew that Sloan, the network's cagey senior television official under Gratton, would never put himself in a position of advising another officer on any matter involving a Joe Gratton meeting. Sloan had not survived at Federal by being a man of initiative; he had fallen into the role of being the network official who could best handle compromising.

When Gratton's secretary ushered Steve into Gratton's plain office, Steve was surprised. All the others who were to attend the meeting were already present. There was an empty chair next to Walter Sloan. Joe Gratton was hunched down in his own chair behind his simple oak desk. To his left was the urbane chairman of the board of Federal Broadcasting, Robert S. Saunders Jr., who sat stiffly tamping tobacco into his Dunhill pipe.

Across from Federal's top brass was an array of United Productions Entertainment toppers, including Jacob Korn, its venerable titular chairman of the board. Thin lipped, professorial, and benign in appearance, he belied his true origins, said by some to have been as a collector of bad debts for a group tied to organized crime.

They were right. The UPE people were a tough group.

Korn had been a collector for a smalltime collection company with a seamy background—there were no Ivy Leaguers in that world—and he used to collect monies owed by people he characterized as sweaty little cheats who tried to pull fast ones on the big guys. After one polite warning and no payup, he and his little team of collectors would wind up cracking kneecaps, and if that message didn't work then the so-called heavy hitters took over. "A cheater never won," Korn had said at one of his meetings with Sam Colman, "so, take it from me, after a kneecap got splintered it made a fellow think hard." He had adopted the same tough policy, though not quite so crudely, at UPE, encouraging his executives to compete with one another. They could lock horns all they wanted, just so long as they made no deals that weren't best for UPE. "Winner takes all," Korn explained bluntly to his executives once. "That's how it works here. No fancy titles, no sweet talk, no promise me this, promise me that. It's the bottom line that counts. You deliver. How? That's your business. I could care less. The results. That's my business."

Seated next to Korn was Sam Colman. He had come out on top in the UPE executive jungle. The final UPE officer was Jerry Moss. Steve had had contact with Moss some years before and knew how hard he was under the surface. Seated alone, his back to the wall, was William Chamberlin, the client, head of Dinsmore & Clark, one of Madison Avenue's fastest growing, innovative advertising agencies.

Steve knew instantly that this was no ordinary meeting. It irritated him that no one at Federal had had the courtesy to advise him in advance of what it was all about, but he smiled politely as Walter Sloan made the proper introductions. Steve had never met Korn and had had only minimal contact with Sam Colman. He'd met William Chamberlin some years before when Chamberlin had put in a short stint at Otis & Meade as a top copywriter when Steve headed its TV operations. In a few moments he knew exactly what the meeting was all about.

Gratton nodded to Sloan, and Sloan, a thin smile on his lips, said, "Steve, we're so glad you could arrange to be here on such short order. You've known everyone in the room for some time—"

"Except Mr. Korn," Steve interjected.

"Except Mr. Korn," Sloan repeated. "Mr. Korn is here because of his long relationship with the Saunders family and, of course, because of the intimate and very happy relationship that's existed for some years between Federal and UPE. As you know, Steve, UPE has been a major supplier of excellent television shows for us. The reason we're here is because of the pilot UPE produced, starring Todd Harris."

That pilot, Steve knew, was one he'd rejected two weeks earlier when he'd written a brief memo to Sloan, copying Gratton and Saunders. There had been no response from any of them until this moment, and Steve immediately realized that he had wrongly concluded that his rejection had been routinely accepted by Federal management.

Quite obviously UPE had elected not to challenge Lane directly, but to voice its vexation to his superiors. He, Steve Lane, had been deliberately placed on the hot seat. Key facts quickly crossed his mind. UPE and Federal had the same connections on Wall Street—it was common knowledge that the two companies working together could benefit each other's corporate balance sheets. It was a fact, well known in Hollywood and Madison Avenue, that the two companies had flourished together and that, in the main, UPE's television product had worked to the benefit of Federal Broadcasting in the relentless battle to corral advertising support.

And there was the rub. When Steve Lane had worked at Otis & Meade, and later at Kane & Shaw, UPE programs were at the bottom of the lists of their media purchases. James Hornwell Otis, some years earlier, along with Tony Gordon, had, in the days when advertising agencies bought whole programs instead of spots, shunned UPE. "Jacob Korn," Otis once said derisively, "is not our kind of people." And although many of their programs had successful runs on network television, it was also the consensus of astute observers and critics that no one could ever accuse UPE of trying to elevate program quality. On the contrary, it was a generally accepted fact that UPE program executives, led by Sam Colman himself, pandered to the lower tastes of the mass audience.

"The Todd Harris program, *The Big Spread*," Sloan was saying "was a show we all had high hopes for. It was a pilot commitment we'd made before Steve Lane joined our company so he had no participation in the initial decision."

"He killed it was his participation," Korn said with icy bluntness.

"Yes, of course," Sloan answered with his customary smile. Then he turned to Jerry Moss. "Jerry? I believe you wanted to discuss our reevaluation of the property."

Steve, containing his anger, recoiled at Sloan's reference to the reevaluation of the show. At once he sensed that he'd been flown in to face a UPE assault, that his rejection of the pilot was not to be the final word. As Jerry Moss glibly laid out all of the presumed virtues of the proposed show, Steve Lane studied Korn. Korn had a strange habit of raising his upper lip, moving it from side to side over his yellowing teeth, exuding an almost primitive sign of animal ferocity. Sam Colman's deeply lined face was a mask of imperturbable, cold indifference. Steve sensed that Colman would be the real champion of the so-called reevaluation in the end, not Jerry Moss. Moss was merely the opening gun, reciting in endless detail the appeal of a new rising star, Todd Harris, and reviewing UPE's long history of success in creating and producing network shows, especially for Federal.

Moss finished his presentation and gestured to Steve.

Steve was now absolutely certain that he'd been set up to take a fall. The top brass of a network and its chief program supplier didn't come together to reason matters out. They'd come together to put things back together again and if a Federal officer had to be the fall guy, so be it. Gratton had been placed at the network by Moss and Gratton knew how to pay off an obligation. Saunders Jr. didn't care, Gratton told Lane, as long as the bottom line went up the hill.

As all eyes turned to Steve, he decided that his best defense would be a strong offense. He'd been designated to be the goat—that was clear, but he was determined to demonstrate that this goat would make a stand.

"Jerry, that was a fine selling job. The problem is that the selling job is over. You did that with great success when you sold Federal on bankrolling *The Big Spread* pilot. As Walter said, that's before I came aboard. Let me be frank." He glanced to his left at Gratton slumped in his chair. "The pilot never lived up to those glowing words you just voiced," Steve went on politely. "The pilot was a dud. Todd Harris is no star. He made no impact."

"How do you know that?" Moss interjected sharply.

"Federal's research, that's how!"

"Research? That's bullshit, Steve, and you know it."

"All of UPE's shows went through the same process. Some scored well. Some were so so." Steve paused for a moment. "When the numbers are good, Jerry, you like our numbers." He stopped again, then shook his head. "*The Big Spread* had the worst numbers of any pilot Federal's bought in years. Not just UPE's—but the pilots of all of our suppliers."

'Tell us what's needed, we'll do it," Moss replied, with a disarming smile.

Steve shook his head. "I wish it were that simple, Jerry. What's needed is a new star, a new premise, a new production team."

Moss was about to respond, but Jacob Korn raised a hand. "A question."

"Sir."

"What gives you the right to tell us, UPE, the company that's helped make Federal a successful network—you think we don't know how to make television shows?"

"Of course you do, Mr. Korn. But not every pilot is successful. Not every pilot becomes a series."

"Every pilot we ever made for Federal's become a series. That's our record, young man!" Korn retorted, acidly.

"And you can be proud of that record," Steve said, coolly. Then looking in turn at Korn, Colman, and Moss, whose smile was fading, Steve added, "This is one that won't."

Moss stood up. "Now you wait a minute, Steve. We're here to make it work. UPE—"

Korn signaled Moss to be seated and then, ignoring Lane, he spoke directly to Gratton. "One man can kill a pilot that has our support? Our hard work? Our record of achievement with you?"

"That's what we're here to discuss, Jacob," Gratton said, placatingly.

Korn pointed to Steve as he looked at Gratton. "He makes your business decisions?"

"No. He's in charge of our entertainment division."

"So?" Korn said, with a sneer.

At that point Sam Colman raised both hands. "Steve, let's look at things this way. Your client, our client, Mr. Chamberlin," he emphasized, "has expressed an interest in our shows. He's bought a major interest in *Speedway*. He likes *The Big Spread*. Am I right. Mr. Chamberlin?"

"I find it an acceptable show."

"Good, good." Colman nodded to Chamberlin and then focused his attention on Lane. "Steve, the client likes our shows. His television buyers like them. As Mr. Korn said, we don't produce pilots to be pilots, Steve. We produce them just to demonstrate an idea. Demonstrate," he repeated. "A pilot. One show. We're not in the business of making pilots. We do it on occasion. But our business is we make series. This is one where your people persuaded us—a new star, a unique premise. Demonstrate it. We sell series—that's our business. This show has a striking idea."

"I couldn't recommend a series without seeing a pilot." Steve countered.

"We've done it for Federal many times, and elsewhere as well," Colman replied, and then added tersely, "I'm not sure we want to make any more pilots."

Steve shrugged. "Your decision, Sam."

Everyone sat in silence for a moment and then Jacob Korn spoke, "What I'm hearing is just one man's opinion—his," he said pointing to Steve. "This against our combined judgment—Mr. Chamberlin's, Mr. Colman's, mine—one man's opinion and it sounds like he's setting a new policy—no series without a pilot. That's bullshit and we don't accept it."

Sloan raised both hands. "Gentlemen, please. This isn't about policy. Policy is Mr. Saunders and Mr. Gratton's area of responsibility. We're talking about one show, how to reevaluate it if that's possible."

"It's possible if you want to make it possible," Korn said angrily. "Right now it looks to me like someone way down the line is calling the shots." Korn turned to Gratton. "Joe, are you putting his opinion—"

Steve stopped Korn short. "Hold it, Mr. Korn. Hold it!" Korn's eyebrows shot up, shocked at the interruption. Steve pointed a finger at the older man. "Mr. Korn, if you don't mind, let me set the order straight. The decision on not to approve *The Big Spread* is not one man's opinion. It's the entertainment division's judgment—the whole program operation was unanimous in rejecting *The Big Spread*. But it could have been one man's opinion, mine—if the whole department voted for it and I disagreed. It's my responsibility as head of the entertainment division to make the final judgment. And my judgment stands. I cannot approve—even with Mr. Chamberlin's endorsement. I recommended against it and I still do. But—" Steve paused.

"But?" Korn stammered.

"Mr. Sloan is my superior. I've made my recommendation. He can overrule me. If Mr. Sloan chooses not to overrule . . ." Steve paused for a moment as he turned to stare at

Sloan's frozen smile, "then Mr. Gratton can overrule Mr. Sloan. And if Mr. Gratton doesn't want this show on our air Mr. Saunders can overrule him." Steve sat back in his chair. The room was silent. Time stood still. Finally, Sam Colman spoke.

"This is a major decision, gentlemen. This show has all the elements to make it a success. If you don't commit we'll put all the strength of UPE to place it on another network—"

Steve broke in. "No one is going to buy that show, Sam."

Korn slapped his knee. "You make their decisions, too, that it?" he said, sarcastically.

"No, Mr. Korn. But when one network passes on a pilot the odds are very much against another picking it up." Steve felt a surging anger at the older man's sarcasm. "You haven't asked my opinion, but I'll go further. It won't even work in syndication as a first-run show."

Korn stood up. "Nice to know, Mr. Saunders, Mr. Gratton, that our arrangement no longer works here."

Sloan raised a hand. "Mr. Korn, nothing's changed. Our relationship is solid—solid, I repeat—this is only one show. One show—"

Moss cut in. "Maybe Mr. Lane should know that if Mr. Chamberlin doesn't get his wish to sponsor part of *The Big Spread* we'll have to reconsider whether we want him—and you—to have *Speedway*."

"Are you suggesting a tie-in—without one the other deal is off?" Steve interjected.

"I'm setting out the facts, facts in the real world, Steve," Moss grumbled.

"Sounds a little like an illegal threat to me."

"There's no threat," Moss retorted.

Steve smiled. "I'll buy that, Jerry. But if you want to renege on your deal, it's okay with me. I don't find anything of value to Federal in *Speedway* either. It was bought before I joined up. We're committed unless you're asking to be released."

Colman slowly got up from his chair. "We're not asking to be released, Steve. Gentlemen," he bowed politely to Gratton and Saunders, "I take it no one's going to overrule anyone." He let a moment slip by. Then he stretched out a hand to Gratton and politely waved to Korn and Moss to join him as he left Gratton's office. Chamberlin hurriedly followed them out.

The four Federal executives sat in silence for a few moments. Then Joe Gratton spoke. "You won a battle, Steve."

"I appreciate your support," Steve replied.

"I detect a touch of sarcasm?"

"Not at all, Joe. You could have overruled my decision."

Gratton shook his head. "That wasn't the issue. When Walter abstained I had no choice. I don't overrule my key executive team in the presence of others. Sam Colman understood that even if he left mad as hell. And don't underestimate this. We have some rebuilding to do. We won a battle of sorts—your battle, Steve. But UPE has been vital to us."

"Putting them on the same level with our other suppliers doesn't seem to me to be a losing proposition," Steve asserted.

"Easy to say, Mr. Lane." Gratton said, and turned to Saunders. "Anything to say, Robert?"

Saunders tapped his pipe. "Couldn't we offer to buy the show—put it on in the summer? Thirteen weeks?"

"Interesting idea." Gratton turned to Steve, "Mr. Lane?"

Steve shook his head. "The show's a loser. Even cable would love to program against it."

"It would help preserve our relationship with UPE," Saunders said quietly.

Steve shook his head. "Sorry. If you're asking me, I can't recommend it in any time slot."

Saunders got to his feet. "Just a thought." He left the room.

Gratton slapped the top of his desk. The meeting was officially over. Steve and Sloan walked down the hall toward Sloan's office.

"You made it tough on us, Steve," Sloan said softly.

"Why didn't Gratton or you tell me in advance what I was being called in for?"

"I think Mr. Gratton assumed you'd get the picture the moment you entered his office."

"Oh? And did you assume that, too, Walter?"

"Not at all. I don't get into these kinds of—shall we call them permutations?"

"Maybe machinations is more like it."

"Machinations, of course," Sloan repeated easily. "That's Mr. Gratton's department."

"So, the net net of all this—to use a Gratton expression—what's your call on this, Walter?"

Sloan smiled and placed a hand on Steve's shoulder. "Like Joe Gratton said, Steve, you won a battle."

"Is that all it was? To stand up and reject an inferior program—a battle?"

"Well, yes, I think that's what's happened. But there are larger stakes than just a show, a pilot. It's the whole relationship. Yes—*you* Steve, won a battle and I must say," he added with his familiar smile, "*we* may have lost a war."

"Explain that."

"It's very simple. Boiled down to its essence—you managed to break a long-standing gentleman's agreement, namely, what's good for us and UPE jointly has worked well—at least well enough in the past. Now, it's a new ball game. That's quite a surprise, thanks to you."

"No, Walter. Thanks to Joe Gratton. He made the wrong assumption. About me. That's the surprise. Think it over."

Sloan smiled. "Time will tell, Steve," he said, then glancing up and down the hall to make certain they were alone, he added, "George Cates knew how to fall on the sword."

Steve tapped Sloan on the shoulder. "Then Gratton should have invited him and not me."

GRATTON'S REVENGE

JOE GRATTON SAT, AS WAS his daily custom, hunched over his desk as early as eight in the morning, taking small sips of his ever present tumbler of vodka, the *New York Times* spread out before him. He was proud, as well as defiant, about his ability to hold his liquor; at the end of each day he made it a point to check in with Saunders, his arms tightly held against his chunky body, making every effort to hold himself straight as an arrow as he walked the sixty feet to Saunders's office and saluted him before leaving, in order to demonstrate to those behind or before him that he was in full control.

And that control was evident in his daily morning briefings when a dozen or so officers of lesser rank reported to his office an hour after his arrival. The ostensible purpose of these meetings was to exchange information so that all of his key executives heading up the various departments of the company were fully informed of each other's activities. But the real purpose was to give Gratton a chance to lavish praise on those few whose accomplishments merited his public approval, but even more so to lash out with tart appraisals at those others whose performance in any given twenty-four-hour period merited public embarrassment. This routine was part of Gratton's calculated way to instill both fear and love among his troops.

On this day, however, there would be a meeting unlike any other ever held at Federal. Gratton had turned his *Times* to the financial section and, even as he raised his tumbler, he suddenly reared up in his chair, the contents of the glass spilling over the paper. His eyes were focused on the two column article with the headline "UPE, A Privately Held Entertainment Corporation Goes Public, Makes Its Key Leaders Overnight Millionaires." There in bold print was the stunning news: board chairman Jacob Korn's estimated stock value was in excess of two hundred and fifty million dollars; Sam Colman, UPE's CEO, was listed as holding at least one hundred million dollars; Jerry Moss was listed as holding at least twenty-five million dollars in corporate stock. The story went on to state that these officers also held stock options worth millions more.

Gratton leaned back in his chair, stunned; he pushed his thick glasses over his crew-cut gray hair, poured himself a fresh stiff drink, gulping it down in one quick swallow, and then picked up the wet newspaper, rereading every word of the article. As he studied the details he muttered to himself, "Bastards, greedy sons of bitches." Abruptly, he pushed himself away from his desk, folded the paper, and rushed down the hall to Saunders's office.

"He in?" Gratton barked to one of Saunders's secretaries.

"Mr. Saunders just arrived," the secretary said politely

as Gratton brushed past her and threw open the door. Saunders, already seated at his desk, looked up as Gratton flung his wet copy of the *Times* on the chairman's desk.

"Feast your eyes on that," Gratton rasped. Saunders lifted the paper as Gratton pulled out his handkerchief to wipe up the damp spot on the chairman's desk. "Sorry about that, Robert. You see that story?"

Saunders pulled out his reading glasses, and, carefully holding the wet paper before him, read the article. A small frown crossed his face.

"Know anything about this? Korn? Colman? Either one talk to you?" Gratton asked angrily.

"Not a word, not a word," Saunders repeated.

"Bastards," Gratton growled.

"We made them rich, Joe. That's for sure."

"And what did we get out of it? Zero. Not even a word! Not even the courtesy of a call. Not an inkling they were going public! They owed us at least that! We were supposed to have mutual interests!" Gratton shook his head. "Jerry Moss. That smart-ass little bastard. He's been to my home a thousand times," Gratton grumbled. "We've gone on vacations together. Europe. The Caribbean. Cocksucker!"

Saunders turned his head. "I always thought of him as your friend. A special friend."

"He was," Gratton replied coldly. "Was," he emphasized.

"Well, they've had their moment, Joe. We can't do anything about that. They chose to play things close to the vest." Saunders smiled. "Their choice. Their call."

Gratton sat in silence for a moment. A cunning smile crossed his face. "We can do something about it, Mr. Saunders. Something they'd never count on."

"Oh? Want to tell me?"

Gratton got to his feat and picked up his copy of the *Times*. "Better I handle this alone for now." He crossed over to the doors. "I've got the staff meeting. This will be topic one."

The word was out on the West Coast, headlines flashing across the front page of *Daily Variety* and the *Hollywood Reporter*.

Nat Ford was the first to read it and rushed into Steve Lane's office.

"This has got to give Mr. Gratton a hangover he never gets from his daily bottle of vodka."

Steve read the headlines. "Why? I'd think he'd be the first to realize he paved the way, all those deals he made with Moss and Colman. He shouldn't be surprised."

Nat ran his tongue across his teeth. "Mr. Gratton's a sensitive man. Very. He makes good money for sure. Very. When he sees this story, particularly Jerry Moss's take, believe me pal, this will rub him the wrong way."

"He shouldn't be surprised considering the business Federal's given UPE."

"Maybe not, Steve. But Mr. Gratton's deal, whatever it is, is small potatoes against Jerry's twenty-five mil. And it has to be chicken feed against Mr. Colman's hundred mil."

"He made it happen. That's the beauty of being an entrepreneur. They take risks. They can lose, they can win. In the case of UPE, they win."

"Okay, Steve, but I'll still wager Mr. Gratton's not going to like feeling small especially next to Jerry Moss." Nat Ford chuckled. "A year ago you got the heat for that little turkey, UPE's *The Big Spread*—now you're liable to get it for what you've been doing since."

"You mean the one UPE show we bought since?"

Nat nodded. "Plus the ones you've okayed for development that are waiting in New York for Gratton's approval, which is something UPE figures he'll do."

"Those are projects I like—and you and Jay and George Cates made enough good suggestions to make them work. Why shouldn't he like them?"

Nat grinned. "Because suddenly you're Jerry Moss's new friend. That's why."

Steve shook his head. "Whether he likes me or not is academic. The show's the thing. Always has been. I think by now that both Gratton and UPE know that I've no prejudice against UPE. *The Big Spread* was a real turkey. The proof is they never sold it."

"Like you said."

"I'm sure Sam Colman had Moss and the others work their tails off just to show me."

"Pal, that's history. Suddenly, well, not too suddenly, it took a year, but now you're their new man."

"Okay with me, Nat, as long as they deliver."

Nat stretched out his long dangling arms. "Don't be too surprised by anything New York does."

"Thanks for the advice." He knew Gratton could be unpredictable. UPE had profited from Federal: Federal had profited from UPE. But this move on UPE's part was unilateral: what was in it for Federal? And if nothing? It would be interesting to see how Gratton balanced the books.

What Gratton's first move would be was soon on Steve's desk: a terse fax that read, "Management Policy—we will take no action on UPE projects. Our position: we're studying our options. You advise Mr. Moss."

Gratton had chuckled as he dictated the message to

Steve and then sat back as his nine o'clock meeting began. He waved the still damp copy of his *Times* before the assembled executives. "I assume you've all seen the news of UPE's going public?" He passed the paper across the desk to those who hadn't. "You all will be asked what this means to our long relationship and the answer is, we're very happy for our coast colleagues. Happy," he repeated.

Balding Bob Colbert, Gratton's chief sales aide, a man who'd moved with him when Gratton wound up at Federal, characteristically struck his teeth with a pencil. "Is that the party line, Joe? That what you're saying?"

"Why not? Sam Colman's done a terrific job for us. A clinker now and then, but if a show can be fixed he's always been there to pour in the money to make it work. That's his credo."

"Plus a willingness to carry those hefty deficits," Colbert added.

"Hasn't seemed to hurt their bottom line," Gratton snapped as he reached out to retrieve his *Times*.

Sid Kaplan, Federal's rotund head of research, who never spoke without raising his hand, asked nervously, "Think UPE's a good buy, Joe, now that they've gone public?"

Gratton rubbed the arms of his chair as he peered out at the group. "Good question, Sid," Kaplan basked in a small moment of glory. "They've made a score, that's for sure, but," he stressed as he leaned forward in his chair, "their success is, shall we put it simply, tied to our success."

"Our stock didn't move," Sid volunteered.

"No reason to. Stock prices discount the future. And while UPE's done well—very well, for them and for us—in the past, who's to say what the future holds?" Gratton's eyes narrowed as he sipped his drink.

The group sat in silence, no one certain how to respond.

"What about the future?" Colbert ventured.

A hint of a smile crossed Gratton's face. "The future. The future," he said, "who can predict the future?"

Colbert persisted. "What I'm wondering," he said, holding up his own copy of the *Times*, "is, does this change anything between us?"

"Why?" Gratton barked, "why would this change anything?"

"I'm thinking about next season—how many UPE shows will we carry?"

"Are you thinking of Federal, Mr. Colbert, or whether to buy UPE stock?"

"Both, Joe. Why not?"

Gratton was privately pleased at the question. He spoke carefully. "What we do is to make certain we have the best schedule Mr. Lane and his program people on the coast can put together. Right now we're evaluating our options. We've always bought a fair share of UPE shows, but everything's on hold. Like always. I want all of us, Steve Lane, management here in New York, to do only what's best for Federal. That's always been our policy. Still is. Clear?"

"No UPE commitments as of the moment, that it?" Colbert asked.

"On target, Mr. Colbert. And remember with no one else, either."

Colbert, the boldest man in the room, asked once again, "Might be a time for a quick short sale?"

"Brother Colbert, I'm not your broker. I don't give advice on stocks, investing, selling short, you name it. My responsibility is Federal. Not Fox, not Paramount, not

UPE." He looked out at the group. "Any questions?" There were none. Gratton slapped the top of his desk. "Remember one thing. This meeting's been confidential. Now let's go to work." Only Tim Harding, a short man who had once been a reporter for the trade papers, his face a road map of fear, lingered behind. He waited quietly until all the others had left Gratton's office.

Gratton rubbed his hands together. Then, in a conspiratorial manner, he winked at Tim. "You got a little job to do."

"Nice finessing, Joe," Tim said, cautiously glancing behind to make absolutely certain the others had gone. "Trade paper? *Times*? TV?" He pulled out a pad and pen.

Gratton stroked his puffy cheeks and sipped his drink. "Maybe Colbert's slant, Tim. The coast."

"Gotcha."

"Just factual statement. No embellishment. No names."

"Natch."

"Federal vamping. No buys. Not even UPE."

"Especially UPE?"

Gratton chuckled. "You got it. Make it a New York story. Clear?"

"Done," Tim said, and with a quick touch of his forehead with his pen, his informal salute to Gratton, he was gone.

The news hit the coast papers the next day. An authorized Federal source in New York was credited with leaking the inside story that Federal was reviewing its relationship with UPE and that executives on both coasts were in sync. Nat Ford and Jay Cummings strode into Steve Lane's office together. Nat pointed to the front-page *Daily Variety* story.

"Wait'll this hits the fan. Be glad, Steve, that the source wasn't credited out here."

Steve read the cryptic piece and looked up at Ford and

Cummings. "Who would do this?" he asked, passing the paper back to Ford.

Nat shrugged. "We're clean. My guess is it's some guy in New York and Gratton will go berserk running it down. That nine o'clock meeting's got to be rough. And one thing's certain, he'll find out."

Cummings shook his head, "Provided he's not the source."

"Gratton? The source? What makes you say that, Jay?" Steve asked.

Cummings smacked his lips. "Because I know the crummy little bastard, that's why."

Steve laughed. He'd learned early on that Jay was about the only executive who spoke out so bluntly about Gratton. Even Gratton, some said, tolerated Jay's sometimes irreverent remarks, usually softened in Gratton's presence by his wit, but Steve was certain he wouldn't accept Cumming's terse comment this morning.

"C'mon, pal," Nat interjected. "Okay. Maybe he's leaked a story now and then, but those are the ones that made him look good." Nat slapped the paper. "This one's going to make Jake Korn and Sam Colman sizzle. How's that benefit Gratton or Federal?"

Cummings shrugged, "Who can figure out a guy who outdoes Machiavelli. It has a purpose, that story. Gratton's purpose."

Steve said nothing, but he reflected on the confrontation over *The Big Spread*. Gratton had let that decision stand. And now the order putting everything on hold after UPE went public and made themselves rich. But what was the purpose of reminding them they were now vulnerable? Federal depended on their shows.

The news was even more aggravating at UPE's coast

headquarters. Sam Colman and Jacob Korn had sat together for over an hour in Korn's elegant office analyzing the puzzling leak word by word.

Korn stood at his floor-to-ceiling window looking down at UPE's vast sprawling stages. "Mr. Gratton could close down half our TV operations."

"More than half," Sam Colman replied as he stood beside him.

"We can't let that happen."

"Mr. Korn, we won't," Colman said. No one at UPE, not even Sam Colman, ever called Korn by his first name.

"He thinks he calls the shots."

"In TV, maybe, he does," Colman admitted.

"Why 'maybe'? He don't buy, we go dry."

"It won't happen, Mr. Korn," Colman said politely.

"You can be so sure, Sam?"

Colman looked into Korn's troubled eyes. "I won't let it happen, Mr. Korn. Mr. Gratton plays his cards, I play ours."

Korn smiled. He'd learned that if Sam had a solution he'd best let him play it out. Sam had won that right. He had confidence in Sam Colman.

Gratton let a day go by without his usual meeting. When the group assembled the following day Gratton squinted once more at his *Times* and smiled as he looked at the market reports. UPE's stock had dropped a dollar and a half from the previous day. He'd asked Tim to check the price while the morning meeting was taking place. He put the paper aside as his executive team arrived. Gratton dealt with a series of minor items, expressing greater vexation than he really felt. He cracked down hard on his station relations chief for changing the compensation paid to a midwest station.

"They're peanuts, Joe." Chris Holden, a Heisman trophy winner said, his heavy body weaving from side to side.

"For others, yes," Gratton growled, "but word gets out then some top ten market's going to claim precedent and how do you handle that?"

"Word won't get out," Holden said. "My guys don't talk."

Gratton's eyes narrowed. "Well, your guys may not talk, but someone in this little group did talk right after our meeting day before yesterday. And curiously it winds up on the front page of the *Daily Variety* on the coast. I thought I made it clear that our meeting was confidential. But one of you sons of bitches couldn't keep the news to himself." He paused to sip his drink. " 'Kay. I don't expect a confession, but let me make it clear—I have an idea of who talked and the moment I can prove it you're out of here." He scanned the room as the group remained silent. "Anyone want to say anything?

Sid Kaplan raised a nervous hand.

"Go ahead, Sid."

"Why would anyone do such a thing. Who benefits?"

"You tell me."

Sid shrugged. "All it does is hurt us—hurt UPE. Hell's bells, their stock's already slipped. They'll blame that leak." Sid looked around the room. "Who else knew except one of us."

There was fear evident on the drawn faces of the assembled group. They all stared impassively at Gratton. To a man they all knew that Gratton had an uncanny knack for tracking down stories that hurt UPE; he'd done it in the past and the culprit was out on a moment's notice. Some figured it was the advertising departments of the press who did Gratton's bidding—Federal's advertising budgets were the largest in the business.

After the meeting broke up Gratton was not surprised to receive a call from Sam Colman, who expressed a desire for a top-level meeting.

"Anything special on your mind, Sam?" Gratton asked, sitting back in his plain swivel chair and winking at Tim Harding who'd hung back from the others.

"I have to be in New York," Colman said, easily. "If you have a few minutes day after tomorrow I'd like to drop by."

"How about dinner in my dining room? Say, six o'clock?"

"That would be fine. I'd like to bring Jerry Moss along, if that's agreeable."

Gratton nodded his head. "You want to talk programming?"

"That's one topic, Joe."

"Then maybe we should have Steve Lane join us."

"Whoever," Colman said politely.

"Six o'clock it is. Day after tomorrow, 'kay?"

"We'll be there." Gratton heard the phone click.

"Bastard never says goodbye, thanks, nothing," Gratton growled as he looked across at Tim. He picked up his carafe and strengthened his drink. "Tim?" Gratton asked, the carafe poised above another glass.

Tim Harding hated vodka, but he never refused Gratton. "Don't mind if I do. But light, Joe."

Gratton sat back, a grin on his face. "Never said a word about the story."

Tim raised his shoulders.

"Hit them in their pocket book and they play it cool."

"Probably figures on checking you when he meets up with you."

Gratton's grin turned ugly. "Taught those bastards a little financial lesson."

"For sure, Joe," Tim said accommodatingly.

Gratton doodled on a message pad. He wrote down a ten-numbered figure. He drained his glass and poured himself another drink. In the privacy of his office, he mumbled, "Lousy bastards. We can make those lousy leeches rich. And we can make them poor."

"You can do it, Joe."

Gratton sneered. "I'm going to teach them manners, Tim."

Harding shook his head. "They had it coming."

"Keeping secrets isn't always so smart, Tim my boy," Gratton said, his words beginning to slur.

"They brought it on themselves, Joe," Tim said.

"You bet your last dime they did. And, Brother Harding, I wouldn't be surprised if Jacob Korn didn't kick some ass himself, starting with Mr. Colman."

"Like I said, one of them should have let you know."

"It would have been the decent thing to do," Gratton said as he slammed his empty glass on his desk. "They had their little secret story, and Timmy, my boy, we had ours."

"Trumped them," Tim contributed.

"Cost them some real moolah," Gratton chuckled. "At least on paper."

"They got the message, Joe."

Gratton stroked his chin. "They got another one coming, a real message, Brother Harding. Day after tomorrow. Wait. You just wait and see."

❁ ❁ ❁

Steve Lane hated the quick orders to be in New York. The conversation had been a bit longer than usual, even conciliatory. Gratton could turn on the charm when it was necessary.

"I hate to drag you in, Steve, on such short notice, but Colman gave me no alternative. Especially when he pointedly announced he was bringing in Jerry Moss."

"I understand, Joe."

"If they want to discuss programming I think it's appropriate to have you on hand."

Steve asked, "Is that the purpose of the meeting?"

"Sam Colman said it." Gratton paused. "If you think your friend Cates can handle things . . ." he paused to let the sarcastic reference sink in.

Steve understood the sly dig; Gratton hadn't given up on ousting Cates. "No, I think this is my call. Cates can handle the fort out here while I'm gone," he added, pointedly.

"You want company, bring in Ford."

"I don't need company, Joe."

There was a slight pause. "Be nice to see the little bastard," Gratton said.

"I don't need him, Joe. You want him in?"

"Two of them coming from the coast. Two of you. 'Kay?"

"Good. Moss'll probably have his New York rep on deck. That sly, gangling Len what's his name?"

"Goldstein, I think."

"Right. 'Kay. See you, six o'clock, my dining room," Gratton continued, "but if you need a little more time, clear your desk, we could push it back to seven. Even eight."

Steve smiled. "It's all right at six. I can be there. No problem."

"Appreciate this, Steve," Gratton went on. "Programming is one thing. Mr. Colman didn't elaborate."

Steve was puzzled that Gratton chose not to refer to the leak in *Daily Variety*. If Gratton wanted to ignore it, he would, too. But he was certain it was a major reason for Colman's demand for a top-level meeting. Machinations.

"That's Sam Colman for you," was Steve's final comment.

"Whatever," Gratton replied. "See you at six, 'kay?"

"Okay." And with that Gratton hung up. Steve fingered the phone. He was certain the meeting was going to be very special. Sam Colman wasn't the kind of executive who had to run off to New York for a holiday.

The dinner meeting opened with casual pleasantries. It was Colman who asked if Saunders was going to be present as the first course was being served.

Gratton shook his head. "You didn't ask, Sam. He's chairing a favorite charity affair tonight. Am I right, Walter?"

Sloan smiled affably. "American Cancer Society, I believe."

Gratton speared a shrimp, a small drop of sauce failing on his lapel.

"Pleasant flight?" Sloan asked Steve amiably as he looked across at Colman and Moss seated opposite him and at Len Goldstein, the toothy, lean New Yorker who sat a bit apart, slightly discomfited in the presence of Colman and Moss, his way of acknowledging his inferior status.

The dinner proceeded with considerable small talk notably contributed, in part, by Gratton, but mainly by

Sloan. Steve was sure Gratton had orchestrated Sloan's cheerful demeanor. Colman paid polite attention, looking occasionally, with a bit of disdain evident in his eyes, as Gratton fumbled with his food and as he proceeded to light a cigarette. "Never could break the habit. Mind, Sam?" Gratton asked.

Colman shook his head. Moss joined in the conversation in an effort to be polite. Len Goldstein played his role with perfect assurance—saying nothing.

As dessert was being served, Colman fired the opening shot. "That was a lousy story, Mr. Gratton." Colman didn't feel the need to elaborate; Steve could read the hostility in Colman's eyes and the pointed formal, even cold, manner in which he addressed Joe Gratton.

Gratton brushed some ashes from his lapel. "We'll find out what little bastard talked, Sam," he said, ignoring Colman's frigid formality.

"That hurt us," Colman added, as he pushed his dessert plate aside.

Gratton nodded. "Us, too, Sam. Our relationship." He pointed to Ford. "That's why I wanted Nat to come in. Knows everyone on the coast, trade papers, everyone. Very good at ferreting out little assholes."

Ford grinned, pleased at what he construed to be a compliment.

Colman lifted a hand before him and studied his well-manicured nails. "We need a vote of confidence."

Gratton shrugged and pulled out a copy of a release he'd had Tim prepare. "You've got it. Read this. If you approve it goes out tomorrow."

Colman pulled out his glasses, read the release, and passed it to Jerry Moss.

"Well?" Gratton asked.

"Words won't do it, Mr. Gratton," Sam said, coolly.

"Hell's bells, Sam, let's not let some lousy little leak come between us. That release covers our whole history."

Sam Colman's tongue darted out for a brief moment—something Steve saw as a sharp signal of an impending attack. It wasn't long in coming.

"Mr. Gratton," Colman said, a touch of venom showing in the insistent formal manner in which he deliberately kept addressing Gratton, "we've got big problems. I repeat—words won't do what has to be done."

Gratton pushed back his chair, his eyes already a bit rheumy from heavy drinking. "So?" he asked challengingly.

At this point Jerry Moss intervened. "Joe, what Sam is saying is that story, which you characterize as some little leak, has been very damaging. We're here to try to arrange some damage control." He looked pointedly at Steve. "Steve's been very cooperative with us." Moss hesitated momentarily. "Maybe cooperative's the wrong word—"

"It's the right word for this meeting," Colman interjected.

"Right, Sam. What I'm saying, Joe—"

Gratton interrupted. "Why aren't you eating your dinner? You hardly touched your dinner. Dessert's there—"

"I'm not hungry, Joe," Moss stated. "We're here to get things straightened out."

"We're listening," Gratton said, pouring himself another drink and waving the carafe toward Moss.

"I'm not thirsty, Joe. Look, we've worked closely with Steve, all the members of his team. They've told us they like our projects for next season. But your system, which is different than any other network, still leaves the final decision to your program board. Saunders is on it. You chair it. In the past—"

Gratton stopped him. "You're forgetting Walter. Walter's a key member. He's in charge of our overall TV operations."

Moss nodded. "I'm aware of that. In the past Len checked in with you after George Cates sent in his recommendation. Len says he can't get any answers. Right, Len?"

Len Goldstein was happy to participate. "Right."

"And he's been trying for some time. I keep bugging Steve. And now that story breaks and suddenly things have changed." Moss, who'd been speaking in an amiable tone suddenly turned hard. "The question, Joe, is—why?"

Sam Colman's eyes also suddenly blazed with hostility. "Yes! Why?" he repeated, sharply.

Ashes from Gratton's cigarette, which dangled on the edge of his heavy lower lip, dropped on his lapel.

"We're doing what we always do. We're looking at our pilots—yours—everyone's—"

"We have a batch of scripts approved by Steve and his people—have you read them?" Moss demanded.

Gratton brushed his lapel. "I don't read scripts, Jerry."

"Then what's holding you up? You have Steve's recommendation. What else do you need?"

Gratton pushed his chair back. "Mr. Moss," Gratton sneered, "what I don't need is a lecture on how I operate Federal Broadcasting."

"If you have your program people's recommendation, if you don't read scripts, how in hell do you decide?"

Gratton flushed, but before he could speak Walter Sloan spoke up. "Jerry, we're not doing anything now that we haven't done before."

"We didn't have to fly in begging for orders, Walter. We got the orders—orders, not just script deals or development deals or pilots. We've gotten commitments. Commitments for series. Twenty-two weeks minimum. Four, five, one season—even six series at a time."

Sloan gave Jerry his familiar easy smile. "It just seemed to management here in New York that with the changes going on in television—new networks, station groups buying first-run, cable, even pay TV—the time had arrived for us to take a bit of time, study the changes, even Madison Avenue's buying methods, before making too many commitments."

Sam Colman looked with disdain at Sloan. "Meanwhile we sit on the coast, our stages empty, our offices filled with tremendous overhead in maintaining a group of the best producers, writers, directors in the business twiddling their thumbs."

"We haven't okayed any of your competitors' shows, Sam."

"I thought we had a special relationship."

"And you do, Sam, you do," Sloan insisted.

"Then prove it!" Colman snapped.

Gratton sat back, enjoying the spectacle of Sam Colman's obvious anger. Sloan turned to Steve. Steve Lane had been trying to figure out Gratton's tactics: was he, as a major buyer, enjoying a little sadistic pleasure at Sam Colman's expense? Did he really want to break up the long-standing arrangements which had given UPE a decided insider's advantage?

"As you know Sam," Steve said, "I'm the new boy aboard and I've worked closely with Jerry and a lot of your creative people. We've put together some very good projects."

"Your authority's limited," Colman said rudely.

Steve absorbed the slight without displaying anger. "Same as George Cates when he was in charge, Sam. I think Joe Gratton and," he added, turning to Sloan, "Walter have a right to take some extra time to do their own evaluation if they feel it's necessary in view of the rapid changes in—"

"Bullshit," Moss retorted. Then, glowering at Gratton, who continued to view his guests impassively, he demanded, "What about the action adventure series with Nelson Porter? We've made a deal with him, a fat one, he gets a majority of the features. That series gives us a chance to do a helluva lot of pilots—he gets to produce some after his big hit—we can't have that hang fire like this so far in!"

Gratton smiled. "We've already bought a series like that."

"You've what!" Moss sputtered. "You've had our concept for over two months," Moss retorted, heatedly. "You've known that's been our number one project—."

"Sorry, Jerry, you were late."

"And you didn't bother to tell us, just let us swing out there in the wind knocking our brains out to pull off this deal? Who in hell's better than Porter?"

Gratton shrugged. "Can't tell you yet—but the fellow who'll star in as many episodes as he wants is big—or as big as Porter. Maybe bigger in fact."

Moss turned to Lane. "You knew about that, Steve?"

Gratton cut in. "No. He didn't. I made the deal with Creative Artists myself."

"What about our comedy block, the four new half hours?"

"Research has them," Gratton replied as he poured himself another drink.

"You never asked us to wait on research before," Moss shot back. "Steve likes the block." He turned to Lane. "Am I right?"

Steve simply said, "Joe has our recommendation. Yes."

Moss turned back to Gratton. "Joe?" he asked, trying to conceal his greater animosity.

Gratton nodded to Sloan. "Walter?"

Sloan hadn't the faintest idea of what the comedy block was, he'd made it a practice to let everyone in the business know that he wasn't a program expert, but he understood Gratton's passing on this question. He'd do his best to finesse the issue.

"A comedy block of interrelated shows is an interesting concept," Sloan said softly. "Could work out nicely. But we're having some internal research done, some viewer focus groups. Our research people should have the results quite soon."

Sam Colman abruptly stood up. "This meeting is over. I flew in to get a vote of confidence."

Sloan tried to wave Colman to his seat. "Sam, we're talking it out. You don't want to rush to judgment—please, sit down. We appreciate your coming in."

"I don't think so," Colman replied curtly. He signaled to Moss and Goldstein who immediately got up from the table.

"You're going away angry," Gratton sputtered.

"I came in angry, Mr. Gratton." Colman started to the door. He turned and looked back at Gratton. "I got the message."

"There is no message, Sam," Gratton insisted. "You don't want to listen, 'kay. It's your call. We're here."

"We'll be at the Plaza tonight if you have a message. We're out of New York in the morning." And with that he, Moss, and Goldstein were gone.

Gratton speared a blueberry in his dessert. "Soreheads. Try to explain what's going on and they act like a pack of dinosaurs. No understanding. No patience." Suddenly he leaned back chuckling. "Mr. Colman—mistering me to death—he got the message all right. Times have changed. Sure. Oh, we'll buy our fair share of their crap, but on our timetable. When we buy it'll be me to Jacob Korn. Mr. Colman will discover how easy it is for me to bypass him, Moss, and Goldstein. To become a supernumerary again."

Sloan raised a hand. "You're sure you want to do that, Joe? Sam Colman's no pussy cat."

Gratton chuckled. "Oh, we made his hair curl," he said, standing up. "You did fine, Walter. You too, Steve." He looked at Nat scornfully. "Mr. Ford, you did nothing but sit on your ass."

Ford's face went white with fear. "Joe," he said, extending his long arms. "What could I say?"

"You were too scared to say anything," Gratton shot back as he walked by him.

"Joe," Nat replied, "I didn't know how to get in the game. I could have talked but I could have said the wrong thing." Gratton eyed him coldly. "Joe," Nat pleaded, "I thought we were in bed with UPE forever. With Sam Colman, Jerry Moss—"

"You read that lousy little leak, didn't you?"

"Sure, but was I supposed to believe it?"

"*Variety* doesn't print gossip, Mr. Ford," Gratton said sarcastically.

"Christ, how was I to know?" But Gratton was gone. Nat Ford turned to Steve. "Am I supposed to get the blame for Colman giving Joe the brush?"

Steve patted Ford on the shoulder. "Forget it, Nat."

"How can I?" He turned in the direction of the door through which Gratton had made his exit. "He never forgets. Worse. He never forgives."

Sloan patted Nat's shoulder, too. "Roll with it, Nat. Joe Gratton's already thinking of tomorrow. Tonight is already history."

"You're used to it, Walter." Nat turned to Steve. "Can we get a drink at '21' before we turn in?"

"Sure, why not?"

Lane and Ford made their way to "21" 's famed bar. As they gave their order Ford nudged Steve. "Look who's in the corner, Steve." Steve turned and spotted Jerry Moss and Len Goldstein.

"Let's join them, Nat. Maybe we can smooth out some of the rough edges." They made their way to the corner of the room. "Mind if we join you?" Steve asked pleasantly.

"Are you allowed?" Moss retorted, as he downed his drink. Steve saw at a glance that Jerry was plainly drunk, something he'd never seen before. "Is he okay?" Steve ventured to Len.

Goldstein cocked his head. "He's plenty P.O.'ed, that's for sure."

"That cocksucker," Moss grumbled. "That goddamn fucking slob bastard!" He lifted his drink to his lips.

Nat Ford reached over toward Moss. "Hey, Jerry, go easy on the soda pop."

"Fuck you, too." Moss said. "You sat on your fat little ass the whole time saying zip."

"You expect me to beat up on Gratton?" Nat replied, with a laugh. "Like you'd beat up on Jacob Korn, maybe?"

Moss ignored him and turned to Steve. "You're okay, Mr. Lane. You were a pain in the ass, too, once—when you killed *The Big Spread*. And to tell you the real truth, you showed guts. That show was A number one lousy. I respected you. You proved you could deal with us and to tell you even more truth you made us toe the line. We've given you some good shows and you've gone with us." He ordered another drink. "But, your Mr. Joseph A.—A. for asshole—Gratton, he'll pay for tonight, you mark my words. I'll make that little bastard eat crow, you'll see!" he said, slapping the table.

Steve gripped Jerry's arm. He'd never seen him drunk and, in fact, he'd been told that Moss had been ordered off alcohol after a heart attack a few years earlier. "Shouldn't you go easy on the stuff, Jerry?"

Moss pushed Steve's hand away. "You know I've gone away with Joe Gratton to Europe—the Caribbean—we've been close. Friends. But he's no bargain overseas. You go away—you want to see the museums, the cathedrals, historic sights—but him? The bastard prefers to sit in his hotel room with his goddamn vodka and a bushel of tapes of shows—the other networks' shows—news specials he's missed. Sits there with his goddamn cigarette and his vodka—never sees one historical sight! Me? I'm in Rome, Venice, Prague. I travel, I'm a tourist, for chrissake!" He took a short sip. "I made his deal at Federal, Mr. Lane, and I can unmake it. One call to your Mr. Saunders! He wants to play hardball he picked on the wrong fellows. Sam Colman and I can take him to the locker room! One call! Take my word for it! One call!" he repeated as he slumped against the wall.

Steve Lane reached out again. "Come on, Jerry. Joe Gratton's your friend."

"Friend!" Moss said, raising his voice. "You call him my friend after tonight? You saw how Sam asked for a vote of confidence? And what did he get? Not one fucking order!

Not one series! Not one pilot! Not even one lousy new development deal! Nothing!" Moss shook his head in disbelief. "Why? I ask you why?"

Steve Lane was embarrassed. He had no answer—none he could give Jerry Moss, at any rate. Gratton had decided to play hardball with UPE.

Suddenly Moss slapped the table again. "I just figured it out!" He shook his head as an ugly smiled crossed his face. "I should have known! It's so goddamn obvious. I know the man better than anyone on earth! I should have known!" he repeated with a smirk.

Nat Ford chuckled. "Okay, pal, fill us in!"

Moss wiped a hand across his lips. "He's jealous, that's what! He can't stand the thought that Jake Korn, Sam Colman and especially me—me, Jerry Moss—got our slice of the pie going public. That put a hole big as a whale right through his ego! And the man is all ego. You two bastards know it! Am I right, Steve?" Moss didn't wait for an answer. "I know I'm right." He leaned in and spoke in a conspiratorial manner. "And that little *Variety* leak—that fits the picture, too. I know the man. It's his story!"

Nat Ford shook his head. "Too obvious, Jerry. Joe Gratton doesn't work that way."

"You don't know him like I do, Nat. Man's jealous of anybody's got more power, more money than he. I know his deal. I made his deal," he emphasized. "And when I call Mr. Saunders I'll unmake that deal."

"Oh, come on, Jerry," Nat said, "You're not going to do anything that stupid."

"Wait and see," Moss replied, as he tried to get to his feet. "I need a little air."

Steve summoned a waiter and picked up the tab. Jerry

Moss stood up, weaving from side to side. Steve signaled Len Goldstein. "C'mon, let's get him out in the fresh air."

The four men made their way to the street. "I'll get a cab," Steve said.

Jerry Moss put up a hand. "I'll walk. Air'll do me good." The four men headed to Fifth Avenue, Len and Nat each holding one of Jerry's arms. Steve walked alongside Len.

"Len," he said softly, "you get him to bed. Don't let him do anything rash."

Moss turned to Steve. "No one's going to stop me, Steve, no one."

"Jerry, you and Gratton are such close friends. You sleep tonight off."

"Balls, Mr. Lane."

As they neared the Peninsula, where Steve and Nat were staying, Steve made one final effort before Len escorted Jerry Moss to the Plaza. "Len, we have to count on you. Don't let him make that call."

Len Goldstein looked at Nat and then at Steve, "I'll try. That's all I can do. Try."

"He'll think better when he sleeps it off," Nat said.

"It's late. I don't think he'll call tonight. If he calls," Len volunteered.

"Work on him," Steve said as Moss grabbed Len's arms. "Good night, Jerry," Steve called out.

Moss waved a hand. "You'll see," he said, enigmatically.

Steve and Nat watched them as Moss weaved unsteadily up Fifth Avenue. "Think he'll make that call, Nat?" Steve asked.

Nat shrugged. "Hard to figure him out in that condition. Never saw him that drunk or that mad. Maybe he'll sleep it off."

"What if he doesn't? What if he does call Saunders," Steve asked warily.

Nat watched Moss and Goldstein in the distance. "The $64,000 question. I've no answer."

"The question is do I tip off Gratton first thing?"

"But what if he doesn't call—where's that leave you?" Nat asked.

"In the bottom of the well, that's where. But if he does call Saunders—and tells him we were with him—I know the answer. Standing here, he could chew out my ass."

"Mine, too," Nat interjected.

"He's already done that," Steve reminded him. "It's a toughie. Everyone knows Gratton and Moss are real close."

"Apparently not always."

"Joe may not be as aware of that as we are after tonight. There are two options: I say nothing because Jerry Moss is too smart to jeopardize his Gratton connection. Or on the other hand, if I tip Gratton off and Moss doesn't call, even sleeps it off, then Joe has to think I'm trying to destroy their friendship. Be my word against Moss who may have forgotten the whole night when he wakes up."

"Do what you think's best," Nat said without conviction as they entered the hotel.

The next morning Steve got a call. It was eight A.M. Gratton.

"Steve, you could have called me," Gratton said icily.

Steve bolted up in bed. He felt the chill in Gratton's voice.

"Get over here as quick as you can." The phone went dead.

Steve Lane dressed rapidly and hurried over to Gratton's office as fast as he could.

Gratton was seated at his desk sipping his usual early morning vodka.

"I never thought he'd make that call," Steve said, frankly. "I thought if I did advise you and Jerry didn't make the call you could quite correctly feel I'd tried to injure your long friendship with Jerry Moss."

"You should have told me first thing."

"And if he didn't call Bob Saunders?"

"The only point is he did, at the crack of dawn."

"Incredible," was all Steve could say.

"*Truth,* Steve, is the only way. You know you had an option. And so you went and chose the wrong one. You should have let me figure out the options."

"I'm sorry, Joe."

Then Gratton grinned. "I owe Jerry. Sure. But, Steve, what you didn't know was Jerry owes me. 'Kay, he placed me here, but I'm the guy who placed him with Sam Colman. And I can make it a condition he goes if I want to trade him out with one series deal."

"Sam Colman would drop him?"

"Sam Colman will do anything for Sam Colman."

"Wouldn't Jerry Moss know that?"

"He's a smart player. He knew how his game plan would end. Checkmate for him, checkmate for me." Gratton chuckled. "And you, Mr. Lane, whenever you have information, no more holding back, 'kay? I always find out. Always. And mark my words, Mr. Lane, I'll find out whoever it was planted that lousy leak. And don't you forget it." He grinned again, then chuckled. "In the meantime, we'll let them stew for a while. Federal has UPE by the short hairs. It's a new experience for them." And he smiled.

Joe Gratton was a happy man.

FIVE O'CLOCK DEADLINE

Steve Lane was barely out of his forties, but this afternoon's tensions made him feel worn and old. He had met every challenge and had risen steadily. He had even, he felt, managed to do so without hypocrisy and without compromising the principles by which he lived. But there was always a new challenge to face. That was television.

He loosened his tie, slumped down into his big red leather chair and glanced at the golden sunburst clock on the mahogany, paneled wall across from him. Five minutes to five. His fingers touched his private telephone which had not rung for almost three hours. The black phone seemed ominously hostile. Lane was waiting for Curly Ames to call back. He knew he had to wait; waiting had its tensions, but to call Ames a second time was to court major defeat.

He knew that upstairs Joe Gratton was also waiting. Gratton had asked him to get a message to Curly. "It's a must," he had said, which meant that if Curly did not comply willingly, Steve had to make him. The question in Steve's mind was not whether Curly Ames but whether he, Steve Lane, was being tested.

The long wait was nearly over. Steve Lane opened his desk drawer and toyed with an elaborate lighter his wife had given him years before. It was designed to look like an antique pistol and when it was new it had been a conversation piece. Now, with cigarette smoking virtually outlawed, it was outdated.

Lane straightened in his chair as the door across from him slowly opened, and put the 'pistol' away. It was his secretary, Anne. The clock outside in her office and the big sunburst were operated by a single mechanism. Steve Lane had a rigid rule that when he was in New York, away from his coast office, last-minute letters to be signed and final instructions for the next day were matters to be taken up at precisely five to five. Anne was a minute late. Steve sensed that she had delayed to give him time and he was grateful. At the first sound of the latch he had taken up a sheaf of papers from his desk and, pretending to be absorbed in them, walked to the Gothic window overlooking Madison Avenue.

Anne came in, placed the letters neatly on his desk, checked his pen, and silently walked out. He knew that she knew. It was even possible that the whole inner executive office knew: Steve Lane was in trouble. For the first time in some years Steve had met his match. And the man who was cutting him down to size was little Curly Ames, idol of millions, an unknown five years before but now high among the nation's top entertainers.

Only a few hours before, Joe Gratton had come into

Steve's office. He announced that he had taken on the chairmanship of the Love Thy Neighbor Week and had promised its committee, headed by Robert Saunders Jr., that he would have *The Curly Ames Show* launch the campaign informally that very night.

"You see, Steve," Gratton had said in his gravelly voice, "the boss hasn't really gotten anywhere on his own with this idea of Love Thy Neighbor and so he's come to me. Now, as you know, a lot of important men, good friends of ours, clients, too, are on the committee; we can't let them down. More important, we can't let the chairman down. We've got to deliver. Tonight. That's why I thought I'd better ask you to take this up personally with your friend Curly. I can't trust this to anyone else. Remember, we must deliver." Gratton closed the door softly as he left for his own office.

Steve analyzed every word Gratton had said, every inflection of his voice. It was his picture together with Saunders's that would be in the morning paper, but it was "we" who had to deliver. And in this case "we" stood for just one person: Steve Lane. Gratton had made that clear by using one of his favorite compliments; he had told Steve he couldn't trust anyone else.

Steve wondered why Gratton had promised the committee that Curly Ames would hail the Love Thy Neighbor Week this very night. Impulsiveness wasn't a part of Gratton's nature. Joe Gratton was a cool, well-oiled machine. Something had prompted this unusual gesture on his part, but what? And why? The very fact that Steve Lane couldn't put his finger on it sent a cold shiver through his body.

Steve glanced at the clock. Three minutes to five. He had told his secretary at two-thirty that he would take absolutely no calls, except from Joe Gratton, Saunders Jr., or Curly Ames, and she knew, of course, that Gratton rarely called—he just popped in. The open telephone, then, was for young Curly. Steve looked down at the crowded street below. None of those people down there gave a damn for him; none of them cared in the slightest about this contest between him and a television entertainer.

But Curly Ames was no longer just an entertainer. He was big business itself. He owned this show that Steve Lane had bought five years earlier. And Mr. Ames was Mr. Big in another, very important, way. Not only was he the company star, he was also a consultant on matters of merchandising and sales to two of the companies that sponsored his show.

Steve remembered how he had stood at this very window exactly five years ago. Curly Ames had just come up from Atlanta where he had created a stir as an unpredictable disc jockey, just as likely to read the fan mail out loud and answer it on the air, even call up some of them, as he was to play records. He had gained national attention when he had taken all the records he was supposed to play one morning and broken them, telling his listeners he would not plug tunes that were inferior, bands that were mediocre, and singers who were machinelike reproductions of bigger names. Then he opened his show to callers and transformed it into a talk show interspersed with iconoclastic, comedic dialogues, and songs from bands Curly felt worth airing. The unusual mix, and his persona, had sent ratings skyrocketing. Steve Lane's network had needed a summer show, and so Steve had decided to capitalize on the iconoclastic young man with an infectious grin and friendly name.

Steve recalled what an incongruous pair they had made that day, Curly so very young, towheaded, almost diminutive, an eager clean-cut young man whose blue eyes were full of absolute wonderment; he, a full head taller, conservative, showing the first signs of gray at the temple. He recalled his asking Curly how he thought he would like network television.

Curly had looked out the window. "Gosh," he said, "I never thought I'd be here, and look at all those people. Kinda scares a guy."

"It shouldn't scare a performer," Steve had said. "After all, in just one performance on television you're seen by more people than you'd be likely to see on this street in fifty years."

"Guess you're right, Mr. Lane. But as a radio disc jockey you never see your audience."

"You'd better get used to it from now on, Curly," Steve said cheerfully.

Curly Ames had frowned and looked up at Steve. "Now I wonder, if we'd been on television the day I busted all those records, would I really have gone and done it."

Steve laughed. "Maybe not, but you're fresh, and we don't want any part of New York or Hollywood ever to rub off on you. Your charm, Curly, is to be yourself—and being yourself is to break the rules, no holds barred."

After that initial meeting, Steve saw Curly Ames on only a few occasions during the first year. The summer show had been a success, strong enough to move it into the regular schedule. The younger man's caution has passed quickly: he felt his way through big time TV with startling aplomb, swiftly gaining assurance, showing he could make the grade.

Curly soon challenged both the producer and the director on the show with the result that both had resigned in a huff. Steve had been angered by this. But when the producer wrote a bitter note directly to Gratton, it was Steve who told Gratton that that was the weakness of an old-line producer; he just didn't understand the dynamics of a fresh, new talent like Curly's. Gratton had accepted Steve's explanation. And Steve had to admit that Curly had a better sense of how to put together his unique blend of talk show interviews, comic and iconoclastic monologues, and live performance. The show cut across the usual demographic lines and drew a huge audience.

By the year's end Curly had emerged as the greatest new attraction television had had in years. And if Curly was surprised by his singular leap into the national consciousness, so, too, was Steve Lane surprised and gratified by his own rising influence.

At the end of that first year, Steve had decided that perhaps the time had arrived when a bit of advice would benefit the young performer. He invited him over to his office. But Steve had to keep Curly waiting for ten minutes in order to handle a pressing matter for Gratton, and then went out personally to usher Curly in from the reception room. "I'm sorry," he said, "sorry I had to keep you waiting. It was just Joe Gratton. . . ." His voice trailed off as he realized he was offering an unnecessary explanation.

Curly waited politely, and then said, "Been a long time since I been here in your office, Mr. Lane." Steve looked at him puzzled. "Last time I was here we had a nice chat about how I was to break all the rules, remember?"

Steve laughed. "You broke enough, Curly. But you've been real smart about how far to go."

"If I'd of broken too many rules I wouldn't be here now," Curly said, chuckling in his half-boyish way. "But maybe now's a better time."

"Don't do anything in a hurry, Curly," Steve replied. "Young men in a hurry tire themselves out."

Curly took out a cigar. "Mind?" he asked, the big cigar looking out of place in his small mouth. As though he read Steve's mind he said, "These don't quite fit me yet. Either they got to grow smaller or I got to grow bigger. And I never heard of cigars growing smaller."

Steve got up from his chair. He had always felt that there was a psychological advantage in standing while a guest sat relaxed, deep down in a comfortable chair. "That's exactly what I wanted to talk to you about, Curly. You are growing up and we're going to grow even bigger." He paused, giving Curly a chance to say something, but the younger man clenched his cigar and looked straight at him. "We want the show to be bigger. Bigger names on it. Bigger bands. Big-name comedy writers to help you out. In short, the works. Curly, you've had an amazing success and we're going to ride right along with you. How do you like that?"

Curly smiled in his strange disarming way. "I like it," he said. "But I wonder how far you'd of ridden along with me if I wasn't out there riding ahead first."

Steve Lane studied Curly carefully. The words had a touch of insolence, and while his face reflected an image of an impudent boy, still there was no trace of maliciousness showing.

"I want to be frank with you, Curly," Steve said. "To be honest, we couldn't have gone very far. Joe Gratton has always said, 'In today's television we rarely have time to build a show. So it's pretty clear that while we can't afford to ride a slow horse—not if we want to play with blue chips—we can ride one that moves ahead steadily.' And in this company we always play with blue chips. Federal Broadcasting's getting pretty big, too, Curly."

"I like that. And I love blue chips, Mr. Lane. And I'm mighty pleased that we've come this far together."

"Well, I always think it's a good idea at the end of the first year to look back to where you start and look ahead to where you're heading." Steve paused to give Curly an opportunity to put anything he wanted on the record.

Curly took the bait. "I've been doing just that, Mr. Lane. I know you're mostly in Hollywood, but New York's still quite a place," he said, looking approvingly around at Steve's office. "People always told me, 'Wait till you get to New York, Curly, and then you'll have a real brawl for yourself.' Well, I sure found out." Curly began to pace the room. "They told me this was the town of culture, the big time, excitement, the top. They were right, but there was something they didn't tell me. You see, where I came from, Mr. Lane, that was a real place with real people, people with real ideas, and ideals, too. I don't mean to be giving you a dose of Georgia evangelism, but New York is pretty far from Atlanta—farther than it says on the map, maybe as far as some place in Africa. And you got to leave a lot behind you when you come here, not just a different style of clothes, but different ideas about what's good. You can't tote around nice ideas in Africa any more than you'd walk around in a tux."

Steve responded good-naturedly, "I'm getting the words and the text, Brother Ames, but not the point."

Curly chuckled. "That's because you've been sitting on top of the mountain for so long that all you see are other peaks. You forgot the trip up from the valley. Now me, I'm just working my way up the slope, easy like. But someday," he said, pointing to the ceiling, "I'll be up there, too."

"I'm sure of it, Curly, positive."

"Yes, sir, this has been quite a year, Mr. Lane," Curly went on. "I found out what this town is really like. A jungle, like I said. Like something in Africa, I guess. And I don't mean modern Africa. I mean like something way back in olden times, back when the good ol' boys sported clubs, back when the choice meat and the choice place to sleep and the choice broads were stuff you conked a few guys on the head to get."

Curly walked over to the window and pointed down to the street. "And that's New York today—at least the part you and I are in. Nowadays the big boys wear those white-collared, white-cuffed striped shirts, crazy ties and pointed shoes; and, brother, they can give you the works in more ways than our ancestors ever dreamed of. And look at the way they fight to get the right address, eat at the right place, drink the right liquor. It's the same old story as the cave man beating his way to the best spot on the side of the hill. And the broads? Well, you pick on one with a juicy bank statement or the right face and figure or the big name, and you're home. That's New York on my side of the fence, Mr. Lane—" he smiled and sat down—"on your side, too."

Steve Lane felt as if Curly had impugned the standards by which he lived and worked. For a moment he resented him, just as he had always detested all of the bromidic people who dismissed the ethics of business as being something divorced from the personal ethics they loudly proclaimed at home or on the golf course or from the pulpit. And what was equally irritating was the fact that Curly, who was now utterly relaxed and had made no specific proposals, was waiting for Steve to speak.

Steve chose his words with care. "I'm not certain that your colorful picture of New York accords with the facts." He caught himself before he added 'anymore than I think you think of your ancestors as Africans.' In a flash Steve realized the younger man was leading him on: one unwise remark would put him at an apologetic disadvantage. His respect went down for Curly personally, but up for his manipulativeness. He wondered how many others in his brief career Curly had gained an advantage over by leading into an embarrassment. All he added was, "But it makes for an entertaining point of discussion."

"Maybe I was speaking too broadly, Mr. Lane," Curly laughed. "I wasn't trying to be entertaining, either, Mr. Lane," Curly said more sharply. "I save that for my show—and for next fall's show."

Steve Lane felt another slight touch of irritation, but Curly went on without pausing. "Spades are spades where I come from and big fish are big fish—and you're a big fish," he added innocently, but Steve did not react. "And there's only one way you become a big fish in this jungle. Or maybe," he said with a chuckle, "I should have said in this aquarium. No matter. You get that way by eating smaller fish."

Steve Lane poured himself a glass of water. "You're getting a bit zoological, Curly, and I'm afraid I don't quite see the picture as—"

"Oh, but there's a reason, Mr. Lane." The interruption jarred Steve. "It's not surprising that you don't see the picture. That's because you've become big enough not to see it the way little fish do."

He tried to imagine himself from Curly's perspective for a moment, perhaps as a shark scattering a school of Curly-size minnows. He found the thought, and Curly, overwrought. Or maybe this was all just the southern exaggeration natural to Curly, like the rolling sentences and inexhaustible adjectives of Pat Conroy.

"Well," Curly went on with a smile on his face, "There it is. You see it. A fact is a fact."

Steve wanted to end this. "I suppose you're looking forward to the new season."

Curly leaned forward eagerly. "Very much, and I need your advice. Who really knows anything about this crazy business? Show business."

Steve smiled. "There are no real authorities. Everyone's always learning. Me, you, everyone."

"I'm glad you feel that way, Mr. Lane," Curly said. "In radio there were a lot of fellows who had it all over me in experience. They know the right words, the right jokes, the right way of emphasizing, the right everything. But in television we're all equals, in the sense anyone can hit, even someone inexperienced in the medium like me. That's why I wanted your advice."

Steve understood him now. Curly Ames had used one of the oldest and surest ways of winning advance support. His eyes narrowed at this new manipulation that reduced his advice to insignificance. He had been an obstacle in Curly's mind, and so Curly had first tried to put him at a disadvantage by luring him into an embarrassing remark, and when that failed, had disarmed him with a calculated innocence and deference. It was plain now that others down the line—smaller fish—had been given the same treatment. Curly got up. "I'm afraid I've taken too much of your time already, Mr. Lane, but the way I had it figured, why shouldn't I get the experience of being my own television producer when there's no one around who knows any more than I do."

"That requires the assumption of considerable responsibility," Steve said.

Curly was at the door. He turned. "Responsibility—that's a big word." He smiled. His cigar had gone out, and he regarded it. The cigar looked big in his hand, too. "I like it. Thanks for the advice, Mr. Lane." And then he was gone.

Steve had stared at the door. Little Curly Ames had come for something and he had got it.

After the spectacular success of the first television season the country clamored for more of Curly's special brand of entertainment. There were a few bad times though—where Curly blithely ignored the program's commercials in favor of more songs or jokes or monologues. Gratton vigorously protested the first such cavalier treatment of the company, but Steve soothed him by showing him the impact of Curly Ames on the sales charts of the advertisers. Even so, Steve talked to Curly, and Curly inquired—showing great concern, whether sales had been dropping. Steve admitted that they hadn't.

"Well, then, Mr. Lane, what's all the complaining about?" Curly asked earnestly.

Now Steve Lane looked down at his hands. Unconsciously he had distorted a delicate lead heron that stood on the bookshelves behind his desk. He looked up—two minutes to five.

At their meeting Curly had once said he was afraid of people. Now Steve thought of all the people who were afraid of Curly Ames; the writers Curly had fired or the bands he had first praised, then humiliated before live audiences, or the personalties he had thrown off his program for supposedly hogging the limelight. And this wasn't all.

The casualties even extended down to members of the production staff and secretaries. At first only the lesser people were affected, but gradually key men were threatened. Some of these lost their jobs, some were shifted to other shows. There were times when Steve Lane scorned himself for having accommodated the young man's growing appetite for authority, but, he told himself, one couldn't overlook the public's amazing loyalty to Curly.

To answer his own misgivings, Steve Lane had his staff compile all of the statistics that might possibly pertain to Curly Ames. Steve wanted to try to isolate Curly's contributions to various sponsors from that of their other efforts in merchandising and advertising. In the end, Steve had to admit that Curly's contributions were substantial.

Steve Lane had become the one man who could deal effectively with Curly. He had not sought the job and he did not like it, but circumstances had put him in the position of sometimes defending, always explaining, the unpredictable attitudes of Curly Ames. It was Steve who was responsible for eliminating personnel objectionable to Curly at the network, at advertising agencies, and even in one or two sponsors' headquarters. Steve had persuaded himself it was all for the sake of Federal Broadcasting, but he often wondered if he hadn't really done it to avoid facing up to Curly's strength.

And yet, never had the company prospered so, and never had he, Steve Lane, gained influence so rapidly. His success with Curly, not his years of loyalty to the company, had propelled him into the executive vice president's chair. That was a fact. And Curly had summed it all up: a fact is a fact.

Now Steve Lane found himself recalling a night when the company had welcomed Curly Ames back from a summer vacation. Everyone vied for Curly's favor, except Steve. While Steve had mastered the art of being ingratiating, on this occasion he held himself aloof, and Curly sensed it.

Curly's retaliation had been to cut in on Steve—or anyone else—who danced with Steve's wife, Susan. Susan's expression had been that of someone pleading for rescue, but no one tempted fate by cutting in on Curly—except for the last dance. Steve moved in brusquely then, and Curly shrugged his shoulders, walked away and laughed. He had had his way.

It was Steve who had sponsored Curly's ambition to take a more active interest in business. Curly was a star salesman, not only of the sponsor's products, but of himself. He knew how many homes saw him each week. He knew how many viewers were buying the products advertised on his show. And so he offered his services as sales-and-merchandising consultant to key advertisers.

Steve maneuvered Curly's desires through more than one agency plans board, while he acknowledged to himself that as Curly's fortunes rose, so would his; but he never forgot that as Curly's fortunes ebbed, his might, too.

Steve assured Joe Gratton that Curly, though without special training or experience, had a business acumen that could be channeled to Federal Broadcasting's advantage. And he pointed out that if the move to bring Curly into the businesses were rejected, Curly might make similar arrangements elsewhere.

It was now one minute to five. Steve Lane looked at the telephone. In one minute Curly Ames would start his rehearsal, and after five o'clock no one could reach him.

No calls were taken. No visitors were allowed. After five on the day of the show, Curly Ames was unreachable. Steve Lane had waited nearly two and a half hours.

Steve had placed his earlier call at exactly two-thirty because he knew that Curly was always in his private dressing room at the theater. Curly would have just finished his lunch, sent over by one of New York's most famous hosts, and he would be using the next hour to review the layout of the show. There was nothing unusual in Steve Lane's calling Curly. It had become a practice of his to call on show day to wish Curly luck and to discuss any details that needed attention.

Steve waited on the telephone as he heard Curly's secretary say, "Mr. Ames's dressing room."

Steve's secretary said, "Hello, Jane. Mr. Lane would like to speak with Mr. Ames."

"Oh, hello," the other girl had said. "Golly, I'm afraid Mr. Ames is terribly busy, Anne."

"So is Mr. Lane," Anne replied briskly. "Would you please tell Mr. Ames that Mr. Lane is calling?"

There was a momentary pause from the other end, and then: "Will you put Mr. Lane on?" In that moment Steve Lane knew that Curly Ames had decided to take his measure. Never before had Curly's secretary hesitated to speed Steve through; never before had there been the challenge of getting him on first. He knew he was Curly's next target.

Anne was well aware of the protocol and subtleties of maintaining prestige, of the position of respect and authority required in telephone etiquette. She knew that her boss must never be put on first. A moment later Steve heard Anne say sharply, "Mr. Lane is waiting, Jane. Now will you please get Mr. Ames?"

This sparring of the secretaries was like the preliminary bout at a fight. Anne had to win for her own prestige. He admired her tact. Then he heard Jane say, "Just a moment, please."

Steve smiled, but he knew the game had just begun. Then he heard Curly's secretary say, "I'm sorry, Mr. Ames is terribly busy at the moment. If Mr. Lane won't mind waiting—"

Steve bellowed: "You get Curly Ames on this line, miss, and right now!" In the same instant he knew he was wrong. Now Curly and his secretary knew. Steve Lane was waiting and Steve Lane was upset.

Curly's secretary said softly, "Just a moment, Mr. Lane." Steve was sure that Curly was listening on the other end, he could feel him, he could almost hear him breathing. And then Jane came back: "Mr. Ames will call you, Mr. Lane, the first moment he's free."

There was nothing to do but hang up and wait.

And he had waited. He had waited all through the afternoon and now it was five o'clock. Curly Ames, he knew, had done this deliberately. Steve Lane had been kept waiting. He had been tempted to call just once more, but he knew Curly would decline to take a second call. Everything would be lost for certain if that happened. He had been challenged. He had faced the silent telephone throughout the afternoon.

And now that the five o'clock deadline was here, Steve Lane knew that Curly Ames was also facing a decision: to return the call or ignore it. He had won the first skirmish. To ignore Steve Lane was to announce open hostility. To return the call at the last moment was, perhaps, to keep Steve off balance.

Suddenly his private telephone rang. Steve was startled,

but he let it ring three times, and then slowly picked it up. "Steve Lane speaking," he said. He had to sound busy and authoritative. He was annoyed to discover the caller was not Curly.

A female voice said, "One moment, Mr. Lane."

He bit his lip. Another skirmish. She must have been given no choice.

"Hello, Steve. Shoot." Curly Ames was ready for round two. He had called back but he was going to keep the upper hand.

"I have something that's got to get on the show tonight, Curly," Steve said.

"It's five o'clock, Steve. We can't begin to make changes this late."

"This is something rather special, Curly," Steve said, setting himself the job of selling Gratton's idea.

"Special or no special. It's too late, Lane. I'm sorry."

Steve was sure now that the younger man intended to take him on. The cue was his first impertinent use of Steve's last name. And worse, he was turning Steve down without hearing him out.

But Steve knew he had to make every effort. Failure to win for Joe Gratton would threaten his own position. He had to use every ounce of strength he could muster to do so, even if it meant using Gratton's authority to supplement his own.

"Curly," he said, "Mr. Gratton made a particular point about getting this change on tonight."

"Gratton? Why didn't you say that in the first place?"

Steve smiled grimly. Curly wasn't ready to take on him and Gratton at the same time. It was cold comfort, but for the first time in hours Lane felt cool and calm. Casually, he explained about Love Thy Neighbor Week. But even as he talked and expanded on the idea he felt, abruptly, the grotesque inappropriateness of the request. And as he gave Curly the essentials of the project, Steve glanced at the top paper Anne had brought in a few moments before, though now it seemed like hours. It was another statistical report prepared by his assistant and it was headed "Report on *Curly Ames,* His Record and Future." He thumbed through it as he had so many others on Curly as he described the basic idea of the campaign to Curly. This report, Steve saw, was different. He felt himself settle down. A number of other points were beginning to fall into place in his mind. He thanked Curly for taking the time and courtesy to call back. He could barely stay focused on their conversation as he took in the report's implications. He couldn't wait to hang up. "I'm sure," he said, "that Joe Gratton will deeply appreciate your launching this project on the air tonight. Love Thy Neighbor is something we can all use a little more of."

Curly laughed. "Are you kidding?"

It no longer mattered to Steve. He had fulfilled Joe Gratton's request. He had delivered. And he had a quiet moment of satisfaction as he beat Curly to the last shot: "That's it Curly. Thanks a lot. Goodbye." He calmly placed the phone on its stand.

It was past five. Steve Lane looked carefully again at the report before him. There was no doubt about it, the figures showed that Curly was a magnificent salesman. Except maybe for the legendary Arthur Godfrey there had never been anything quite like him in the business. But great as he was, he had now stopped climbing. The figures revealed that Curly Ames had reached a plateau.

Curly could continue to do well if he stayed on the plateau, but he was through doing wonders. The plateau that he had leveled off at was nothing to dismiss lightly. Curly Ames was formidable, even on paper, but the charts clearly indicated that he was also vulnerable. At that instant, Steve Lane knew that part of his own vulnerability lay in the fact that he had allowed himself the luxury of ignoring these indications, which had heralded themselves months before in earlier analyses. He had wanted something more certain.

Unconsciously, Steve drummed his fingers on his desk, but stopped when he grew aware of the trite gesture. He had minimized Curly's temperament, his indiscretions. He had been credited with discovering Curly Ames, and so he had always been loath to disown him. Even when it became clear what a piece of work Curly was personally. Looking at the evidence in this report, he knew he could probably cover up again. He was an old hand at talking away figures. But blue-chip business could not afford rationalizations based on emotional relationships.

There had been times when he had placed his own judgment on the scales, and he had seen it triumph over so-called facts. That was the big gamble a business leader had to take, staking his judgment against the facts. But some facts could neither be talked away nor contested after a reasonable period of time. And now danger signals were flying. Nor did he feel any desire to talk away anything. He made his decision. He had to look where the company was going. Curly Ames might stay on top a time, and he might go down, but Steve was sure he would not go higher.

Gratton was still in his office and Steve concluded that he had thrown this assignment at him deliberately; Gratton was the only other man who could have called Curly. Steve sometimes suspected that Gratton had fallen for Curly Ames's line—it was no secret that Curly was wooing him—but to Joe Gratton everyone was expendable. It was only necessary to decide who and when, and he may have decided it was Lane and now.

Steve Lane stood up, adjusted his tie, walked to the stairway, climbed the steps, and a short time later entered Gratton's office.

"Sorry to bother you, Joe," Steve said casually. "I wasn't sure you'd still be around."

"No bother at all, Steve. Just getting set to call it a day." He looked up at Steve and waited.

"You remember you asked me to get a message through to our young friend, Curly Ames?"

For the moment Gratton frowned. "Oh, that!" he said, as though he had just recollected.

"Love Thy Neighbor week."

Gratton gave him a quizzical look. "Have any trouble?"

"No trouble at all," Steve replied easily.

Gratton rubbed his hands, obviously pleased. He had promised the chairman that he would promote the idea that very night and he had delivered. He pushed his chair back, and then rose to his feet.

Steve was about to start to his own office, then stopped, his hand gripping the door knob tightly. If he felt agitated he gave no other outward sign. He knew his critical decision could place his fate in the other man's hands. "There's one other situation we ought to look into Monday morning, Joe," he said.

Gratton was putting on his coat. "What's that?" he asked.

"Might be that the time has come when we ought to reexamine Curly. I hate to put it quite so coldly, Joe, but otherwise I wouldn't be faithful to my responsibility to the company and to you. We ought to take a look at where Curly's going."

"Steve," Gratton said softly, "I think that would be very wise. We could be complacent about our success with Ames and just ride along: on the other hand, it might be just about the smartest move we ever made—next to hiring him in the first place—to let him out when he's reached his peak."

"That's just it, Joe," Steve said, indicating the papers in his hand, "he's already reached it. It's all here in the latest analysis."

"You sure?" Gratton asked.

"Yes," Steve said. "I'm sorry if it comes as a surprise. I should have seen it months ago myself. But I wanted to be sure. These figures speak for themselves. I should have been their spokesman; instead they're mine."

"Well, now," Gratton said stroking his chin, "there's no damage done anywhere. The fact is you know his time is up and that's the important point. You've put yourself ahead of Ames and you've put Federal ahead of yourself. Sometimes it's hard to do what's right, but what's right is always best. We get off of Ames while we're still on top. Of course, we'll stay up for quite a while on the momentum alone, but you'd better start looking for a new horse."

"This will take a bit of delicate handling."

Gratton smiled. "You've had tough ones before, Steve. There'll be a few squawks. But take my advice; when you have to operate, Steve, don't spend a lot of time telling the patient all about it. Just go ahead and do it. Surgically.

And," he added reassuringly, "we can handle all the squawks on this one together." Gratton smiled and left the room.

Steve felt a release of tension. So Gratton had been waiting for him to come to terms with himself. He supposed, had he failed, he might have been dropped, too, but Gratton had precipitated a decision by asking him to achieve a difficult assignment.

His secretary was waiting for him. "Anything else before I leave tonight, Mr. Lane?"

"Nothing else, Anne," he said, "except Monday, first thing, let me have copies of our contracts with Curly Ames." Anne smiled as she turned to the door. "You're looking rather pleased, Anne. Have a good day?"

"Looks like Monday will be even better," she said. "That contract comes up for renewal in three weeks."

Steve thought for a moment, then he nodded. "You're right, Anne. I hadn't realized it was so soon." He looked down at Madison Avenue and said softly, "I guess Curly was right after all. Facts are facts." He felt vindicated. Ultimately, unprincipled success laid itself bare, and faltered.

Anne said, "I'm sorry, Mr. Lane, I don't quite understand."

He turned and said, "That's all right, Anne." She started out and he added, "Oh, and one more thing. From this moment on—when the phone rings I will not be in to Mr. Ames."

ENVOI

SHORTLY AFTER CURLY AMES WAS picked up by another network Steve Lane took the train down to Philadelphia for one of his periodic visits home. His father, John Lane, was retired from his one man real estate business, but still watched his son's career with great pleasure, while his mother, Evelyn, filled one scrap album after another with his accomplishments. Steve always felt constrained in their presence, his easy-going, well-meaning father, the modest but comfortable surroundings, his quick-to-criticize mother who to this day still disliked anyone poorer than herself, or ethnically different. She had been poor once, and it was a favorite saying of hers, "The rich are a different race, and so are the poor. I know. Take it from me."

Evelyn had loved *The Curly Ames Show* since the moment Curly had focused one program on welfare mothers and turned on them devastatingly, as right wing as one could imagine, and then embarrassed a struggling rap group who provided some of the live entertainment. It had been a disagreeable but still very popular show. She had ignored his next show when Curly had turned on right wing Republican critics of welfare and affirmative action: he had put himself in her good graces forever with the earlier show. The rest, she knew, was just a necessary bow to appease the liberal media that she was sure he hadn't meant.

"Evelyn was sure unhappy when you let Curly go," his father had laughed at the time. After a rival picked him up, his mother had sarcastically commented on his judgment.

"He could still be yours!" she insisted. "How could you let someone that influential, and *right,* go?" She was not interested in his explanations. What was the saying about being a prophet at home? But, then, he couldn't think of a time his mother had ever admitted she was pleased with him. If Steve hadn't known about the scrapbooks she kept from his earliest days he would hardly have guessed the depths of love she felt for him.

Steve reflected it was all part of a narrow, constrained world he had left behind even before he went to Penn.

But it wasn't his parents he was primarily interested in, this trip. Ever since his novel had been published Helen Merin, now Leopold, had been back in touch with him. He had immediately recognized her handwriting when he received her letter: as he opened and read it he could imagine her presence, hear her voice. Susan had been with him and seen his reaction, so he had had to explain.

"Oh, your first love," she smiled. "How nice. What does she want now?"

Steve heard every inflection, every phrasing in Susan's voice. He was careful to explain how long it had been since he had seen Helen, how young they had been, and that Helen had been happily married for many years, and, apparently, as he read further in the letter, had become the mother of three children.

"I don't even remember what she looked like," he added.

"Probably a very nice Philadelphia matron," Susan said.

Steve made a point of never opening a letter from Helen again at home, and suggesting Helen write him at the office in the future once he was at Kane & Shaw, then Federal.

Now and then Helen had, too, not to say she missed him, or to pry into his privacy. They were direct, friendly letters between adults who had known each other in their youth, and he responded, now and then, in kind. He suspected it was just her way to soften some of the changes inevitable with time and, perhaps, to renew what had always really been just a friendship.

One of Helen's recent letters had suggested they meet for lunch next time he was in Philadelphia, just for "old time's sake." Aldo, her husband, knew they wrote once in a while, and wouldn't be put out at all, she assured him. Steve hesitated through several letters, then accepted.

Helen was at the restaurant before him, with Aldo, a nice man their age now growing the paunch Steve had so far avoided. His wiry hair was already full of gray. He shook hands amiably with Steve, and for a time they chatted: they had known each other at Penn, and it was pleasant to remember those years as well as dip into the stream they had fed into. Then Aldo got up gracefully, wished them a good lunch.

"Good to see you again, Steve."

"And you, Aldo." They shook hands again, and Aldo strode off.

"Well," Steve said, sitting down.

"Well!"

"This is very unexpected," Steve said, "but I'm happy you had the idea."

"It's been such a long time. I always felt it was too long."

"Have you been happy?" He knew how abrupt that was: how could she answer that except with an 'of course!', unless there was something else on her mind? He wanted to find that out right away.

"I married my best friend," she said softly.

"Ouch."

"I have been happy with Aldo."

They were both silent for awhile.

"And you? With Susan?"

"Yes," he said simply. Helen could see it was true. She scrutinized Steve's face carefully: still as handsome, still as fair, still topped by a head of black hair barely touched by white, only a little thinner. Time had treated him well. Steve's eyes still had that look of intensity and intelligence she had loved as a young woman, except now he was not a young man trying to look more mature than he was. Steve looked every bit the accomplished executive he was.

For a time they talked about children, hers, his son, and their inevitable hopes and fears as parents. The appetizer came and went, and then the main course. Steve relaxed: the luncheon was well on its way to being an unremarkable, anti-climactic meeting. He wondered if he would ever see Helen again. They didn't really seem to have anything to say to each other. He wasn't sure what he had felt concern about, why he had hesitated to see her. He sat back, told her amusing stories, and took in the restaurant, high in one of Philadelphia's new buildings, with a fine view of the older part of the city.

"I was so impressed with your novel," Helen said, changing the direction of the conversation. "I always thought you had so much talent as a writer."

"Thanks."

"It really is very good. But you don't have much time for more of that, do you?"

"No. I'd like to—"

"Really?"

"Well, maybe not enough to take it from other things."

"You always knew what you wanted."

"While you seem to have the best of both worlds. You're still an editor, and a good one from all I hear—and there's the family."

"Yes." She looked at him reflectively. "Aldo was my best friend."

"Yes, you said that."

"It took me a long time to fall in love with him."

It was suddenly very still between them. Steve's tension soared, and he realized how much there was, indeed, to talk about. Almost helplessly his mind flashed back to how Helen had said goodbye to him at the railroad station so many years ago, her hand held out, her voice as set as her face. He remembered how she pronounced each syllable of "Good bye, Steve," still amazed at how much those three syllables had communicated.

Finally, he asked, "Why did you say 'good bye' like that?"

"A woman can put up with many things. Even being second to many things. But not to her need to be needed."

"I needed you."

"No," she said smiling. "I found that out our last night together." He was frowning. "I was comfortable for you."

Steve nodded slowly. He had known his share of women since then, some that he had simply regarded as conquests, some he felt he had had to have—for a moment—and one he really had no desire to do without. Whom he couldn't have enough of. Helen had been none of those. It was as she said: there had been a time and place, and a certain comfort, before the world began. Steve nodded again.

"We were very young."

"Much younger than people now."

"Yes."

"Even so." Her brown eyes were locked on his now. In that moment he took Helen in very clearly: still trim, still attractive, not actually all that pretty, her intelligence more obvious now with some of the twenties softness gone. She had the lines that went with her age, only mildly compensated for with makeup, with no disguising facelift which so many women in his circle seemed to think was necessary as soon as they reached forty. All in all hers was the same open, bright and honest, if now somewhat matronly, face he thought he had loved, then. A real person. Steve felt intensely how close they had been, once. And wondered as intensely what he had meant to Helen, or how little, or how comfortable he had been, in turn, for her, that she could shake his hand like that and walk away so calmly.

"You were my great love." The words went through and through him with a revelatory power. "You hurt me, Steve."

It was the first time she had used his name; he felt as if she had driven a spear through him into the wall behind. He could say nothing. He only took her hand, and held it while she let him, while he struggled to control his breathing, she her tears, that never fell.

As they walked out later he hailed a cab for her.

"Will you still write?" he asked. She flashed him a dazzling smile.

"Oh yes. Now and then," and she was gone.

The sun beat down on him, and the humidity was oppressive. But he stood unwilling to move in any direction, musing as the traffic moved past, and the citizens of the city he had rejected surged about him, as if he was one of them, as if he was not irreducibly strange in their midst, as if they were all not irreducibly strange and unpredictable beside one another, everywhere, as they moved about within the world, hunter, or hunted, in jungles of their own choosing.

The mood didn't last long, and soon Steve Lane hailed a cab and started his long journey, eager to be home.

www.ingramcontent.com/pod-product-compliance
Lightning Source LLC
Chambersburg PA
CBHW020613310726
48979CB00008B/1456/J

* 9 7 8 1 5 7 3 9 2 2 4 5 6 *